"This smells like real cowboy coffee."

"It'll float a spoon," he said.

"Just how I like it." She took a sip. "Perfect."

Her eyes were as dark as her hair, fringed with thick lashes. Her face was slender, cheekbones high, lips curved in a smile. In the dim confines of the tent, after that plunge in the icy river and the mighty struggle with the canoe, she should have looked like a scrawny wet rat, not a sexy fashion model.

"Why are you here?" he said, blunt and to the point.

She shook her head, took another swallow of coffee. "My boss dropped me off up at the lake so I could canoe downriver and deliver a message from your sister." She ran the fingers of one hand through her wet, shoulder-length hair, sweeping it back from her face, and gazed at him frankly. "She's very worried about you. I spoke with her on the phone yesterday. She told me what happened to your dog, and she feels bad about it."

He made no comment. He had nothing to say to this girl about his dog or his sister.

His life was none of her business.

Dear Reader,

Like many fictional stories, *A Soldier's Pledge* found its origins in real life. One segment of a documentary was being filmed at my workplace. The documentary was called *Searching for Home: Coming Back from War*, and one of the soldiers being filmed for the documentary had lost his leg while serving a tour of duty in Iraq.

I am deeply indebted to Sergeant Brandon Deaton for his personal insight into a wounded warrior's difficult journey back from war. Any inaccuracies are my own. This story is about a fictional character, but is dedicated to all soldiers, past and present, who served and sacrificed to protect our nation, and to those who served and didn't come home.

Nadia Nichols

NADIA NICHOLS

A Soldier's Pledge

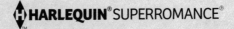
HARLEQUIN® SUPERROMANCE®

Recycling programs
for this product may
not exist in your area.

ISBN-13: 978-0-373-64011-9

A Soldier's Pledge

Copyright © 2017 by Penny R. Gray

Printed in U.S.A.

Nadia Nichols went to the dogs at the age of twenty-nine and currently operates a kennel of twenty-eight Alaskan huskies. She has raced her sled dogs in northern New England and Canada, works at the family-owned Harraseeket Inn in Freeport, Maine, and is also a registered Maine Master Guide.

She began her writing career at the age of five, when she made her first sale, a short story called "The Bear," to her mother for 25 cents. This story was such a blockbuster that her mother bought every other story she wrote, and kept her in ice-cream money throughout much of her childhood.

Now all her royalties go toward buying dog food. She lives on a remote solar-powered northern Maine homestead with her sled dogs, a Belgian draft horse named Dan, several cats, two goats and a flock of chickens. She can be reached at nadianichols@aol.com.

Books by Nadia Nichols

HARLEQUIN SUPERROMANCE

From Out of the Blue
Everything to Prove
Sharing Spaces
Montana Standoff
A Full House
Buffalo Summer
Across a Thousand Miles
Montana Dreaming

Visit the Author Profile page at Harlequin.com for more titles.

CHAPTER ONE

SHE FIRST SAW him through the smoke of a forest fire. He was standing on the end of the dock where the smoke jumpers waited for the planes, backpack and rifle case resting at his feet, staring off across the river. Normally the ferry landing could be seen on the opposite shore, but with the wind out of the west, smoke roiled over the water like thick fog that glowed a dark molten red in the sunrise. Cameron took a second sip from her first cup of coffee and squinted out the window of Walt's cluttered office.

"That him?" she asked, leaning forward until her nose almost touched the grimy, fly-specked pane. Stupid question. Who else would be standing there at dawn? Her brain was muddled from lack of sleep and three beers at the pool hall the night before.

"That's him," Walt said, his voice as rough as hers from breathing smoke for days on end. "Said he drove all night to get here and there's a big storm front right behind him. Been waiting there pretty near two hours."

"Well, he'll have to wait a little longer, smoke's too thick to fly. Jeez, Walt, I can't believe you called me at oh-dark-thirty to get me down here. This was supposed to be my first day off in over two weeks."

"Wind's going to shift pretty quick. I listened to the forecast. You'll be able to get him where he wants to go."

"Where's that?"

"Kawaydin Lake, headwaters of the Wolf River."

"He's taking a fishing trip in the middle of a forest fire?"

"Didn't see a fly rod or a kick float. He's traveling light. His total kit weighed under fifty pounds."

"When's he want to be picked up?"

"Doesn't. Says he's going to walk down the Wolf to the Mackenzie."

Cameron laughed aloud. "You're kidding, right?"

"Says it'll take him eight days, and he'll send us a signal on his GPS transmitter when it's time to pick him up."

"He might be standing on that dock for eight days if the wind doesn't shift. By the way, this coffee's terrible. When and if Jeri ever comes back, give her a raise. A big one. Then tell her if she leaves again you'll fire her, and if she stays you'll marry her."

Walt looked like he hadn't bathed, shaved or slept in two weeks, which was just about how long the fire east of the park had been burning out of control and just about how long Jeri had been gone. The first two weeks of August had been fourteen miserable days of nonstop work and bad coffee.

"Plane's all gassed up, ready to go," Walt said.

"I thought the park service closed the area down to nonessential personnel."

"They've okayed this because it's way outside the fire area and it's not inside the park. Don't complain. This works out good for us. He's paying a lot of money to get flown out to that lake."

"Speaking of flying, the plane was running rough enough to spit rivets yesterday, Walt. She's overdue for a checkup."

"He's paying a *lot* of money," Walt repeated. "That plane's not up for inspection for another month. She'll get you there and back, and you know it. It's three hours' flying time, round-trip. You'll be napping in your rusty old trailer by noon. Look, see that? The wind's already shifting out of the south, just like they said it would."

Cameron glanced at her wristwatch and thought about how dog tired she was. If she'd known about this job in advance, she wouldn't have played pool until 2:00 a.m. "What about Mitch? Can't he do it?"

"He ferried a big crew of smoke jumpers out to Frazier Lake yesterday to fight the fire, then he was going to drop another crew back in Yellowknife. He won't be back till late this afternoon. C'mon, Cam, it's an easy hop. I'll throw a bonus at you for flying him out there."

"How much?"

"Hundred bucks."

She took another sip of stale, bitter coffee. It was no better than the first. "Walt, that's your second joke of the morning. You're on a real roll."

"Hundred fifty."

"Two hundred fifty and a week off, *paid*, or I'm going back to bed and you can fly him out there yourself."

Walt hesitated. "Hundred fifty and two days off if we get the heavy rains they're predicting tonight. If not, you'll have to keep flying the jumpers. I don't have any other pilots right now, you know that, and you also know we need the money."

Cameron tugged on the brim of her Gore-Tex ball cap and sighed in defeat. Walt's expression instantly brightened. "Good. I've already loaded supplies that you can drop over to Frazier Lake after you get the Lone Ranger situated."

"That's wasn't part of the bargain."

"Mitch's plane was overloaded with smoke jumpers. He didn't have room for any provisions. Those jumpers have to eat, and you can swing over there easy as pie on the way home."

"Easy as pie. Right." She attempted another swallow of coffee and looked out the grimy window. The sky was brightening as the wind shifted and pushed the smoke to the west. The old red-and-white de Havilland Beaver tied to the dock rocked gently on small river swells. Cameron thought about the past four months, moving up here after an ugly divorce, living in a battered old house trailer two miles from the airstrip, flying as much as she could because when she was flying she could outrun her past, and if she flew fast enough and far enough, who knew? She might catch a glimpse of the future, and maybe it would look good.

"What's the Lone Ranger's name?" she asked.

THE WONDERFUL THING about the red-and-white Beaver, tail number DHC279, was the tremendous amount of noise it generated in mid-flight, that great big Wasp engine roaring away, metal rattling, wind whistling through all the cracks. The noise made conversation impossible, which suited Cameron right down to the ground. She had no desire to make small talk with clients when flying them to their destinations. She hid behind her sunglasses and liked to be alone with her thoughts. She never tired of studying the landscape, the rivers and lakes, the mountains and valleys, the wilderness that appeared so pristine, so untouched by human hands. This wild landscape was a balm to her spirit. She liked to daydream about building a cabin in this valley, or maybe that one, down where those two small rivers converged...or that next valley wasn't bad, either; it had a natural meadow that would make a good garden spot.

And hey, was that a wolf down there? No, *two* wolves, trotting along the riverbank. The spotting of wildlife from the air never ceased to thrill her.

Her passenger made no attempt at conversation but seemed equally content to watch the world slip beneath the plane's wings. The forest fire's destruction was visible west toward the park. Thick plumes of smoke nearly obliterated the dark bank of clouds advancing from the south. If this front brought the promised rain, two intense weeks of flying smoke jumpers in and out of the park would come to a welcome end.

The plane touched down on the lake just past nine thirty after a one-and-a-half-hour flight. Cameron taxied toward the shore, cut the engine, popped her door open and climbed down onto the pontoon. When the bottom shallowed up, she lowered herself carefully into the water, well aware of how slippery the smooth stones could be underfoot. Bracing her heels, she caught hold of the wing rope to pivot the plane. A second rope hitched to the pontoon acted as a tether, and she hauled the back of the floats toward shore.

Her passenger opened the side door and climbed onto the pontoon, hauled his pack out of the door behind him, slung his rifle case over his shoulder and closed the door. He waded ashore with his pack and rifle case, and leaned both against a big round rock near the shore's edge. She hadn't noticed his limp when he was getting into the plane back at the village. She'd been too busy prepping the plane. He straightened, turned to look at her and took off his sunglasses. Good-looking man. Well built. Short military-style haircut. Squint lines at the corners of clear hazel eyes that had seen too much, maybe. Strong features. Early to mid-thirties. But there was something about him that made her uneasy. Not many chose to be dropped off alone in such a remote spot, with so little gear.

"Thanks," he said.

"You're welcome," Cameron replied, hiding behind her shades. "My boss says you're planning to follow this river out to the Mackenzie?"

"That's right."

"It's rough going through there. Wild country. Going solo's pretty risky, and what you're carrying for gear isn't much."

"It'll get me there."

"Did you hurt your leg jumping out of the plane?"

"No," he said.

The wind gusted, and the plane tugged at the tether rope like a balky horse. Cameron tugged back. "This is grizzly country. They can hang along the rivers like brown bears this time of year, and they can be territorial."

He leaned against the rock, half sitting, and folded his arms across his chest.

"We're the intruders here," she continued. "A brown or grizzly will bluff charge. If you get into a Mexican standoff and the bear charges, wait until he crosses the point of no return. Chances are if you stand your ground he'll stop twenty, thirty feet out or better. No need to shoot him. Of course, if it's a sow with cubs, all bets are off."

"I'll try to remember that."

She felt a twinge of annoyance. Most guys enjoyed talking to her. Most guys actually came on to her. Something about young women pilots really got them all hot and horny. This one spoke politely, but she had the definite impression he just wanted her to go away. "Most people who get flown into this lake want to fish for char or canoe down the Wolf, or both. It's a beautiful stretch of river. Not too many people know about it." Why was she trying to make conversation with a man who didn't want to talk? He'd brought a weapon. Clearly he understood about the bears. "What's your contingency plan if you get into trouble, say you break your leg or something?"

"I have a GPS transmitter. When I reach the Mackenzie, I'll request your flying service to pick me up."

"You really think you can make that distance in eight days?"

"Yes."

"Well, in case you don't, we fly year-round. If you signal us six months from now, we'll pick you up, and if you get into any trouble, I guess you know how to hit an SOS button." Cameron flushed from the effort of anchoring the plane and making awkward conversation. "Well, it's your party. I'll leave you to it. Have a nice hike."

She unfastened the tether from the pontoon, wrapped it neatly, climbed back into the cockpit, slammed her door harder than necessary, put on her safety harness and fired up the old Beaver. She taxied slowly back out into the lake, taking her time and casting frequent frowns toward the shore, where the man still leaned against the large smooth rock, watching her depart. This remote lake was large and deep enough to make a good place for floatplanes to drop clients, though not many came up here. Most wanted to be flown to the Nahanni, or to Norman Wells. Cameron had never been to this lake before, though she'd dropped adventurers at other lakes with their gear and canoes. Cheerful adventurers, too. Totally the opposite of the taciturn Lone Ranger.

His name was Jack Parker, and he hailed from a place called Bear Butte, Montana, according to the contact information left at the plane base. After the Beaver lifted off the surface of the lake, she banked around for one last glimpse of him sitting on the rock beside his rifle and pack. He lifted his arm in a slow wave, and she dipped one wing in reply. She felt uneasy leaving him there, a loner with an untold story, and wondered if the world would ever see him again.

THE FLIGHT TO Frazier Lake was uneventful, and the provisions were off-loaded enthusiastically by the crew there. They were glad to get the supplies. She lifted off immediately afterward, declining an invitation to lunch because she didn't like the look of the weather rolling in from the south. "Gotta go, boys, I'm flying right into that stuff."

Ten minutes later she changed her flight plan, radioing Walt. "I'd be home napping in my rusty house trailer by now if you hadn't sent me to Frazier," she said. "Ceiling's dropping like a rock, and I'm heading back to Kawaydin Lake. I'll wait there till conditions improve."

"Roger that," Walt said.

"You owe me two weeks' paid vacation," she said. He squelched the radio twice, and she laughed aloud. "Cheap bastard."

Thirty minutes later Cameron was back at the lake, and it was just starting to rain. She landed the plane and taxied to the place where she'd dropped off the Lone Ranger, who was predictably nowhere to be seen. She waded ashore with the tether rope after pivoting the plane, and tied off to the nearest stalwart spruce at the edge of the lake. If the lake got rough, she'd have to taxi back out into deep water and drop anchor to protect the floats from damage, but right now it was fairly calm and she was curious to see how far the limping Lone Ranger had walked. She pulled off her waders and laced on her leather hiking boots while sitting on the same rock her passenger had used, then folded over the tops of her waders to keep them dry. She strapped a holstered .44 pistol around her waist, shrugged into her rain gear, switched her ball cap for her broad-brimmed Snowy River hat and shouldered a small backpack she always carried in the plane with her own emergency gear.

It was raining hard now, big drops hammering like bullets onto the lake's surface, each impact creating a small explosion. The sound was deafening. She'd reached the lake just in the nick of time to set the plane down ahead of the bad weather, so she was feeling pretty good about things. This heavy, soaking rain would drown that forest fire once and for all. If it rained hard for two days, all the better. It had been a dry summer.

The Lone Ranger's tracks were quickly being erased by the rain, but they were still easy enough to follow along the shoreline. They made a beeline for the wooded shore on the north side of the headwaters of the Wolf

River. She followed them, intending to walk a few miles or until the wind came up and she had to return to the plane. With his pronounced limp and the rough terrain, she figured she'd catch up to him before too long.

When she saw the tent set up on a small bluff, set back from the edge of the river and not one hundred yards from the headwaters, she came to a surprised halt. For a man whose agenda was to hike nearly eighty miles in eight days, he'd set up camp a good twelve hours early. He could have covered five miles, easy, ten if he pushed hard. It was a blue tent with a darker blue fly, made all the gloomier by the rain, which created such a racket bouncing off the fly she could walk right up to the tent without being heard, so that's what she did.

"Hello the camp!" she said outside the tent's door, which was zipped up tight. There was no response from within. Her sense of uneasiness built. Why had he come out here all by himself? Perhaps he had no intention of walking to the Mackenzie. Maybe this whole trip had been a suicide mission. Had he already done himself in? Was he lying inside the tent, dead? "Hello the camp!" she shouted.

"Hold your horses," a man's voice said, rough with sleep. The door unzipped. He looked out at her, fatigue shadowing his face, and motioned for her to enter. It was a small tent, hardly big enough for the both of them, but she shrugged off her pack, left it in the vestibule created by the fly, and crawled inside on her hands and knees. It was more than a little odd making her way into the Lone Ranger's tent, but it beat conversing in the pouring rain.

His pack and rifle case took up the rear wall. His sleeping bag was laid out. He doubled it onto itself and sat on it, one leg straight out, the other drawn up to his chest. She sat down cross-legged on the sleeping mat. The door of the tent was open, and the dark blur of river tumbling past the door made her dizzy.

"Sorry to bother you, but the weather closed in and I had to turn around," Cameron explained before he could question her unexpected visit. "Since I have to wait out the bad weather, I thought I'd just make sure you were on the right trail."

He grinned wryly at that. They both knew there were no trails except those made by wild animals in this land. "You're wondering why I made camp when there's a good ten hours of daylight left."

Cameron removed her hat, which was dripping water onto the floor of the tent. "None of my business how far and fast you travel," she said. "You can camp wherever and whenever you like."

"I've been on the road three days and drove all night to make the floatplane base first thing this morning after hearing the weather forecast. Figured I had a narrow window of opportunity to get flown in."

"You figured right," she said.

"My plan is to rest up today and get a fresh start in the morning."

"Good plan."

They sat and listened to the rain pounding down on the flimsy tent. Cameron hoped the tent pegs held under the strain. "Well," she said after a long awkward moment, "I'll get back to the plane, and as soon as there's a break in the weather, I'll head home."

"Good plan," he said.

"I probably could've made it okay, but my father always told me that optimism has no place in the cockpit."

"Sound advice."

Once again he'd succeeded in making her feel foolish. Last night at Ziggy's, three men had hit on her while she was playing pool. She could have gone home with any one of them, if that was her game. It wasn't, but she liked knowing that she could have her pick. She enjoyed the attention of men when she wanted it, and was used to flirting, having her drinks paid for, then spurning her admirers, holding them at arm's length and sometimes breaking their hearts. This guy annoyed her. No ring on his finger, not married and not the least bit interested in her. Wanted her to leave so he could go back to sleep.

Cameron pulled on her hat. She loved her Snowy River hat and thought it made her look especially sexy. To most guys, anyway.

"Well, okay then, I'll head back to the plane," she repeated. He made no response.

She crawled back out of the tent and into the torrential downpour, pushed to her feet, gave a small wave to the Lone Ranger and headed back toward the plane. "What a weirdo," she muttered to herself as she trudged away, not sure if she was talking about Jack Parker or herself.

CHAPTER TWO

AFTER SPENDING A miserable cramped night sitting in the plane, sating her hunger with four granola bars and her thirst with water from her kit, Cameron was relieved when morning brought a higher cloud cover, lighter rain and the welcome opportunity to head home. She pumped water out of the plane's pontoons—they both had slow leaks—then pushed the plane into deeper water and hopped back on board. She wondered if the Lone Ranger had already broken camp as the Beaver's pontoons rocked free of the lake and the plane roared into the air. Would he hear her taking off? Was he still asleep or was he already on the trail? What did she care? Why was she even thinking about him?

All she cared about right now was getting some coffee. Not Walt's coffee. His wasn't fit to drink. When she got back, she was heading to the diner. She was going to order a huge plate of ham and eggs and toast and greasy home fries, and a bottomless cup of very strong hot

black coffee. Her stomach growled in antici-
pation. A stiff headwind slowed her progress,
but even so she was taxiing up to the dock by
7:20 a.m. Walt came out to tie off the plane.

"You owe me," she said as she climbed out.
"Big time."

Walt was wearing one of his expressions.
"Listen," he said slowly as they walked down
the dock toward the office. "Got a phone call
yesterday after you left. It was from that guy's
sister. Lori Tedlow was her name. I couldn't
follow her conversation too good, she started
crying, so I told her you'd call her back just as
soon as you returned."

Cameron halted abruptly and rounded on her
boss. "What? I have nothing to tell her. She already knows where he is, right? You told her
where I dropped him off, right? What more
could I add to what she already knows?" She
felt another surge of annoyance at this latest
development.

"She was upset. Crying. You're a woman.
Women are better at handling stuff like that.
She's waiting for your call."

"Walt, I'm starving. I haven't had any coffee, I'm crippled from spending the night in the
plane and I want my bonus money."

"Yeah, I heard you lost a bundle at Ziggy's,
playing pool the other night."

"Hank cheats. So does Slouch." Cameron entered the office, tossed her ball cap on the desk, pulled the band from her ponytail and finger combed her dark shoulder-length hair. "One of these days they'll pay, soon as I figure out how they're doing it. I'm missing way too many easy shots I could make blindfolded when I was twelve."

"I won't be able to get your money till the bank opens. Coffee?" Walt asked, lifting the pot from the hot plate.

"No way. The coffee you make should be banned. I'm going to the diner for a real cup of joe and a big breakfast, and then I'm going to take a long hot shower in my rusty old trailer, and *then* I'm going to come back here and collect my bonus, so you better have it ready. Bank opens at nine. I'll be back at nine thirty sharp."

"If I have your bonus ready, will you make the phone call?" Walt asked hopefully.

"Nope. *You* talk to the Lone Ranger's sister. I'm just the pilot who flies the plane. You're the boss. You get the big bucks for handling all the drama. Tell her he was fine when I left him yesterday. I can't vouch for how he is today. Wet, probably." Cameron pulled her hat on and started for the door.

"I know how Hank and Slouch are fouling your shots," Walt said as she reached for the doorknob. She paused and looked over her shoulder. "If you make that phone call for me, I'll let you in on their dirty little secret."

She hesitated just long enough to make Walt squirm before nodding. "Deal."

TWO HOURS LATER she was back at the floatplane base, clean, well fed and dialing the number Walt had provided her. A woman's voice answered on the third ring, and Cameron studied the words she'd carefully drafted on a paper napkin while she ate her breakfast at the diner.

"Mrs. Tedlow?" she said, speaking slowly. "This is Cameron Johnson. I'm a pilot for Walt's Flying Service, and Walt asked me to call you when I got to the office this morning." She read the words aloud over the phone to the Lone Ranger's sister in Montana. Writing her opening had been clever. She had a tendency to get tongue-tied on the phone, so she'd made extensive notes in preparation for this call.

"Thank you so much for getting back to me, Cameron," the woman replied. "I really appreciate it. I'm afraid I wasn't very coherent when I called yesterday. I apologize for that. I was just so relieved to have finally located my brother. And please, call me Lori."

"Walt understands completely how upset you were yesterday." Cameron shot a glance at Walt, who gave her an encouraging nod and two thumbs up. "He's a very understanding man." She scanned her notes and continued reading. "I just wanted to let you know that I saw your brother yesterday afternoon, and he was just fine. He'd set up camp and was going to get a good night's rest and start his hike today. It's not raining nearly so hard now, so it won't be bad going at all."

"It's raining up there?"

"First real rain we've had all summer, and it was coming down cats and dogs yesterday."

"Oh no!"

"It's not a bad thing. We needed the rain. We've been fighting a big forest fire up here, and thanks to this downpour it's just about out." She was getting way off script. She turned over the napkin and continued reading from her notes. "Your brother told me he was carrying an emergency transmitter, and he's programmed our number into it. If he gets into any trouble at all, we'll get him out. We have good search and rescue up here, what with the park being so close to us and all."

There was a frustrated sound on the other end of the line. "My brother wouldn't signal for help if he was being eaten by a grizzly. He's an army ranger, and they all think they're invincible. Look, Cameron, I'm going to be blunt. He checked himself out of Walter Reed—that's a military hospital near DC. He was in rehab. He was badly wounded in Afghanistan and needs medical supervision and treatment. He can't be wandering around in the wilderness. He has to be brought back before he gets into trouble. He could die out there in the shape he's in."

Cameron shot Walt an exaggerated frown. "I guess I'm not following you. You expect us to find your brother and bring him back? That's not our job."

"I know that, but you have to understand, this is all my fault. I'm to blame. This has to do with his dog."

"This is about a *dog*?"

"I should have told him about his dog last summer after it happened, but I didn't want him to freak out or be distracted when he was still deployed and doing dangerous soldiering stuff. I knew he'd be really angry at me, so I just kept putting it off. I kept lying to him and telling him everything was fine, and then when I went to see him in the hospital last week, I told him what happened and he just…" Her voice squeezed off and ended in a high pitched, mouse-like squeak.

Cameron waited a few moments for the woman to collect herself. She covered the phone and mouthed to Walt, "I bet she's a blonde."

"I'm sorry," Lori continued shakily.

"No need to apologize, Lori. I think I understand the situation. You were taking care of your brother's dog while he was deployed and something bad happened to it, and when you finally told him, he freaked out and took off."

"It's worse than that." She paused, and the sound of her blowing her nose came over the line. "This wasn't just any dog. This dog saved his life in Afghanistan. *Twice.* They featured the story on the national news down here in the States. We held fund-raisers to get the dog home because Jack was so attached to her. It took forever and three thousand dollars, but we finally got her flown back here a year ago last June.

"My fiancé and I had been planning for two years to do this paddling trek in Northwest Territories last July. My mother offered to take care of the dog, but she was really sick from her chemo treatments, so we thought we'd just bring the dog along with us rather than put her in a boarding kennel, you know? She'd gotten to know us and was well behaved. We traveled up where you are to take a canoe trip down the Wolf River to the Mackenzie, and then to Norman Wells." There was a snuffling noise, another squeak or two, and then Lori resumed. "Everything went fine until a huge bear came into our camp on the second night. It walked right in while we were cooking dinner. The dog chased the bear off and she never came back. We waited there awhile, then moved a short distance downriver to get away from our cooking spot and stayed for two days hoping she'd return."

"The bear probably killed her," Cameron said. "Bears don't like dogs very much."

"That's what we figured. Still, we didn't know. Maybe she got lost, couldn't figure out where we went, or maybe she was hurt and just lying out there. We waited for two days, looked around as best we could, then left her there. That's the bottom line. When I told my brother about it in the hospital, he told me to leave. Wouldn't talk to me, he was so upset. It was awful, the worst moment of my life. The next morning when I went back to see him again, he was gone. They told me he got up in the night, got dressed and walked out."

"So now he's up here, searching for a dog that's probably been dead since last summer," Cameron said. *What a cheerful story*, she thought to herself.

"There's more," Lori continued amid another round of sniffling, nose blowing and mousey squeaks. "Like I said, my brother got all shot up in Afghanistan. That's why he was at Walter

Reed. He was wounded four times and lost the lower part of his left leg. He spent the last two months in the hospital. At first they weren't even sure he was going to make it. He was only recently fitted with a prosthesis and had just started physical therapy and rehab."

"I'm sorry to hear that, but I'm not sure how I can help."

"Don't you see? He'll die out there if you don't go get him!"

"*Me?* How'm I supposed to rescue someone who doesn't want to be rescued?"

"He's depressed. There's no telling what he'll do. He probably brought a gun with him, too." Cameron thought about the rifle in the case. "He could be planning to kill himself. Lots of veterans do. Twenty-two veterans commit suicide every single day, *twenty-two*, and I don't want my brother to be one of them. I don't want him to become a statistic because of something I did. This is all my fault. We shouldn't have brought Ky on the canoe trip. We should have put her in a boarding kennel."

"Ky's the name of the dog?"

"Yes." Loud sniff. "That's what he named her because she looks so much like a coyote, but she looks more like a small wolf to me. They have wolves in the mountains of Afghanistan, where he was deployed. He really loved that dog. I mean, she was just a pup when she followed him out of the mountains. She bonded to him, and he got really attached to her."

Cameron gnawed on what was left of her fingernail. All her fingernails were short and chewed. The past year had been a hard one on her nails. Walt moved into her line of sight, eyebrows raised in question. She shook her head and blew out a sigh. "Look, Lori, I'd like to help, but I don't know what I can do. He has an emergency GPS with him. He can signal if he gets into trouble. Tell you what. If you come out here, I'll fly you back to the lake and you could try to catch up with him. He's probably not traveling very fast."

"Believe me, I was going to fly up there yesterday but my husband Clive—we got married last August, right after our canoe trip last summer—said he wouldn't let me go even if I hired a guide because I'm eight months pregnant. I told my brother where the bear came into our camp. It was just above a trapper's cabin on the north shore of the Wolf. It's the only cabin on that entire river."

"Let me guess. You want me to look for your brother there."

"He can't make that kind of walk on a prosthetic leg. No way. He'll die out there. If you could just find him and tell him how sorry I am about his dog and how much he's needed back home, if you can just bring him back out, I'll pay you good money."

"Why don't we give him the eight days he asked for? If he doesn't show up, we can go look for him."

"Because we're afraid he might be suicidal," Lori said. "Eight days is way too long to wait, and besides, there's something else. My mother's really sick. She didn't want him to know how sick she was. She didn't want me to tell him about the cancer. She didn't want him to worry about her while he was in Afghanistan, and then when he got hurt and was shipped stateside, she made me promise not to tell him, but he really needs to know. He has to come home. You have to find him."

Cameron gnawed on another fingernail. "What if he won't come?"

"He will, if you tell him how bad things are with our mother," Lori said. "Will you do it? I'm begging you."

"Why didn't *you* tell him that his mother was so sick when you saw him at the hospital?"

"I was going to, but he got so mad at me when I told him about his dog. He wouldn't even look at me. I couldn't add that awful news to what I'd just told him. I was going to give him time to calm down and tell him when I came to see him the next day, but he'd already gone."

"I don't know how much time I can spare," Cameron hedged. "I have my job to consider."

"Then consider this," Lori said, her voice suddenly all steel with no trace of a mousey squeak or sniffle. "My husband Clive and I have some money in our savings account, money we were going to put toward our baby's college fund, but we'd spend all of it to get Jack back safe and sound. I'll pay you five thousand for getting him off that river and back to a town where we can pick him up, and a generous bonus if you can find him fast enough so we can get him back to Montana just in case my mother takes a turn for the worse. She's holding her own right now, but that could change. What do you say? Do we have a deal?"

Cameron glanced out the window at her rusting eighteen-year-old SUV with its bald tires, badly cracked windshield and crumpled front bumper, thought about the leaks in her rusting house trailer rental, the carpet and furniture that reeked of old cigarette smoke and the moldy ceiling tiles that dropped onto the floor when it rained, and wondered how far into the future five grand would carry her. She thought about Johnny Allen's sexy red Jeep that he'd just listed for sale. She didn't have to think on it for long. "Okay, I'll do it."

After she hung up the phone, she met Walt's questioning expression with a thoughtful frown. "Looks like our Lone Ranger really is a ranger, an army ranger, and I just went from being a bush pilot to a bounty hunter."

CHAPTER THREE

THE FOLLOWING MORNING she and Walt were flying the old red-and-white Beaver through a moderate rainfall back to Kawaydin Lake. Strapped to one of the Beaver's struts was an eighteen-foot beat-up canoe they'd borrowed from one of the villagers. Behind her in the cargo compartment were provisions enough to feed an army for a week. She'd hashed out a reasonable plan for getting the Lone Ranger out to the Mackenzie River where the plane could pick him up. Walt would drop her off at the lake. Cameron would take the canoe down the Wolf River, stopping periodically to check for his tracks, and when she caught up with the wounded soldier, she'd seduce him with the idea of traveling by canoe. She figured he'd be easy to persuade after two days of bushwhacking along the river's edge in the cold rain. By the time she found him, he'd be all over his depressing search for that long dead dog and be ready to head back to soft beds and civilization.

"They're a critical part of my strategy,"

Cameron explained when Walt questioned the amount of high end foods, including several bottles of decent red wine and three pounds of freshly ground Colombian joe.

"You must've shelled out a small fortune on all this fancy food and wine."

"I only spent what I won last night at the pool hall, after shoring up that rotten section of flooring from underneath. Wish you could've seen those two pool sharks trying to make the floor sag and the pool table tilt without being too obvious about it. I skunked 'em in six straight games, made enough for all these groceries and then some.

"This is going to be the easiest money I ever earned," she told Walt. "In four days, I'll have this soldier roped, tied and delivered to his sister and that five grand will be in my bank account."

"Better not spend it all before you earn it," Walt advised her at the lake while helping her load the heavy cooler into the canoe in a cold dreary rain. "You might not find him, and even if you do, he might not want to come out with you."

"Oh, I'll find him, and I'm pretty sure he'll jump at the chance to travel with me." She held up two bottles of wine. "In my experience, men only care about two things. Food and sex, and wine goes good with both."

"Did you bring handcuffs in case your strategy doesn't work?" Walt asked.

"Duct tape," Cameron said, stashing one bottle inside her tent bag, the other inside her sleeping bag duffel, then tucking both into the tight folds to protect them from the river's tossing. "Duct tape works for everything. There's a lot of money riding on this, Walt. You can count on hearing from me in four days."

WITHIN THE HOUR the tethered canoe was loaded, and she was ready to set off. She helped Walt push the plane away from shore, waited while he taxied out onto the lake and then watched him take off and head south into a wet overcast. It was 4:00 p.m. If she started paddling now, she might overshoot the Lone Ranger before dark. Her travel time would be much faster than his, just drifting with the current down the river. The smartest thing might be to spend the night where he had first pitched his tent, then get on the river by dawn before he had a chance to break camp. He'd be easy to spot that way. His tent fly was blue and highly visible, assuming he was camped right at the river's edge. But setting up camp right away would mean just sitting there for hours while the rain came down, waiting for the bears to find her cooler full of goodies and rip it apart.

Maybe she should just plan on deliberately overshooting the Lone Ranger and wait for him to catch up to her. If she spotted him stumbling along the shore while she was drifting effortlessly by, all the better; she'd put ashore slightly downriver of his position to give herself enough time to tidy up, get pretty and pry the cork out of one of the bottles of wine.

Then again, she'd spent a late night at the pool hall, fleecing those cheats Hank and Slouch out of all the money they'd taken from her. Hitting the sack early and drifting off to the soothing sounds of the rushing river and the rain pattering on her tent had a certain appeal. She could always haul her food up into a tree to keep it from the bears.

Whatever she decided to do, the Lone Ranger would eventually drag his bruised and battered body into her cozy comfortable camp, and she'd have him. That much was certain.

WAKING UP WAS the hardest thing; those first few moments between sleep and full consciousness, when reality came back with a sickening rush. Mornings meant remembering over and over again, on a daily basis, all the bad things that had ever happened to him.

Mornings meant losing his friends all over again. Mornings meant losing his leg all over again. Mornings meant looking at that alien contraption that now substituted for his lower left leg, lying within arm's reach on the damp tent floor. Mornings meant fitting the socket carefully over the liner and socks covering the stump of his left leg, those eight inches remaining below the knee. Mornings meant pain. The stump was raw and inflamed from yesterday's long struggle, and even after adjusting the number of socks over the liner, the suspension socket went on hard. It was a routine he'd never once imagined would be a part of every morning for the rest of his life, but he knew he was one of the lucky ones. He'd seen plenty of soldiers less fortunate.

He could hear the river rushing past, the light drumming of rain on the tent's fly. He could smell the damp earth and the resiny tang of spruce, the wetness of his gear. The rain would keep the insects down, but a few more days of it and his gear would be moldering. He lay back on his sleeping bag until his breathing and heart rate had steadied. Then he did situps. Fifty of them. Numbering each one under his breath. He used to do one hundred effortlessly. Now he could barely manage fifty. He needed to get fit because he was going back to

Afghanistan, and he was going back as a fully functioning soldier. When he was done with the sit-ups, he rolled over and did push-ups.

The pain was everywhere. There was no place he didn't hurt, but he had learned to ignore it, to live with it. They'd given him drugs for the pain at Walter Reed, but the drugs had messed up his head. He preferred the pain. It kept him focused. He needed to stay focused on his mission.

He had to find Ky because he knew she was alive. He knew this as surely as he knew that he was alive, even though by all rights they should both be dead. He'd allotted himself eight days to find her, but he'd take twice that if he had to. He wasn't going to leave here without her.

He rolled over, sat up, reached for his pack and dragged it toward him. Inside were his provisions, and they were minimal. Dried food, first aid and personal supplies, spare clothing, tool kit, his four-pound spare prosthesis. He pulled out a protein bar and ate it, drank the water he'd purified last night. Shifted enough to open the tent door so he could see the river. Yesterday's progress had been slow. The water levels were high from the rain, and any shoreline he might have been able to walk on was underwater. He'd had to bushwhack inland, away from the choking tangle of alder and willow that grew along the river. Each step was a conscious effort, a struggle. He'd only recently been fitted with his prosthesis. The specialist at the rehab center had told him he'd need weeks of physical therapy to learn to use it properly.

He much preferred the physical therapy of the wilderness. If he hadn't learned to use the damn thing after eighty miles of rough walking, they could have it back and he'd whittle himself a peg leg. He figured he'd barely made three miles yesterday, three long hard and painful miles, which left seventy-seven more ahead of him, but he wasn't going to look that far ahead.

One step at a time was the measure of all journeys.

Breakfast over, he zipped on his left pant leg, laced the leather hiking boot on his right foot and called himself fully dressed. The cargo pants with removable legs had been a good investment. They were made of a lightweight, tough and fast-drying cloth. He could get the prosthesis off easily at day's end, and even if he slept in the rain-wet pants, they dried quickly. Taking his kit, he crawled out of the tent and into the drizzle. He made his way to the river's edge, crouched and splashed water on his face, washed his hands, brushed his teeth, finger combed his close-cropped hair. Didn't bother to shave. Nobody to scare with his five o'clock shadow. Stuffing everything back into his kit, he was about to return to camp when movement on the river caught his eye.

A canoe came around the bend from upriver, a battered red canoe with one person seated in the stern, using the paddle as a rudder.

For a moment he could scarcely credit what he was seeing, because this early in the morning and in this wilderness setting he shouldn't be seeing anything even remotely human. But as the canoe drew closer, he knew beyond a shadow of doubt that the person in the stern was that same girl who'd flown him out to the lake. The girl who'd looked too young to be driving a car, let alone flying a big bush plane in the far north. There was no mistaking that Aussie hat and the slender boyish figure that not even the orange life jacket could hide.

Before he could rise to his feet she spotted him, and he caught the flash of a smile. "Good morning!" Her cheerful greeting floated loud and clear over the rush of the river and the patter of rain. "Fancy meeting you here!"

She ferried the canoe across the strong, swift current like a voyageur, paddling with short strokes from the waist and using her upper body for leverage. It was pretty obvious she knew what she was doing in a canoe. She came toward him at a good clip, and was almost to shore when the canoe fetched up hard against a hidden rock, swung broadside to the current, spun backward in a tight arc around the submerged rock, backed hard into the downstream eddy and pitched sideways, spilling her into the river with a loud, undignified squawk.

To her credit she came up swiftly, paddle in hand. She flung the paddle onto the riverbank, grabbed the nose of the canoe and began hauling it ashore. The river swept her along, but within ten yards she got her footing and lurched backward out of the water, both hands clamped to a snub line fastened to the nose of the canoe. By the time he reached her, she had things pretty much under control, but the canoe had taken on water and was heavily loaded with gear, securely lashed in place or it would have been floating down the river. She was having trouble finding a spot to haul the canoe out. She had her heels braced against the pull of the river, and tossed the slack coils of rope to him when he came near.

"Tie her off to something, anything," she ordered. "And hurry, this current's strong." She struggled to keep it from ripping the canoe out of her grasp.

He plowed through the dense tangle of alder and willow with the rope, hauled himself up the bank, found a black spruce that looked up to the task and snubbed off to it. When he returned to the river, she was watching for him over her shoulder.

"Okay?" she said.

"Okay."

She relaxed her grip on the rope, and the canoe remained obediently tethered to shore. She was soaking wet from her swim and out of breath from the struggle to hold the canoe. Her hands flew to her head, then she stood staring downriver, stricken with shock.

"You all right?" he asked from the riverbank. "Did you hit your head?"

"I lost my Snowy River hat. I loved that hat." She stared downriver through a veil of rain, as if it might be floating just out of reach or stuck on an overhanging branch. Her shoulders slumped, she dropped her hands and looked back at him. "I didn't see that rock. I was too busy looking at you. Stupid of me. Now I'll have to unload the canoe and bail it out."

"When you're done bailing, my camp's just a few yards upriver. Coffee's on."

Her expression brightened. "Thanks," she said.

He made his way back to the camp. The coffee was boiling over. He shut off the little multi-fuel stove and poured himself a cup. A part of him felt guilty not staying to help with the job of unloading the canoe, but he was equally annoyed that she'd invaded his morning and literally crashed his party uninvited. What was she doing here? It obviously had something to do with him, and he didn't like that one bit.

Forty minutes later she tramped into his campsite. Her hair had come loose from the ponytail and was dripping with river and rainwater. She crawled into his tiny tent on her hands and knees, and took the insulated cup he offered with a grateful smile. She sat crosslegged and inhaled the steam.

"Thanks. This smells like real cowboy coffee."

"It'll float a spoon," he said.

"Just how I like it." She took a sip. "Perfect." Her eyes were as dark as her hair, fringed with thick lashes. Her face was slender, cheekbones high, lips curved in a smile. In the dim confines of the tent, after that plunge in the icy river and the mighty struggle with the canoe, she should have looked like a scrawny wet rat, not a sexy Abercrombie and Fitch fashion model.

"Why are you here?" he said, blunt and to the point.

She shook her head, took another swallow of coffee. "My boss dropped me off up at the lake so I could canoe downriver and deliver a message from your sister." She ran the fingers of one hand through her wet shoulder-length hair, sweeping it back from her face, and gazed at him frankly. "She's very worried about you. I spoke with her by phone yesterday. She told me what happened to your dog, and she feels bad about it."

He made no comment. He had nothing to say about his dog or his sister. His life was none of her business.

"She wanted me to tell you how sorry she was that she didn't tell you right away, when she got back from the canoe trip last summer, and she wanted me to try to make you understand that the reason she didn't tell you when you were in Afghanistan was because she was afraid you'd be upset by the bad news, and you'd get hurt because you were distracted."

He pulled his pack toward him and began stuffing his sleeping bag into the bottom compartment.

"I mean, I can understand how bad your sister feels," she continued. "And I can tell you, she was genuinely upset on the phone. She wanted me to find you and bring you out by canoe. She also said to tell you that your mother is really sick, and you need to come home right away."

"My mother's fine. I talked to her on the phone every day while I was at Walter Reed. I talked to her the day before you flew me out here, and she was fine. She'd have come to visit me herself when I was in the hospital, but she's afraid of flying. My sister just told you to tell me she was real sick to get me to quit looking for a dog she thinks is dead. She feels guilty about leaving Ky out here, and she should. How much did my sister's rich banker husband of hers offer you to find me?" he asked, not pausing in his work.

"I don't know what you mean," Cameron said.

"Sure you do," he said. "You've wasted your time, and now you're wasting mine."

She finished the coffee in the mug and sat dripping quietly onto his tent floor. "I figured that's what you'd say, but I promised her I'd try." She watched him in silence for a few moments. "Listen, I could help you look for the dog. We could travel downriver until noon, beach the canoe, then I could walk back to this campsite, looking for tracks while you set up camp. We'd cover a lot more ground that way."

"Tracks?" His flinty gaze locked with hers. "You know as well as I do there's no tracking anything along this shoreline. Right now this journey is all about leaving my scent and hoping Ky gets downwind of it."

"Well, leaving a scent trail won't work worth a damn until it stops raining," she said. Her eyes dropped from his, and after a brief pause she scrambled out the door and went down to the river. He watched her crouch there and wash the metal mug. His guts were churning. His sister shouldn't have put either of them in this awkward position. It wasn't the young pilot's fault that she'd been sent on an impossible mission. He shouldn't take his anger out on her. He finished packing his gear. The only thing left to do was pack up the tent, lash it to his pack and keep walking.

CAMERON TOOK HER time washing the mug, reflecting on her next move. His hostile response to her arrival hadn't been unexpected. What she hadn't anticipated was ramming the canoe into that submerged rock, getting all her gear wet and making a fool of herself, but that wasn't altogether a bad thing. At least she'd found him, and rather easily, in fact. The rest of her job would be much simpler. It was just a matter of wearing him down, and the rough country would do that for her.

By the time she returned to the campsite, he'd taken down and packed up the soggy tent, donned his rain gear, shouldered his pack and picked up his rifle. They faced each other, separated by five feet of steady rainfall. "Thanks for the coffee," she said, handing him his mug. "I'll be heading downriver as soon as I get the canoe repacked."

"Good," he said.

"There's a trapper's cabin about a day's easy paddle from here. Maybe twenty miles, by my calculations. That's near the place where the bear came into your sister's camp. I figure that's the best place to start searching, so I'm going to find that camp, off-load most of my gear and wait for you there. You're welcome to join me right now. We could make day trips up and down the river from there."

"Walking this river's my best shot at finding her, and I prefer to do it alone."

"Suit yourself." She stuck out her hand. "My name's Cameron Johnson, by the way. I don't believe we've ever been formally introduced."

It took him a moment, but he returned the gesture. His hand clasp was brief and firm. "Jack Parker."

"I have a satellite phone in my canoe, if you want to call your sister and ask her how your mother's doing."

"I don't."

"Suit yourself."

She turned on her heel and retraced her path back to the canoe, where her small mountain of gear was piled untidily on the rough bank. The canoe, relieved of the weight of water and provisions, was safely hauled up on shore. She slid it back into the water, secured snub lines front and rear to the most stalwart of alders, and commenced repacking. There was a skill to packing a canoe, and Cameron knew it well. It took her less than thirty minutes to accomplish the task and lash the gear securely. During that time, she'd rethought her plan of action.

The wind was shifting out of the west. By nightfall the rain would have stopped, and she'd have a chance to dry out her gear. In the meantime, she'd drift downriver four, maybe five miles and set up camp in as nice a spot as she could find. She'd build a good cook fire, plan a hearty supper, get things ready for his arrival, then walk back upriver to meet him. She had three more days to land her man, but in spite of them getting off on the wrong foot, she didn't think it would take nearly that long.

THE RAIN STOPPED before noon and the wind picked up, shredding the heavy overcast and providing brief, promising glimpses of blue sky. Jack had made poor progress. The walking was so rough along this stretch he'd had to bushwhack farther inland than the day before. At one point he'd gotten so turned around in the thick undergrowth he'd had to pull out his compass and take a bearing to navigate back to the river. The protein bar he'd eaten for breakfast had long since burned off, and he was hungry. He found a fallen log to sit on and ate another protein bar between swallows of water. His leg was really sore, but he didn't see the point in examining it. There was nothing he could do except clean it well at night and keep the socks and liner as clean and dry as possible. The doctors had told him it was going to take some time to get used to the prosthetic limb, and adjustments would need to be made. This was just part of the breaking-in period and it was bound to be painful.

During his lunch break, the mosquitoes arrived in a hungry swarm and had him rummaging in his pack for gloves and mosquito netting. The netting had an elastic hem, and he pulled it over his hat and down onto his shoulders. The gloves were leather gauntlets. The swarm would have to find their lunch elsewhere. He rested only ten minutes, then pushed off the log and continued his journey downriver.

CHAPTER FOUR

CAMERON'S CAMPING SPOT was picture perfect, situated on a raised point of land overlooking the river. A nice breeze kept the blackflies and mosquitoes at bay, and a stately spruce with a sturdy branch about ten feet up provided the anchor point for the peak of her tent, making the pole unnecessary. Along the river's edge, she gathered enough partially dry driftwood to build a fine campfire come evening. On the downriver side of the peninsula, she'd beached the canoe in a calm backwater eddy. Because the river curved around this point of land, the site offered good visibility both upriver and down.

Cameron felt quite pleased with the efficient way she'd set up camp. She took her time because there was no hurry. She built a functional stone fire ring for cooking, then erected her thirteen-pound center-pole Woods Canada nine-foot-by-nine-foot tent with its deluxe midge-proof screening on the doors and windows, blew up the thick air mattress, laid her sleeping bag atop it and set the novel she was reading on her pillow next to her little LED headlamp. It was a very homey nest and something to look forward to, come bedtime, plus it was plenty big enough for two people, which might end up being a distinct possibility if she played her cards right.

Gathering kindling from the nearby woods, she laid the fire in the ring then set up two camp chairs flanking it. When all was completed, she stood back to admire the campsite. Everything was shipshape, almost as if she did this on a daily basis. Almost as if she knew what she was doing. The thought made her laugh out loud.

FOR LUNCH SHE fixed herself a peanut butter and jelly sandwich and ate it sitting in a camp chair, admiring the river views. The sun swept out briefly, warmed her skin then vanished behind scudding clouds. Amazing how just a little dose of sunshine bolstered the spirits. She finished her sandwich and drank some tea from the thermos she'd filled the day before. The tea was still vaguely warm, strong and delicious. Earl Grey.

Afterward she sat with her kit in her lap, pulled out the small mirror, leaned it against the backrest of the second chair and brushed then braided her hair. She deftly applied eye-liner and mascara, some lipstick, a little foundation to hide the freckles over the bridge of her nose. It took minutes and completely transformed her. She smiled approvingly at her image. "Not bad."

She had earlier contemplated taking a post-prandial siesta but decided to scout upriver instead, in order to see how much ground the Lone Ranger had covered, how far he had left to travel and then figure out when to plan supper for his arrival. The wine, a nice organically grown 2011 Les Hauts de Lagarde Bordeaux, really should breathe awhile before being served.

She checked the pistol on her hip, pulled on her ball cap and shouldered her day pack. Hiking would feel good after being cramped in the canoe. A few hours should be plenty of time to find Jack Parker and shepherd him back here. She hadn't come that far downriver from where she last saw him. She checked her watch and started out.

TWENTY MINUTES INTO the upriver slog, she stopped to don her mosquito netting. Once away from the river and the breeze, the bugs were fierce. She'd already inhaled enough to qualify as an appetizer before supper. She was sweating from exertion. Her eyes stung from the makeup. Everything she brushed against was wet. Rainwater still dripped from the spruce trees, and having left her rain gear at camp, she was soon as drenched as she'd been after her morning swim, and the temperature was dropping.

The walking was tough, but she'd known it would be. She didn't bother looking for signs of a lost dog because she knew that Ky was long dead, and searching for a dead dog, as far as she was concerned, was a complete waste of time.

One hour into the hike, she paused for a break. She should have found Jack by now. Even with the tough going she was probably covering at least a couple miles an hour, and he had to have made two miles since leaving his camping spot. It was entirely possible she could have missed him. They were both bushwhacking inland, away from the river, and the undergrowth was thick. Maybe he'd reach the campsite before she did.

She beat her way out to the river to get her bearings and was grabbing two handfuls of alder branches to steady herself on the riverbank when she heard the whistle from upriver. At first she thought she might be hearing the wild, territorial whoop of a pileated woodpecker, but then she heard it again. Definitely not a woodpecker, and ravens made all kinds of noises, but that wasn't one of them.

Was the Lone Ranger signaling for help?

She balanced herself carefully, released her grip on the alders, pushed up her mosquito netting and returned the finger whistle with a high-pitched, shrill one of her own. She thrashed through the alders and moved away from the riverbank where the walking was easier and the sound of the rushing river not so loud. She took off the mosquito netting and stuffed it into her jacket pocket, rearranged her hat, smoothed her wet hair. Then she whistled again, just in case he hadn't heard the first signal. In this whistle she tried to convey a calm reassuring signal that she'd soon be there. *No need to panic. Help is on its way.*

There was no response to her second whistle, which was odd.

Cameron waited a few moments, then pushed onward. It wasn't long before she spotted him working his way slowly along with his backpack and rifle case, and wearing a veil of mosquito netting pulled over his hat. She had to get pretty close before she could read his expression behind the netting. He didn't seem too pleased to see her, but she was getting used to that. He most certainly didn't look panicked.

"I heard your whistle, and I thought you might be in trouble," she said.

"I'm not."

"Do you always whistle when you walk?"

"Isn't there someplace else you'd rather be?" he asked.

"Not particularly. I haven't had a vacation in years. It's a beautiful day, and I'm enjoying myself. It's nice to get out of the canoe and walk a bit."

"Then maybe you should turn around and walk back to your canoe."

Cameron blew out her breath. "Look, all I'm trying to do is help you out. You're looking for the dog, I'm looking for the dog. If we both look, that's twice the search power."

"The only thing you're looking for is to make some money."

She started to voice her indignation and inhaled a mosquito instead. By the time she'd coughed the insect out of her lung, he'd walked past her and continued on his journey. She turned and followed after him, fumbling her mosquito netting back out of her jacket pocket and spitting out pieces of wings and proboscis.

"I've set up camp about a mile downstream from here," she said, pulling the netting over her head. She was past the point of trying to look sexy. "It's a real nice spot, good breeze, no bugs, high and dry. I've got a couple steaks marinating and a nice bottle of wine ready to go."

"They must be paying you a lot of money." He didn't turn around when he spoke, just kept moving forward at that slow steady pace.

"Your sister's worried you might be suicidal."

"If I was going to commit suicide, would I torture myself first by trying to walk down this river?"

"How should I know? I've never been able to figure out why men do the things they do," Cameron said, adjusting the netting over the brim of her hat. "My ex-husband was a complete mystery to me."

He paused and half turned toward her. "I came out here to find out what happened to my dog. That's all."

"What if you don't find him?"

"*Her.* I plan to keep looking until I do. She's out here somewhere. She wasn't killed by that bear. Hurt, maybe, but not killed. She was wild when I found her in Afghanistan, and she knows how to survive. She's a fighter. She's smart and she's tough. I came out here to find her and bring her home, and that's what I'm going to do."

He resumed walking with his stiff, awkward

limp. She matched his pace, keeping three steps behind. "Where's home?"

"Northern Montana. A place near Bear Butte, on the Flathead Reservation."

"Aha! No wonder you're so tough. You're not only the Lone Ranger, you're Tonto."

"Just because you live on the rez doesn't make you an Indian. Whites can own land there. The *Allotment Act* of 1904 gave every Flathead Indian a certain amount of land on the reservation. The rest of the reservation land was sold off to whites in a typical government scam, half a million acres. One of the settlers who bought a holding was my great-grandfather. He married a Kootenai girl and had a bunch of kids. My mother has the place now, but it's falling down around her. She should just give it back to the Indians. It rightfully belongs to them."

"But you're part Kootenai, so that makes it your home, too."

"I only call it home because I was born and raised there."

"You said when you find your dog you're going to bring her back there, so it's more than just the place you were born. You must want to go back."

He kept walking and didn't respond.

"What about your army career?" Cameron

asked after a respectful interlude of silence. "Don't you have to go back and finish that up first? How many years have you been a ranger in the army?"

"How many years were you married?" came his curt reply.

"Too many," Cameron said, ignoring the jab. "Getting married to Roy was a big mistake. He liked women. All women. He said he liked me best, but I got sick of sharing him with all the others about a year after saying 'I do.' I didn't know what I was agreeing to when I said my vows. How could I cherish and honor someone who was screwing around with every willing female north of 60?"

Each step was a study of caution, navigating the tangle of underbrush, fallen branches and mossy logs.

"Anyhow," she continued, "Roy was a real sweet talker. He could charm the pelt off an ermine. My father raised me while working in a string of backcountry sporting camps, so I was brought up among men, but those men were all too respectful to be anything but polite to me.

"Then along came Roy. He was hired by the same big outfitter me and my daddy were working for at the time, so that's how I met him. He was flying trophy hunters and fishermen into the bush, same as we were. Roy was dashing and handsome, and he was the first man who made me feel pretty. He told me I had a smile that could light up New York City. I think I fell in love with Roy on our very first date. He took me to the village dump so we could watch the bears pawing through garbage, but that was just an excuse to get me alone in his pickup truck. He was the first man who ever kissed me, and holy boys, could Roy ever kiss."

"How would you know?"

"How would I know what?"

"How would you know Roy could really kiss if he was the first man who ever kissed you?"

Cameron laughed at the silly question. "Either a man can kiss or he can't, and any female worth her salt can tell the difference between a good kisser and a bad one right off the bat. She doesn't have to kiss a thousand men to know something as simple as that. Anyhow, I finally figured out how Roy got so good at kissing, and when he wouldn't give up his philandering ways after we got married, I divorced him. I suppose we'll run into each other from time to time, we're both still bush pilots flying in the north country, but I won't be kissing him, that's for sure. I've learned my lesson."

"Where's your father now?"

Cameron focused hard on the ground at her

feet. "Oh, Daddy flew his plane into a mountainside about a month after I got married. He was a real good pilot, careful. It was an unexpected turn of real bad weather, rotten luck and mechanical failure that killed him."

"I'm sorry."

"Me, too," she said. It still twisted her up inside to talk about it. She guessed it always would. "Were you ever married?"

"Nope."

"Smart."

He was having more and more trouble getting his leg over obstacles. Finally he stopped. "You go on ahead. I'm just slowing you down."

"Tell you what," she said. "I'll go start the cook fire. You can't miss the camp. Just follow the river. It's not much farther. We're almost there."

Cameron took it as a very good sign that he didn't put up any argument about sharing her camp. It had been a hard slog, and he was ready for a break. They both were.

This was only day two, and things were working out just the way she'd planned.

By THE TIME he reached the camp, the sun was angling into the west. Cameron had started the campfire and opened the bottle of wine. The steaks were nicely marinated, the potatoes were all dressed and wrapped in aluminum foil jackets, ready to be nestled into the coals, and she'd made a salad, courtesy of the well-stocked cooler. Best of all, the breeze was still stiff enough to keep the bugs down. She had removed her mosquito netting, changed into dry clothes and touched up her makeup. The stage was set.

He didn't say anything when he arrived at the camp site, just looked around, laid his rifle case down, shrugged out of his pack and dropped into one of the folding camp chairs. He pushed the mosquito netting back over the top of his hat and sat there, looking completely wrung out. Cameron poured a glass of the bordeaux into one of the fancy polycarbonate nesting wineglasses that were a wedding gift she'd never used, and handed it to him, then poured a second glass for herself and sat in the other chair.

They gazed at each other across the small cook fire, which was already settling into a nice bed of coals. She took a small sip of wine, wondering what she should say. His pant legs were soaked from walking through the wet brush, and she wondered if he had a dry pair in his pack. She wondered if she should suggest that he change into dry clothing because the evening was shaping up to be a chilly one.

She pondered why she was wondering if she should say these things when normally she would just say them. She'd never been bashful when it came to speaking her mind, and Walt had told her more than once that she was downright bossy, yet all she could do was sit with her wineglass clasped in both hands and watch him and wonder what to say.

"I have a plan," she blurted out, startling herself because she hadn't thought to speak aloud, not while he was looking at her that way. He raised his wineglass and took a taste, still watching her over the small campfire.

"You give me the clothes you're wearing," Cameron continued, "I put them in my laundry sack, and tomorrow morning first thing I take them down to the trapper's cabin. I'll leave them there, hanging all around the outside of the cabin. Then I come back up here, pick you up and we leapfrog our way back to the cabin. You can walk a bit, or I can drag something of yours and do all the walking while you take the canoe. We'll cover a lot more ground and lay a good scent trail that way. If your dog survived that run-in with the bear, chances are she stayed in the area. That cabin is the only human structure along this whole river. She'll pick up your scent and home in on it."

He took another swallow of wine. His eyes never left her face.

"My daddy had a couple hunting dogs when I was little," she said. "Bang and Vixen. Every once in a while they'd run off on a hot trail, and when they hadn't come back by dark he'd leave his wool jacket there on the ground. Sure enough when he went back the next day those beagles were right there by his jacket, waiting for him."

She set her wineglass on a flat stone, put another chunk of driftwood on the fire, raked out a bed of coals, nestled the potatoes on it and covered them with more coals. "I hope you like steak and potatoes," she said. "That's tonight's special." She used a piece of driftwood to nudge the live fire to one side of the fire ring, then laid the grill over the narrower end and the exposed bed of coals. "I won't do a dirty steak, don't like the grit. I prefer throwing steaks on a hot grill." She rose to her feet, fetched the bottle of wine and topped off his glass. "There's an old saying, 'Wine gives strength to weary men,'" she said. "Sometimes when I'm really tired, the only thing that gives me the strength to cook and eat my evening meal is sipping a glass of wine first. That's good wine, isn't it?"

She sat back down in her chair, cradling her own glass. "Bet I could catch us a char for breakfast right off this point when the sun sets." She gazed out at the river. "See that riffle halfway across? Right below it. Bet there's a beauty or two just laying there in that back eddy. Do you like trout? Rolled in cornmeal and fried in bacon fat, it's the best breakfast ever." She took a taste of the wine and congratulated herself for choosing so well.

"Roy didn't like fish," she continued. "He liked to catch them, but he wouldn't eat them. How can anyone trust a man who won't eat a wild caught trout?" She stretched her legs toward the fire, flexed her ankles and admired her L.L.Bean hunting boots. "These Bean boots are good boots for this kind of travel," she said. "They sure are good for tramping in the woods and canoeing. If I'm lucky, I can get four months out of a pair."

She cast a covert glance from beneath her eyelashes. Was he falling asleep on her? She pushed out of her chair, retrieved the steaks from the cooler and laid them on the hot grill. The steaks hissed. Fragrant smoke curled up from the bed of coals. "Maybe you could tell me a little something about your dog," she said. "Like how you found her in Afghanistan."

He shifted in his chair, pulled off his hat and laid it on his knee. "I didn't find her," he said. "She found me."

CHAPTER FIVE

SHE FOUND HIM in the Hindu Kush, in the rugged mountains along the Pakistan border. He was on advance patrol, the only American in the group of four. They were scouting for a possible Taliban training camp in some of the roughest, wildest mountains they'd been in north of Hatchet. For over a week they'd had little contact with the outposts to the south, and they'd been unable to find the rumored camp. He kept to himself when they bivouacked that night, preferring to keep his own company. Ever since the outpost attack at Bari Alai, he hadn't really trusted Afghan soldiers.

He ate a cold MRE, drank from his water bottle, eased the small of his back against the side of the mountain. The sunset illuminated a jagged wall of snow-covered peaks to the west. If he hadn't been living so long in this place of war, he would have thought this country was beautiful, but it was hard to admire the mountains when each and every day was a struggle of straight up or straight down, carrying gear that weighed close to seventy-five pounds, and wondering when and from where the next attack might come, and if he would survive it.

There was enough light remaining to work on a letter to his mother he'd been writing for the past week. He pulled it out of his pocket along with the pen, used his thigh as a paper rest and added a few sentences. "These mountains at sunset remind me of home. If this war ever ends, I could be looking right at the future ski and snowboard capital of Pakistan. Hindu Kush could become a popular tourist trap. This mountain range is part of the Himalayas, and the mountains are rugged and wild. Hard traveling. We camp when we can go no farther."

He could hear the three Afghan soldiers talking and laughing quietly, and he could smell pot on the faint updraft. They smoked it every night in spite of rules and regulations.

"Ask Danforth for help with the haying this summer," he wrote. "Offer him half the crop if he'll cut it all and put your half in the barn for you. That should be enough for you to winter what's left of the cattle and horses. Use the money I sent you to cover the missing mortgage payments. I'll send more next month. The bank shouldn't be hounding you like that. Clive should keep that from happening. Never mind what Otis Small tells you about anything.

Otis likes to stir up trouble. Keep counsel with Kootch. He'll steer you straight every time."

A high yelp of pain jerked his head up. All three Afghan soldiers were picking up stones and flinging them down the slope at a running animal. There was another yelp as another stone struck home and tumbled a leggy dark-colored creature head over heels. It ran off and vanished. It looked like a dog.

"Knock it off," he commanded just loud enough for them to hear.

The Afghan soldiers laughed, but the stones fell from their fingers and the fleeing animal escaped. Dogs weren't treated as pets in this country, and they weren't treated kindly. Sometimes they were used for target practice. In Kabul, herding dogs were used for dog fighting, their tails and ears cut off at a young age. They ran in packs, usually, and struggled for survival.

Jack returned to his letter home, and with what little remained of the daylight, finished it. He was folding it to slip back into his pocket when he noticed movement to his right. His eyes focused on a pair of canid eyes watching him from a clump of brush in the mountainside, perhaps twenty feet distant. The eyes were dark and wary. The animal's coloring, thick fur, pointed muzzle and upright ears gave it the appearance of a western coyote or brush wolf. He thought it might be the same animal the Afghan soldiers had been stoning, and his hunch was proved correct when the animal moved a few steps and he saw that it was limping.

It was just a pup, maybe four months old, with that big-pawed, leggy clumsiness that had made it such an easy mark for the stone-throwing Afghans. Hip bones and ribs jutted through thick fur. It was starving. Jack reached inside his jacket and pulled out a strip of jerky. He tossed it toward the pup, who vanished the moment he raised his arm but reappeared moments later to snatch up the piece of beef. It disappeared again temporarily, then peeked warily from cover. He tossed a second strip of jerky.

There was only one reason he could think of that a stray pup would be on this mountainside. The Taliban and insurgents often used packs of dogs in their camps as an early-warning system. It was highly probable they were near an enemy training camp. In fact, one might be just over the next ridge, and this half-wild pup may have strayed from there. He glanced to where the Afghan soldiers lounged with their pipes, and a few moments later, moving in a crouch and carrying his weapon, he joined them and shared his observations with Maruf.

"Could be," the senior platoon leader agreed, nodding. "Tomorrow we will find out."

"I'm going up the ridge now, under cover of dark," Jack told them. "You stay put. Post a guard. I'll have a look into the next valley."

He left the radio with them, a decision he was later to regret, then stashed his pack carefully beneath a clump of mountain brush. With the last of the fading light, he picked an almost vertical path up the mountainside, moving from cover to cover. At one point, the slope became so steep he was crawling upward on his hands and knees. By the time he'd ascended to the top of the ridge line, a good half mile above where he left the Afghan soldiers, he was sweating profusely and struggling to catch his breath in the thin air.

He moved cautiously forward in the gloaming, keenly attuned to any sounds or movements that would have hinted at the enemy's presence, but there was just the cooling sweep of wind from the glaciated mountains to the east. The wind was not in his favor, but it shifted as darkness thickened. He flattened himself on the rough, stony ground and looked through his night scope into the deep valley below him.

A jolt of adrenaline quickened his pulse when he spotted several small mud-walled houses at least one mile distant. Tents flanked both sides of a small river that divided the narrow valley. There were twelve tents in all, and three buildings. Unbelievable that way out here in this impossible terrain he'd find a Taliban training camp. The rumors had been true.

Excitement coursed through him. It was too dark to return to his men, so he crawled back down as far as he dared in near darkness, then spent an uncomfortable night beneath the sheltering foliage of a big clump of vegetation, dozing off and on, uneasy with the noises that seemed to originate from every direction. The loose rattle of a stone, the sudden tug of wind hissing through brush, the faint murmuring from the distant river. Every small noise brought him from the edge of sleep to a state of instant adrenaline-fueled alertness, but there was no attack. No swarm of insurgents creeping stealthily over the ridge line to knife or shoot him in his sleep.

As soon as there was enough light to move, he returned to his former position. His pack was where he'd stashed it. The three Afghan soldiers were sleeping in a row where he'd left them sitting the night before. No guard posted. That sort of careless behavior could get them all killed, and he felt a surge of anger at their flouting of his orders. He checked the coordinates of his position in the GPS unit inside his pack. All he had to do now was rouse the Afghan soldiers and radio those coordinates to his commanding officer. The scouting mission would be a success, and the Taliban encampment would be eliminated within hours.

Jack shrugged into his pack and descended toward the sleeping Afghan soldiers. His furtive approach went completely undetected. As he drew near, he paused uneasily, focused hard and realized with a jolt of shock that they weren't sleeping. They were dead. Their throats had been cut and their weapons, packs and his radio had been taken. He scouted carefully before moving closer, and for a few moments he crouched beside them, assessing how much time had passed since they'd been killed. Several hours at least, long enough for them to stiffen. Those noises he'd heard last night had not been his imagination. He was a dead man, too, if they caught him out in the open like this after sunup.

Crouching low and hugging the cover of brush, he raced the sunrise and angled down the steep slope toward the river valley far below, where he would find better cover. He moved slow enough to keep rocks from tumbling noisily down the slope, fast enough to make his thigh muscles cramp and burn. At every moment he expected a bullet to slam into him and push him into the abyss.

He was well over thirty miles north of a friendly outpost, and that mileage was measured in straight line distance. He knew from experience how hard mountain miles could be. The valleys were easier to travel but more dangerous in terms of potentially hostile encounters, and hostiles were all around him. Still, there were brown trout in that river, and timbered forests and drinking water, all powerful incentives for taking the risk. He had no other options, really.

In two hours of furtive travel, he'd gained the cover of the timber, and another hour later the river. There had been no sign of the enemy, no hint that his presence had been detected. Perhaps they thought the scouting patrol had consisted of only the three Afghan soldiers. He'd cut no fresh human sign, not even down near the river. When it became too dark to travel farther, he found a place to hole up, away from the river, tucked back into the slope in a shallow cave created when a big pine toppled toward the water. The massive tree truck gave him good cover in front. Nobody could sneak up on him from behind and cut his throat.

He shrugged out of his pack, took a long drink of water from his bottle and pulled out an MRE. He was halfway through eating it when he lifted his gaze and realized, after a few beats, that he was gazing straight into the eyes of that same stray pup he'd encountered the evening before. The pup was flattened beneath the brush to the right of the tree trunk, blending nearly perfectly with its surroundings. Its ears were erect, muzzle pointing toward him, eyes bright and wary. He took a scoop of food onto his fork and flipped it toward the pup, who waited several long moments before darting out, snatching the mouthful of food and retreating.

Jack was uneasy knowing that the pup had followed him all day and he hadn't spotted it. The sky above him had been active with large birds, but he'd seen nothing on the ground, and he'd been checking his back trail continuously. Had he missed the enemy, too? He finished the MRE, sharing every other mouthful with the pup, who darted out immediately and snatched it off the ground. He could have eaten another meal, but there was a long journey ahead. He rummaged in the pack for the GPS unit and calculated his position. He was a little over twenty miles from the outpost. He'd only made ten straight line miles since finding his dead soldiers. Twenty more miles didn't seem that far, but when moving carefully and trying to avoid detection, those miles would be long and slow.

He slipped the GPS onto his belt next to his water bottle, wanting to keep it near. He was exhausted but unable to relax. He rested sitting up, using his pack for a backrest, draping his sleeping bag over his shoulders like a blanket and cradling his weapon in his lap. He closed his eyes but knew he wouldn't sleep. He couldn't get the image of those three dead Afghan soldiers out of his mind.

A noise roused him in the middle of the starlit night, a low, almost inaudible warning growl coming from the pup. He gathered his legs beneath him and let the sleeping bag slide off his shoulders. He was lifting his weapon and preparing to rise to his feet when the night exploded around him and all hell broke loose. Lightning and thunder, muzzle-flashes and bullets, an ambush on his position and no place to go except straight into it. He dove forward, rolled and came up all in one motion, firing at the nearest spit of flame, then raking the muzzle to the right and triggering another burst. He jumped over a fallen form, crashed through the brush and ran like a jackrabbit, zigzagging and dodging.

How many were there? Four? Five? He wasn't going to stick around to find out. Another movement to his right, and he swung his weapon and fired another short burst, kept running. Felt something sting the calf of his leg and pushed on. He'd always been a good runner, and he ran now as he'd never run before. He could hear shouts coming from behind him, nothing up ahead. He dodged among trees. Slowed down when the canopy closed out the starlight and the darkness became too thick. Sped up when he could see the ground again.

He ran as if his life depended on it, because it did. He ran until he had to slow down, catch his breath, and even then he kept moving, walking fast, pausing from time to time to listen for sounds of pursuit over the pounding of his heart. He heard nothing but that meant nothing. They could be right on his heels. They were stealth fighters, and they were very good at it.

For over two hours he pushed hard. He paused only once, to check the burning in his calf. His pant leg was soaked, his boot full of blood. He had no idea how bad the wound was, nor was there time to find out, but he knew the bone wasn't broken and counted himself lucky. If the bullet had struck bone, they'd have had him, and he'd be dead right now. He tied his bandanna around his calf to try to staunch the bleeding, then angled toward the river, and when he reached it he walked in. The water was frigid. He continued downriver in the shallows along the water's edge. This wouldn't slow his pursuers much, but they might think he'd crossed the river. He'd walk like this as long as the night covered his movements.

Too soon the sky began to brighten, and he lost the cover of darkness. He scouted ahead, searching for places where he could leave the river without leaving tracks. He stripped off his jacket and wrapped it around his lower leg when he came to an outcropping, and then climbed onto it. The ledge ran back far enough to get him off the immediate shoreline before ending in a choke of brush. He kept his jacket around his leg while he was on the ledge to prevent a blood trail, and removed it only after he was well into the brush. He moved back into the woods and kept moving, but his head wasn't as clear as it should have been, and he could feel his strength failing him.

They could be right behind him, but he had to hole up. He found a place where he could make a stand if he had to, and he pulled his jacket back on because he was cold, really cold. He thought he'd just rest a while, listen and watch his back trail and be ready to fight if they caught up with him. He would stay alert because to sleep would be fatal. Disciplined vigilance was his only chance.

Don't fall asleep.

That was the order he gave himself just before he passed out.

HE OPENED HIS eyes on the bright dawn, and the sight of the grayish-colored pup lying beneath the brush with him, almost within touching distance, head on its paws, watching him. "Back in Montana the ranchers would use you for target practice," he muttered. "They don't care for coyotes."

His calf was throbbing, his head ached, he was desperately thirsty and sick from all the adrenaline, but he was still alive and the enemy hadn't caught up to him. Yet. He ate some jerky for breakfast, drank water from his bottle, tossed the last three strips of dried meat he fished out of his pocket to the pup, figuring he'd make it back to the outpost within hours. He left the bandanna tied over the wound, pushed awkwardly to his feet, took up his weapon and started out. He could barely hobble, but he was sure once he got moving his leg would limber up and travel would get easier. When he looked back over his shoulder, the pup was following him, no longer trying to hide. That day the hours passed in an endless and painful blur, but there was no sign of the enemy.

Or the outpost. He was traveling far too slowly.

That evening he made his way back to the river to refill his water bottle. He drank his fill crouched by the river, knowing that would be the only supper he got. That night was colder than the last. When he awoke, stiff and aching and chilled to the bone, the pup was within hand's reach, lying right beside his injured leg. When she saw he was awake, she raised her head off her paws and tensed, ready to flee at the slightest aggressive move from him. He extended his hand slowly, and she sniffed it. He touched her for the first time, a light stroke that brushed the black-tipped hair along her back while she remained rigidly motionless and watched him steadily with those dark golden eyes. He stroked her for some minutes, slowly and gently, and as he did the wary caution left her eyes and was replaced by something else entirely, and from that moment she was his.

That day his progress was slow and halting, and he rested often. If he was still being followed, the enemy would have picked him off by now as he hobbled slowly along. That evening he drank his fill again at the river and wondered if the pup would stick with him when he had no food to offer. The temperature dropped and snow fell during the night, and in the morning, the pup was lying on top of him, her nose tucked beneath his chin, warming him with her body. That day his progress was slower than the day before. His strength gave out, and he collapsed at dusk. He could travel no farther. He knew he was within striking distance of friendly territory, and his last conscious thought was how important it was that his unit get those GPS coordinates.

His discovery by a scouting party the following morning caused quite a stir, not only because he'd been out of radio contact for so long that they'd just about given him up for dead, but also because he was being so fiercely guarded by the wild pup who refused to let anyone approach. It took some doing by one of the scouting party to drag her away. He made a noose from a belt, attached it to a long pole and slipped it over her head. Two of the party returned to the outpost and brought back a stretcher. By that time Jack had roused enough to tell them about the pup and make them remove the noose from her neck. They loaded him onto the stretcher, and she dogged their heels all the way back to the outpost. She shadowed him in the medic's tent and followed him when they transferred him to a waiting truck. He was barely aware of any of it.

"The medics say your leg's infected and needs surgery," Lieutenant Dan Royce said as they slid the stretcher into the bed of the truck. "We're transporting you to Hatchet. They have a better setup there. That wild dog can't go. You know the rules," he said when the pup tried to climb into the bed of the truck.

"Sir, that dog's the only reason I found that Taliban training camp. She saved my life."

"I didn't make the rules, Parker, but I have to enforce them. You can't keep the dog."

Ruben Cook, who had helped carry Jack back to the outpost and was standing with a group of soldiers, said, "Don't worry, I'll take care of her for you."

Jack looked at him, dizzy from the morphine. "She saved my life," he repeated. "Treat her good." He reached out one hand to the pup as she gazed at him with that intense golden stare.

"I'll be back," he told her as Ruben replaced her makeshift collar and pulled her out of the truck.

It was over sixty rough road miles to the next outpost. Jack didn't remember much of the journey itself or the surgery that followed. When he woke up, he thought he was still out in the bush, hiding from the enemy, and an experienced army nurse talked him back to reality. The following morning the same nurse roused him gently and said, "Sergeant Parker? There's something you should see."

She helped him out of bed into a wheelchair and pushed him to the door of the tent. Outside the mobile hospital, a crowd of medical staff had gathered to stare at a starving, half-wild pup who had just limped into the camp. "One of your men forwarded a message for you yesterday," the nurse explained. "He said that your wild dog got loose and chased after your truck when you left the camp. None of us ever thought it would make it this far."

Jack spent five days at the mobile army hospital unit. His "wild dog" stayed under his cot, shared his meals and accompanied his every movement. When he returned to his unit, the pup's presence was discreetly ignored by his commanding officer, especially when less than two months later she alerted the outpost to a hostile intruder wearing an improvised explosive device. Her growling caught Jack's attention, and he exited the mess tent just as she sank her teeth into the intruder's leg. Jack tackled the hostile, who was subdued, arrested and later tagged as a Taliban trainee. He was sixteen years old and wearing an IED that had failed to detonate.

From that point on, Jack's wild dog became the camp's highly regarded mascot. Jack worked to teach her basic commands, which she picked up quickly, but she never took to any of the other soldiers. They nicknamed her "Ky" because she looked like a coyote, and tempted her with the choicest of tidbits to gain her trust, but her loyalties belonged to Jack. She would answer to no other.

Jack began to worry about her fate, should he be killed in action or shipped stateside. While his unit was on leave in Kabul three months later, he contacted his sister and began the arduous process of getting Ky safely back to the United States. It was a process that took months but was ultimately successful. When he last saw her, Ky was huddled in a dog crate at the airport awaiting shipment to his sister in Montana. Her intense yellow gaze was fixed on his face, and her expression was one of fear and anxiety.

"You'll be okay," he reassured her. Those words had haunted him ever since his sister's visit while he was at Walter Reed.

"So, THAT'S WHY I'm here," he said, returning to the present and looking across the campfire at Cameron, who had listened quietly while he told the story of a soldier and his dog. "I told her she'd be okay. I lied."

CHAPTER SIX

CAMERON REFILLED JACK'S wineglass a third time while he told her his story. The wine, after a long and challenging day, had loosened his tongue. The man who had been so aloof, so silent, had revealed a side of himself that she suspected few had ever seen.

"You didn't lie," she said. "You did what you thought was right. You couldn't have known what would happen. Your sister did her best, too. A bear came into their camp. Your dog chased it out. That was nobody's fault."

The sun had set and the air was chilly. She forked a big steak and a potato onto his plate, buttered and seasoned both, added a generous side of dressed salad, nestled a knife and fork on the plate and handed it to him.

"No more talk," she ordered. "Eat."

Cameron fixed her own plate and sat. She was ravenous. The steaks were grilled to perfection. They ate in silence while the river rushed past and the deepening twilight brightened the campfire. When they were done, she

covered the grill with coals, threw a few more
pieces of wood on the fire and let the heat burn
the grate clean. In bear country, one kept a
clean camp. One also camped a good distance
from the cook fire, but she was stretching the
rules in this instance due to Jack's exhausted
state.

"Now," she said, "you go into the tent and
get out of those wet clothes. I'll put your pack
inside, and you can set up your sleeping bag
in there. No point in setting up two tents. I'll
wash these dishes in the river."

She gathered the supper dishes and went
down to the river's edge to give him time and
privacy, and to think about her next moves. He
was exhausted but well fed, and he'd drunk half
a bottle of wine. Things were going pretty well.
It baffled her that anyone could be so attached
to a dog, but people were funny about their pets.
Some put more value on a dog than a human.
Her father's hunting dogs were good hunting
dogs, but they'd been focused on two things:
her father and hunting. To them she'd been an
ancillary figure in the family pack. By the time
she was fifteen, both had died of old age and
they'd had no other dogs. The life of a bush pilot
in the far north was unfavorable to owning pets.

The river water was cold. Years of traveling
in the bush had taught her to carry all essen-

tials on her person, so when the supper dishes had been scrubbed clean she fished her toothbrush and a tiny tube of toothpaste out of a pocket and brushed her teeth and washed up as she crouched on her heels beside the river.

In a few days she'd be rich. She'd buy Johnny Allen's red Jeep with the money. It was flashy and bold, with a good stereo and aggressive tires. The guys would think that was sexy.

When she'd finished with her nighttime routine, she walked quietly back to the tent, unzipped the door and eased inside. Darkness wrapped around her like a thick blanket, but she could make out a long shape lying prone against the far wall, darker than darkness. She stripped down to her camisole and panties and slipped into her sleeping bag, only then switching her LED headlamp on low, providing just enough light to read by. She picked up her book, nestled into her comfortable bed and cast a secretive sidelong glance toward her quarry. In the dim light she could see only that he was there. Awake? Asleep? She didn't know. It was a shame he hadn't seen her matching black and very sexy underwear, but tomorrow was another day.

"No talking in your sleep and no snoring," she said softly, and turned the page of her book.

"No worries" came the low reply.

WHEN JACK OPENED his eyes, it was already light and Cameron was up and gone. Her sleeping bag was rolled neatly into its stuff bag and sitting on the cot. He could smell wood smoke and coffee. He dressed in clothes that were still slightly damp from the day before and moved to the door of the tent. She was nowhere to be seen, but a small fire burned in the fire ring, and the coffeepot was off to one side where it would stay warm without boiling. A cup had been placed thoughtfully beside it. He exited the tent and filled the cup, taking a long appreciative look at the predawn wilderness that stretched away from him in all directions; the river, the mountains, the forest; mist rising from the rushing water into the cool morning air. He spotted her down on the riverbank, fly casting to that spot below the riffles she'd spoken about last evening. Her movements were practiced, graceful. The girl could also fly-fish, among all her other talents.

He took a sip of hot coffee. Rich and delicious. Perfectly brewed. He expected nothing less after the meal she'd served him last night. He carried the coffee down to the river, upstream of her, and washed the sleep from his face. He contemplated shaving but discarded the idea. The last thing he wanted was for her to think he was trying to look good for her.

The sooner they parted ways, the better. In the meantime, he'd add to his scruffy look.

He returned to the campfire, poured more hot coffee into his cup and walked down to where she was fishing the river.

"Good morning!" She greeted him with a bright smile after making an impressive double haul and delivery, the fly settling clear across the river from her. "You must be raring to go. You slept like the dead last night." She watched the fly drift quickly toward the big boulder.

"Did I talk in my sleep or snore?"

"If you did, I didn't hear you. I was tired, and the sound of the river was nice." She was fishing the drift, watching the fly. "I hope you're hungry. I caught three trout while you were sleeping."

"I could eat."

She smiled, and at that moment a trout struck her fly. Within five minutes she'd landed a fourth trout, an eighteen-inch arctic char. She walked into the water to release the fish without lifting it out. "What a beauty," she said, watching it swim away, tired but uninjured. "I file the barbs on my flies. Makes catching them a little harder but hurts them less, especially if you release a lot, like I do."

"Admirable," he said.

She reeled her line in and cast a glance in his direction. "You don't like me much."

"Not true. You're a great cook, and your coffee is excellent."

"But you think I talk too much," she said, bending to lift the stringer of cleaned trout out of the cold water. She gave him a critical up and down. "I see you're wearing the same clothes you had on yesterday. What am I supposed to ferry down to the trapper's cabin?"

"Three stinky socks. I draw the line at backpacking in the nude, especially when it's buggy."

"You didn't bring a change of clothes?"

"I brought a set of long johns, spare socks and underwear."

"Three's an odd number of socks."

"I have an odd number of feet," he said.

She flushed and dropped her gaze. "Well, I'll fix you a good breakfast before I leave. You'll need it." She marched back to the campsite, and he followed at a slower pace. In jig time she had bacon frying and the trout prepped and ready to slide into the bacon fat while he studied the map she handed him. He unfolded it over his knee and tried to figure out their location.

"The black circle halfway down the Wolf is where the cabin is," she told him. "It's a little farther than I thought. And that other mark upriver of it is where I think we're camped right now. I don't know how long it will take me to reach the cabin." She forked the cooked bacon onto a plate. "Calculating distances on a twisty river can be tricky. I'll unload the heavy gear, most of our food into the camp and then ferry the canoe back up here. That'll take me considerably longer. You can keep hiking downstream, so I won't have to come back so far." She thought about her plan for a moment and frowned. "What if we miss each other on the river?"

"Why don't you just stay at the cabin, and I'll meet you there."

She thought about that suggestion briefly, then shook her head. "We should stick together. That's the safest way. You should come with me."

"No, thanks. I've seen the way you handle a canoe."

She lifted her chin. "I'm good with a canoe. I just didn't see that rock because I was distracted by you."

"Not my fault I have that effect on women."

"If you took the canoe down to the cabin, I could do the walking," she offered, ignoring his comment. "I'll drag your socks behind me on a piece of parachute cord and lay down a good scent trail. I could make ten miles easy before dark, camp the night and meet up with you at the cabin tomorrow. Have you ever paddled a canoe?"

"Hell, I'm part Indian, remember? I can paddle, and shoot a bow and arrow and my tomahawk skills are unmatched. It's a genetic thing."

Cameron took a slow breath. "There's no need for sarcasm. I'm only trying to be helpful. I think we'd make better time if I did the walking and you did the paddling."

"Backpacking along this river with no trail brushed out is tough work. My sister must be paying you a small fortune."

Her expression turned to stone as she slid the three char into the frying pan. Bacon fat spattered. The edges of the trout curled. His mouth watered. He figured if there was a grizzly within ten miles, they'd have company for breakfast, but any bear would have to tackle him first to get a bite of that fish.

"I'm offering to help you," she said. "It was a genuine offer. Do you want to find your dog, or don't you?"

He had no response for that. They sat upwind of the small cook fire and ate the three trout and finished off the pot of coffee. He thought of Ky when he tossed the fish bones into the coals. Thought about how she'd shadowed him, slept beside him, watched over him, protected him, loved him. Depended upon him. He thought about how he'd let her down. He had to find her. Ky was out here, somewhere, and he had to find her.

Cameron was offering to help. Why did she irritate him so much? Was it because he was sure she was being paid handsomely to guarantee he made it out to the Mackenzie? Was it because he didn't like being chaperoned? What red-blooded man wouldn't want to keep company with a great-looking gal who could cook and clean and set up camp and drive a plane and paddle a canoe and fly-fish with such panache?

"Who taught you to fly a plane?" he asked as he ate the last of his bacon.

"My father. I use to fly everywhere with him, and he taught me to work whatever controls I could reach. I soloed as soon as my feet could reach the rudder pedals, but I'd been flying since I was six. That's when my mother left. It's how we get around up here, and my father couldn't leave me alone, so he took me with him whatever job he was on."

"What happened to your mother?"

Cameron glanced up from her plate and gave a little shrug. "She went bonkers, living way out in the bush. Some people just can't stand the isolation. She had two miscarriages after she had me, so I never did have any siblings. One day this wealthy dude from back east came to shoot himself a trophy bear. My mother was cooking for the sporting camp then, and he stayed for ten days. He killed his bear and when he left, she went with him and that was that."

"Do you ever hear from her?"

"Nope. I have no idea what city she's living in, but I bet it's a big one and I bet she doesn't miss the wilderness."

He studied her as she concentrated on her breakfast. She was beautiful, really, even dressed in a well-worn sage, violet and pink plaid flannel shirt, synthetic zip T-shirt, cargo pants and L.L.Bean boots. Her glossy black hair was pulled back in a short braid, and she wore no jewelry, sported no piercings or tattoos. Her skin was clear and glowed with health. He couldn't imagine any mother turning her back and walking away from her only child, leaving her to be raised in remote hunting and fishing camps way out on the edge of nowhere. But her father had done a good job raising her. She was unpretentious, down to earth and completely at home in the wilderness.

"Cameron's an interesting name for a girl."

"It was my mother's maiden name."

"Did you go to school?" he asked.

"Sometimes. I can read and write, if that's what you're wondering. We'd winter in Fort Simpson, and there was a school there. My dad was pretty lax about it. Said I could learn more in the out-of-doors than I could ever learn inside four walls. The only thing he demanded of me was that I learn to read because he said knowing how to read was the most important thing. He taught me math, though, because it was essential for flying." She finished her breakfast and licked the grease off her fingers before wiping them on the napkin. "I thought school was boring. I graduated, passed all my exams with flying colors even though I hardly ever went to class. My dad said that's because I read so much."

"If you don't mind my asking, how old are you?"

"Twenty-four." She smiled at his expression. "You're not the first person who thought I wasn't old enough to legally drink. What about yourself?"

"Thirty. Old enough to drink."

"But never married. I think I know why."

"Enlighten me."

"You're afraid of rejection, so you never dared ask."

"Wrong."

"Then why isn't a good-looking guy like you married?"

"I asked my college sweetheart to marry me before I was shipped out on my first deployment. She said yes and promised she'd wait forever if she had to. I gave her a ring. My deployment lasted nearly a year. When I got back, she was six months pregnant. She gave the ring back and married another guy." Were Cameron's eyes dark blue or brown? He couldn't tell, even though he was looking right into them while he spoke.

"Wow, that's pretty bad," she said. "Did she break off the engagement before you got back home?"

"No, for the same reason my sister never told me what happened to my dog. There's this perception that bad news will drive a soldier off the deep end or cause him or her to get careless and get killed. So I wrote her letters weekly while she was romancing another man."

"Sounds like your girl might have been related to my ex-husband, Roy."

He laughed, and she smiled in response. Her eyes dropped from his, and after an awkward moment she rose to her feet and gathered the breakfast dishes and carried them down to the river. While she was there, he rolled up his sleeping bag and packed his gear. When she came back to the camp, she was wearing a pensive expression.

"Five thousand dollars," she said, staring him straight in the eye. Her eyes were blue. Very dark blue. "That's what I was offered to get you safely to the Mackenzie River. And a generous bonus on top of that if I could do it real quick, because your mother's so sick."

"Five thousand dollars? That's what my sister offered you?" He shook his head in wonder. "I hate to tell you this, but my mother's fine. She'd have told me herself if she wasn't. She's a real straight shooter, tells it like it is. So it looks like you've lost your generous bonus. No need to rush things. As for the rest of the reward money, you'll have to earn it. I've decided to take you up on your offer of the canoe. I'll paddle down to the cabin and wait for you there. You can drag my three stinky socks. You're so quick you'll probably beat me there."

"Fair enough," she said after a surprised pause. "The camp's on the north bank of the river. Your sister said it was impossible to miss. It's on a point of land just like this site."

"Good."

"Be sure to wear that personal flotation device while you're on the water," she said. "If you should fall out of the canoe, it won't do you any good unless you're wearing it. The water's cold. Even if you're a good swimmer you'll probably drown."

"Right."

He carried his gear to the canoe, acutely aware of how slow his pace was compared to hers. She was quick and strong, and she had that tent down and packed in minutes, the canoe loaded and lashed, the campfire thoroughly doused with water from her canvas bucket. She had a routine, and it was an efficient one. It was hard not to be impressed. He'd grown up in the out-of-doors and knew how to handle himself, but his skills didn't hold a patch to hers. He was annoyed that she regarded him as a way to earn some extra income, but her life wasn't an easy one. The money his sister offered her must've been a strong incentive.

"What?" she asked as she straightened from lashing the last of the gear in the canoe and caught him watching her.

"Nothing."

"You're worried about something. I can see it in your face. Now listen, there are rapids, but they're below the camp. You should have smooth sailing. The canoe has float bags, everything's tied down and the critical gear is all in dry sacks. If you capsize, stay with the canoe and get it ashore unless you're about to get caught in a strainer. That's a tree that's fallen into the river. I'm sure you already knew that. Very dangerous, those strainers. The river level should drop some during the day, but the wind's apt to come out of the west this afternoon and slow you down. You'll probably make the cabin well before dark. Spend the night there. There's tons of food in that cooler, and if the camp's a mess or a bear's living in it, you can always set up the tent. That'll keep you dry and out of the bugs."

"You're worried about me?" That floored him.

"Of course," she said. "If I don't get you safely to the Mackenzie, I won't get my five grand, and I have my heart set on buying Johnny Allen's red Jeep."

She straddled the bow of the canoe to steady it so he could climb in. "Wait a minute," she said as he reached for the paddle. "You're forgetting something."

"What's that?"

She held out her hand. "Your three stinky socks."

CHAPTER SEVEN

Cameron was still holding out her hand when he handed her the paddle instead of the socks. "I'm not getting in, you are. I wasn't really going to make you walk. I just wanted to see how bad you wanted the money."

She took the paddle from him with a frown and watched as he shrugged into his pack. "But I can walk four times faster than you can."

"Thanks for that compliment, but walking's not part of your job. It's mine. It's how I learn to use my new leg. It's how I'm going to find my lost dog. Your job is to find the trapper's cabin and hang up my dirty socks." He fished them out of his jacket pocket, enclosed in a zipper storage bag, and tossed them into the canoe. "There you go, guaranteed stinky."

"Take the canoe," she said. "I'm packed light and I can walk fast."

"I exaggerated about knowing how to handle a canoe. You probably think my genetic memory would fill in the gaps, but if I lost the canoe, how would you get me out to the Mackenzie?"

"How can anyone not know how to paddle a canoe?"

"Are you really willing to risk losing that red Jeep?"

Cameron blew out her breath. Arguing with him was futile. They were burning daylight. "Okay, you win. I'll be back for you as soon as I can. If you wolf whistle your way down the river like you were doing before, I'll hear you. When you hear me answer, make for the river's edge."

"Sounds like a plan. You'd better get going."

Once again, she'd been summarily dismissed. She untied the snub lines and climbed into the canoe, fuming inwardly. She pulled on the life vest and zipped it up. He had his rifle and his camping gear, but she still felt uneasy leaving him behind. "It could be late tomorrow before we meet up," she cautioned him.

"I'll try to be all right on my own."

His sarcastic words sparked another quick surge of anger. "Fine, then. Have a happy and healthy day."

She paddled away and didn't look back. Her anger gave her strength. The canoe fairly flew downstream. For an hour she paddled steadily, keeping a sharp eye out for boulders that might be submerged in the high water, but water levels had dropped rapidly in the two days since the rains ended, and she had no problems navigating the river. Nearly three hours into the journey she spied something hung up in the branches of a tree that had toppled off the eroded riverbank on an inside curve and into the river. She leaned forward, squinting intently.

Was it? Could it be?

Yes! It was her coveted Snowy River hat. By sheer luck it had been caught by the stampede strings in the very tip of a big spruce tree that was blocking two-thirds of the river. She was tempted to try to retrieve the hat immediately but decided against it. She'd unload the heavy canoe at the cabin and rescue her hat on the upward ferry, or maybe on the way back down with Jack in the bow. He could snag it with a long pole while she handled the canoe.

Just before noon she rounded a river bend and spotted the trapper's cabin. Jack's sister had been right. Nobody could paddle past without seeing it. The structure was in better shape than she expected. She'd spent many a night in moldering old camps where a tent would have been a better option. This one was laid up of peeled spruce logs, weathered to a silvery gray. The roofing was sound, there was a stovepipe that looked serviceable, a door and window facing the river, and another window that she could see facing upstream, both tightly shuttered against marauding bears.

The small cove on the downstream side of the peninsula was the perfect spot to land the canoe. She heaved the bow onto the gravel spit, tethered it to a spruce, hiked up the knoll to the cabin, unlatched the door and peered inside. A quick scout and she was reasonably sure nobody had stepped foot inside since the trapper left in late winter. Everything was as neat as a pin. The wood box was full, a fire had been laid inside the woodstove and was ready for the strike of a match, the dishes were all washed and put away, the floor was swept. Whoever trapped in here was a real woodsman.

She carried the gear up the steep knoll one armload at a time and stashed it inside the cabin. The cooler was the heaviest thing. She had to unload it, carry it up and then refill it once it was inside. It took her over an hour to get everything situated and organized and to hang Jack's three stinky socks from tree branches outside the cabin, as promised.

When all that was accomplished, she fixed herself a peanut-butter sandwich and ate it sitting on the cabin steps, resting and admiring the view. She left a note on the table, just in case, took a long drink of water from her bottle and closed the cabin door. When she returned to the canoe, she had only her emergency gear, food for the night and the tent for ballast, all of which was lashed into the bow. She'd already traveled four fast hours on the river, and knew that paddling back upstream was going to be demanding work, and much slower, but there were hours of good daylight left, and she should be able to make it back as far as her hat before running out of strength. She'd pitch camp there.

She worked the currents and eddies as efficiently as possible. On straight sections of river she hugged the bank where the current was slower, and on twisty sections she ferried back and forth, constantly seeking slower water. The afternoon wind was westering at her back, which helped some, but her arms and shoulders burned from the effort, and every half hour she stopped for a long drink of water and a ten-minute rest. By 4:00 p.m. she had reached the spruce tree on the undercut riverbank that had uprooted, toppled into the water and snagged her hat. Her timing was impeccable. She was tired and hungry and ready for a long break.

But first she'd retrieve her hat. It was hung up on the very tip of the half-submerged spruce. If she kept the canoe straight into the current and paddled past the end of the strainer, she could reach over in one quick moment and snatch the hat. Strainers were dangerous, and a paddler never wanted to get crosswise of one, but Cameron was sure if she just maintained a straight course up to the very tip of the tree, and didn't go beyond it to the upstream side, she'd be all right.

She drew a few deep breaths before flexing her arms and shoulders and taking a fresh grip on the paddle. If she'd had a client in the canoe with her, she'd never have attempted this, but she'd use extreme caution, and if there was even a remote chance she could get into trouble, she'd abort the plan.

She ferried across the river and approached the spruce from downstream. The hat was dangling in midair from a branch near the very tip, as if the tree was holding it out to her, but she knew it was only because the water level had dropped since the hat had gotten hung up. She kept the bow straight and paddled strongly into the current, drawing almost abreast of the hat before making the grab. To make sure she had time to reach for it, she gave one more strong push forward with the paddle. She didn't lean much at all, just reached with her arm, but when she tugged on the hat, the stampede string didn't come free, and so she reached a little farther. The second, stronger tug caused just enough of a deviation in the bow that the current snatched hold of it. The canoe snapped around so suddenly she lost the paddle, lost her balance, and in that awful moment she knew she'd made a terrible mistake.

The bow was pulled hard against the upstream side of the strainer, the canoe tipped sideways, filled with water and was sucked beneath the tip of the tree by the powerful current in a matter of seconds. She made a desperate grab for the upper branches to pull herself out of the canoe, but the current grabbed hold and pulled her under. Instantly she was suctioned into the deadly tangle of branches beneath the water. She struggled to fight free, but the branches were thick and strong, and she was pinned against them by the powerful current.

The canoe was right beside her, a smooth solid object pushing against her. It was moving forward and downward, being pushed beneath the strainer, and she caught desperate hold of a thwart and pulled herself down and half under the overturned canoe. Her lungs burned as she reached blindly for the next thwart and tried to haul herself ahead. The canoe jerked forward again, pulling her with it, but something snagged her life vest and held her back.

She struggled to wrench herself free and couldn't. Her lungs were burning and for a moment panic overwhelmed her, then a strange calm prevailed. She unzipped the vest and stripped out of it one arm at a time, never losing her grip on the thwart, and as soon as she was free of the PFD, the canoe was pulled down farther until it wedged between the river bottom and the tree. She wriggled alongside of it, flattening herself against the smooth stones of the river bottom and hitching herself along the gunnel until she had cleared the strainer.

The moment she was free of the tree branches, the current swept her downriver. She thrashed to the surface, gasping air into burning lungs, then struggled to reach the shore as she was slammed against a submerged rock and sucked into an eddy. She choked on mouthfuls of water, felt gravel underfoot and lurched to her feet, fell again and was tumbled farther downstream. By the time the river straightened and the current slowed, she was more than half drowned. With the last of her strength, she dragged herself onto the bank and lay there, legs still trailing in the river, coughing and retching up swallowed water.

At first she was only vaguely conscious, then she became aware of a strange, high-pitched sound and realized the noise was her lungs struggling for air. She lay motionless until her breaths came easier. Her hands were clutching at the vegetation along the riverbank. She unclenched her fingers with great effort. She heard the river rushing past, the wind in the trees, felt the warmth of afternoon sunshine on her hands. She was alive. She shouldn't be. By all rights she should be dead, but she was alive.

She pulled herself forward until her legs were out of the water and then rolled over and sat up. She was bleeding from half a dozen wounds caused by frantically clawing and forcing her way through the submerged branches in the strainer, but she was more focused on how close she had just come to drowning.

She sat for what seemed like hours on that riverbank, looking back up to where the tree lay halfway across the river, her hat still dangling like the brass ring on a merry-go-round, dipping back and forth into the water. Somewhere under that tree was her canoe and her warm fleece jacket and all her food and emergency gear, including Walt's satellite phone in the waterproof case, her pistol and the tent. But she wasn't trapped under there with her gear. She was sitting right here in the afternoon sunshine, breathing in and out.

Alive. She was alive. It was a miracle, considering her stupidity.

Jack would be all right on his own. He had everything he needed to camp out, but she was soaking wet, badly beat-up and needed to get back to shelter. She unlaced and pulled off her boots, emptied them of water, wrung out her wool socks, replaced socks and boots on her feet, got up and started walking back down-river. Her clothing would dry as she walked. If she was lucky and didn't break an ankle, she'd reach the cabin well before full dark.

JACK HAD SPENT nearly three years in the mountains of Afghanistan, participating in countless forced marches carrying packs and ammo weighing upward of seventy-five pounds. Those years had made him tough. But the long weeks lying in a hospital bed when he was shipped stateside had eroded his strength. At the end of the day, he figured he'd made ten miles, maybe twelve. He was halfway to the cabin. Maybe. This was good progress. He felt his strength returning for the first time after his long hospitalization, and could only attribute this to the excellent meal Cameron had cooked for him the night before.

He found his thoughts straying often as he hiked, and the paths they traveled always began in Afghanistan with his men and Ky and always ended with Cameron Johnson. He would wonder if his unit was preparing to depart Afghanistan as was rumored before his final ill-fated patrol almost a year after Ky had been shipped stateside. That patrol had nearly killed him and had killed several of his men, or he'd probably still be over there. He wondered if Ky could possibly have survived the bear attack and the long bitter winter, and then pushed away his nagging doubts. Of course she had, and he would find her. He wondered if Cameron had made it safely to the cabin. She'd probably reached it before noon, if her pace starting out this morning had held.

She was very strong and a good paddler. It was possible she'd already started back for him, and could in fact be nearby. He began listening for her wolf whistles about the time he found a good place to camp near the river's edge. It wouldn't surprise him if she showed up before dark, and truth be told, he wouldn't mind if she did. She'd bring food, real food, and that big comfortable tent of hers. He'd slept well last night. No nightmares. The nightmares had been a constant torment ever since the brutal firefight that had cost him three men. No therapy was going to cure him. No prosthetic leg was going to make him whole again. The army psychologist had talked to him about how to deal with the flashbacks, the nightmares and the lack of sleep, but it was pointless being counseled by someone who'd never been there, done that and then had to suffer the hellish aftermath.

Last night, sharing Cameron's tent, he'd had the first good night's sleep in many months. No coming awake in a heart-thumping panic, his own shout startling him in the dark.

Jack set up his little tent, cooked two packages of ramen noodles over his tiny camp stove, then boiled a quart of really strong tea. He ate his supper, drank his tea, imagined Cameron was dining like a king and either warm and dry in that trapper's cabin or equally comfortable in her canvas tent. He'd never met any woman as capable and self-reliant. There was little reason to worry about her, so he didn't. He was still hungry when he rolled up in his sleeping bag, but he had no trouble falling asleep.

CAMERON PUSHED HARD to reach the cabin. By sunset she was certain she must be close. When she rounded each bend in the river, she wasted time pushing through thick brush to the riverbank in hopes of seeing it there on the point of land, but all she saw was another wild lonesome stretch of water. She kept pushing because she thought for sure the cabin was just around the next corner, but as time passed and darkness began to thicken, she realized she'd be spending the night out. Her clothing was still damp, and she had no jacket and no food, but she had a river's worth of water to drink, and around her neck where she always wore it, tucked inside her shirt, was her plastic orange whistle. On the butt of the whistle was a tiny compass, which screwed off to reveal a waterproof compartment full of waxed matches.

Her father had taught her as soon as she could toddle to always wear this "necklace" whenever she was in the woods, which was most of the time. He'd been strict about compliance, and she'd grown up thinking the most valuable piece of jewelry any woman ever wore was an orange plastic whistle with a compass and waterproof match case.

She was glad for that orange necklace now, because her other fire starters were in her emergency pack and her jacket. As long as she had the means to make a fire, she knew she'd be fine. She found a cut bank along the river that offered shelter from the wind, and kindled a tiny fire in the river gravel, which would reflect heat back against the bank. While enough light remained, she gathered armloads of driftwood and dragged a few dry snags to the campsite. When it grew too dark to safely move in the woods, she returned to the fire and stripped out of her damp clothing, draping her pants and flannel shirt over the mountain of firewood where the heat would dry them. She kept her underwear, synthetic T-shirt, boots and socks on and then gathered nearby stones to build a heat reflector behind the fire while her clothes dried. As long as she kept moving she was fine, but the night air was chilly, and every now and again the cold night wind would tug through the spruce and bring goose bumps to her skin.

She checked her clothing and turned it over as if she were grilling a steak. By midnight it was almost dry. She donned it gratefully and then huddled, exhausted, in the warmth of the fire. For the first time she felt her face, hissing in pain when her fingers traced the deep gashes and scrapes. There was a tiny reflector mirror on the cap of the match case, but she really didn't need or want to see what she looked like. She knew her face was a road map of bruises and cuts inflicted during her struggle through the branches of the spruce tree, and her left eyelid was almost swollen shut, but she wasn't complaining. She was painfully aware how lucky she was to be alive. Spending an uncomfortable night crouched beside a small campfire was a small price to pay for her stupidity. By all rights, she should have drowned.

DAWN BROUGHT MIST rising off the water like smoke, trout rising in the eddies, the clear yellow band of light over the dark forest to the east. Cameron was on the move as soon as it was light enough to see. She'd run out of firewood, and the embers of her little fire were cold. So was she. Moving forced warmth into aching muscles, and the stiffness gradually left her. She hadn't walked thirty minutes before she came to the cabin. At first she couldn't process the idea that, had she kept walking just a little farther last night, she'd have slept warm, dry and well fed.

She had a fire going in the woodstove within five minutes of her arrival, and within half an hour had breakfast cooking. She ate ravenously: six eggs, three pieces of buttered toast and three mugs of strong hot tea. When she was finished eating, she cleaned up, made three thick peanut-butter sandwiches and put them in an empty bread bag. One of the dry bags had a shoulder harness, and she loaded it with enough gear to be able to hike upriver toward Jack without starving or facing another night without shelter. The pack, when she shouldered it, weighed twenty-five pounds. Two hours after she had arrived at the cabin, she was re-tracing her steps upriver.

By noon she had reached the fallen tree that had almost claimed her life. Her hat was still dangling from the tip of the spruce in midair, swinging back and forth in the light breeze, taunting her. She paused long enough to eat one of the sandwiches and drink some hot tea from her thermos, then she pushed on. She had no way of knowing how much progress Jack had made the day before, but she figured she had a ways to go before finding him.

The faint sound of a whistle over the rush of the river, less than an hour later, surprised her. She blew a long answering blast on her orange whistle, listened for a reply and felt weak with relief when it came. Tears stung her eyes as she blew once more on her whistle and heard the answering response. Her legs grew wobbly. She sank down in a heap, shrugged out of the heavy pack and surrendered to the sudden rush of emotions that overwhelmed her. She was still cradling her head in her hands when she heard approaching footsteps. She wiped her face on her shirttail and struggled to her feet just as Jack limped into view, pushing his way through the brush that choked the riverbank.

He stopped short and stared when he spot-ted her standing on dry land, not paddling upriver in the canoe. "What happened? Where's the canoe?"

She shook her head. Her eyes stung, and her throat cramped up. He crossed the distance between them, and when he reached her, he tipped her chin up to look directly at him. He studied the cuts on her face, her swollen eye. He gently turned her head first to one side, then the other before letting his hand drop away.

"What happened?" he repeated. "Are you all right?"

She blinked and swallowed hard. "I lost the canoe." With her palms she blotted the tears that stung the scratches on her cheeks. "I'm okay. Just tired, that's all."

"We'll find a good place to camp." He gave her another up-and-down appraisal, then glanced around. "This place looks perfect."

"I can walk," she said. "The farther we go today, the easier tomorrow will be. It's only an hour's hike to where I lost the canoe."

"You sure? You look like hell."

She nodded and struggled to her feet. "I'm sure."

"I'll carry your pack," he said.

"No, you won't."

This time she followed him, and fell behind. He had to wait for her twice. By the time they reached the downed spruce tree that had nearly killed her, she was on her last legs. She let the pack drop from her shoulders for the second time and sat on it, pointing to the tree lying half submerged in the river, and to her hat suspended just over the water, like an ornament. "The canoe's pinned under that tree," she said.

Jack shrugged out of his own pack and lowered it to the ground. He studied the tree for a long, silent moment. She didn't have to explain how it all happened. He was plenty smart enough to figure out what she'd done.

"Most paddlers don't survive something like that," he said. She waited for him to tell her how foolish she'd been to risk her life just to retrieve a hat, but he didn't. He could have made any number of "I told you so" comments, knowing she'd almost drowned trying to do something very, very stupid, but he didn't. Her throat cramped up again and she looked away, blinking hard and struggling for self-control. She wasn't going to start bawling again. She was done with that.

JACK SET UP camp on the best spot he could find. His tent was small and didn't need much level ground. The bugs were bad, and they had both donned their head nets. He unrolled his sleeping mat and bag inside the tent, then crawled out and sat beside her. She reached inside her dry bag and brought out two sandwiches, handing him one.

"Supper," she said.

They ate awkwardly, lifting mosquito netting for a bite, letting it fall again.

"Romantic," he commented, and she laughed in spite of her pain and misery. They drank water from their bottles. Not a fancy supper, nor was it enough, but considering the circumstances it was more than he'd expected. "Thank you, that hit the spot," he said when he'd finished. "Well, the way I see it, your canoe's pinned under that tree, and we have to cut the tree to free the canoe. I have a folding saw. I'll start on the tree trunk. You go inside the tent and get some sleep."

"We won't both fit in there—it's too small."

"We'll fit. You're used to a condo, that's all. You've gotten spoiled."

"You can't cut a tree that size with a folding saw."

"I'd use an ax if I had one, but I don't."

"There's an ax at the cabin."

Jack's glance was sharp and questioning. "You made it there?"

She nodded. "Yesterday, around noon. It's a nice cabin, too. I unloaded most of the gear there, all the food and the cooler, before starting back upriver with the canoe. There's an ax behind the woodstove."

"When did you lose the canoe?"

"Late yesterday afternoon, on the way back to meet you. I tried to make it back to the cabin, but I ran out of daylight. My clothes were wet. I'd have frozen to death if I hadn't had matches on me."

"Remind me to thank your matches," he said. "Get some sleep. Take my sleeping bag. It's warmer."

"Don't worry about me. I could sleep on a bed of nails," she mumbled, unzipping the tent door, pushing her blanket and fleece through, then crawling inside. "Hurry up. The bugs'll fill the tent. You can cut the tree tomorrow after we get the ax."

Jack didn't need a second invitation. She was right. The bugs were bad, and he was tired. Within moments they were situated head to toe like two sardines in a can. "I apologize in advance if I talk in my sleep," Jack said, but there was no response. Cameron was already out.

CHAPTER EIGHT

SECONDS LATER, IT SEEMED, her voice woke him and her hand was on his shoulder.

"Jack. *Jack*, wake up. There's a bear right outside the tent! Where's your rifle?" For some reason she was whispering.

"My what?"

"Your rifle!" she said urgently. "You brought it in here last night. I saw you."

Jack struggled to sit up and shrug out of his bag. The tent was so cramped he could barely move. She was crouched at the door, looking out.

"Where's the bear?" he asked, crawling up beside her.

"It's right *there*, right in front of you. Can't you see it?"

Jack stared out the screen door into the darkness. He saw something big moving nearby, a very large, bulky object that appeared to be approaching the tent. He heard the roll of gravel under its huge paws and the lung-deep breaths of a very large animal.

"You're right, it's a bear," he said, rubbing his hand over his face. "But they're mostly all bluff. Isn't that what you told me?"

She made a noise of frustration and crawled to the back of the tent as the bear approached the door. Jack shouted, "Hey bear! Hey, go on now, leave us be," and clapped his hands together, but the sounds didn't prevent the bear from seizing Cameron's dry sack in its jaws and dragging it several paces away. She crawled up beside him with his guitar case in hand.

"If this is a rifle, it's mighty light, and keeping it inside a case is dumb," she muttered as she struggled to open it. He heard the zipper being jerked open, then another noise when her hand encountered the contents. *"What the hell's this thing?"*

"That's a Martin classical backpack guitar."

"A *guitar*? You've been carrying a *guitar* on this trip? *A guitar*? You've got to be kidding me." She thrust it into his hands. "What use is a guitar when a grizzly bear's tearing our camp apart?"

"There's a can of bear spray in the side pocket of my pack. Get it, in case this doesn't work," he said. Then he unzipped the door of the tent and crawled just outside. The bear was a mere ten feet away, enthusiastically plundering her dry sack and ignoring the two of them. He remained on his knees for balance, tucked the guitar against his hip and drew a deep breath.

CAMERON HAD A healthy respect for bears. She'd seen firsthand what they were capable of, the speed at which they moved, the aftermath of their brute strength when combined with fear, aggression or fury. That's why she carried the .44 Magnum pistol, which she'd have in her hands right now if it weren't inside the dry bag that was lashed in the nose of the submerged canoe, along with her cans of bear spray and the noisy bear bangers.

When Jack crawled out of the tent to confront the bear with nothing but a guitar in hand, she dove for his pack and started searching frantically in the side pockets for the can of bear spray, but before she could find it, he created a blast of noise with strings and belted out Elvis's "Hound Dog" in a deep tenor voice, a very impressive voice, matter of fact, that drove her back on her heels. *"You ain't nothin' but a hound dog, cryin all the time…!"*

The bear lifted its head, startled by the sudden outburst of noise, then reared onto its hind legs, making it appear at least nine feet tall in the darkness. Jack never paused, just kept belting out the song and thrashing hard as he could on the guitar strings. He hadn't finished the first stanza before the bear dropped to all fours, wheeled and ran off so fast it ran head-first into a small spruce, flattened it and kept on going. He played and sang a few more stanzas before stopping and looking over his shoulder to where Cameron cowered inside a tent that was rapidly filling with mosquitoes. She was holding the can of bear spray in her hand, arm extended and pointed toward the door.

"You're crazy," she managed.

"You complaining?"

"No."

"Good. We should've hauled that pack of yours up into a tree when we made camp, but I don't think that bear'll be back. It didn't like my singing."

"I'd haul it now if I had some rope."

Jack crawled back inside the tent, and she zipped the door behind him. He opened a side pocket in his pack and came up with a roll of parachute cord, which he handed to her. "You sure you want to go back out there?"

"Stand by with your guitar and the bear spray." Cameron crawled out of the tent, crossed to the duffel, tied one end of the cord to the straps, tossed the roll of cord over the nearest high branch and hauled the bag aloft, tying it off to the base of the tree. She wasted no time returning to the tent and zipping the door behind her. "At least if that bear comes back, it'll be focused on getting that pack out of the air and not eating us."

They hunched side by side in the gloom. Jack rested the guitar by the door. "Just in case," he said, then flopped back onto his sleeping bag. She heard him slapping at mosquitoes as she lay on her stomach, propped on her elbows so she could keep watch out the door. She was still holding the can of bear spray.

"Well, you were right," he commented casually, as if a giant grizzly hadn't just invaded their camp. "Most bears are all bluff."

"Except the ones that aren't, and I've met a few. That's why I carry a gun."

"Speaking of which, where is that big elephant pistol of yours?"

Cameron peered out into the darkness, watchful. "In the canoe. I lost Walt's satellite phone, and the canoe wasn't mine. I borrowed it. It'll take a bunch of money to pay the owner back."

"How much is a bunch of money?"

"A lot more than I have in my bank account."

"What would you do if you had more than a bunch of money, as much money as you could ever want?" he asked.

Cameron contemplated the question while

watching for the bear to return. "I'd buy a brand-new red Jeep instead of Johnny Allen's scratched-up mud runner. Who knows what he's done to that transmission?"

"That's it?" he prodded. "A new red Jeep is all it'd take to make you happy?"

The darkness was beginning to ebb as the short northern night slowly gave way to the arctic dawn. Cameron saw no movement on the edges of the campsite. The bear was gone, scared off by Jack's impressive Elvis imperson-ation. She rolled onto her back, laid the can of bear spray beside her, laced her fingers over her empty belly and drew a slow breath, let-ting it out just as slowly. "I worked at a sport-ing camp a few years before Roy came along. It was a beautiful set of camps over in Yukon. I loved that place, everything about it, includ-ing the folks who owned it. Minnie and Marl. It's for sale right now, and if I had the money I'd buy it, and if there was enough money left in my treasure trove I'd buy a new plane to go with my new red Jeep. I'd run that business like an eco-lodge because I'm sick of ferrying tro-phy hunters around, and if I was rich I wouldn't need to cater to them anymore."

"And you think that would make you happy?"

"That would make me self-employed. Self-reliant. Independent. In charge of my own destiny. My own boss. And yes, I'd like that. Who wouldn't?"

She heard a soft laugh in the darkness. "You just described the polar opposite of a soldier's life."

"Did you always want to be a soldier?"

"I wanted a good education, couldn't afford one. The army was my ticket out of Montana and my path to an engineering degree. But I liked the army, and I'm up for another promotion. That's why I'm planning to return to active duty, as soon as they'll have me."

"Would you go back to Afghanistan?"

"If that's where my unit is, yes."

"My father spent fifteen years in the military," Cameron said. "That's where he learned to fly and that's how he met my mother. He was thirty-six when he headed north. He loved the bush pilot's life. Never cared much for having fancy things or lots of money. He liked to hunt and fish. He'd have been happy living in a tent."

"Guess that's where you get it from."

Cameron laughed. "It sure didn't come from my mother. My father's only sibling was an older sister who lived in Vancouver, a librarian, never married. Esther Johnson. Just what you'd picture when you think of a spinster librarian, the reading glasses on a chain around her neck, cardigans and skirts in gray wool. Flat-heeled sensible shoes. My father sent me to stay with her when I was twelve so I could attend a hoity-toity private school, courtesy of Aunt Esther, and live in a big city with lots of culture. I lasted about four months before I was expelled."

"What crime did you commit?"

"The spoiled rich girls would pick on me because of my backwoods ways, and I'd beat them up. Anyhow, Aunt Esther was very nice. She really tried to show me the benefits of civilized life. Took me to the theater, operas, art museums, the zoo. Took me to high tea once at a place so formal we had to wear hats and white gloves, and I expect if a lady ever burped or farted inside that teahouse she'd be a social outcast for life."

Another low laugh came from the back of the tent. "Was she tough to live with?"

"Not at all. We got along great. She was quiet and shy, but while I was living with her she'd do things and visit places she'd never have done otherwise. She'd have kept me even after I got expelled, but when she came into my bedroom to ask me to stay, I told her I just really wanted to go back home, and she respected that. She told me my father missed me so much he was glad I'd gotten expelled in time to get home for Christmas."

"Do you keep in touch with her?"

"Yes. I think a lot of Aunt Esther. She came to my father's funeral, which was more of a big backwoods drunken potlatch than a funeral, but she showed up, all proper in her dark wool skirt and cardigan, and she even got a little tipsy. Her being there meant a lot to me." Cameron's empty stomach let out a growl. "I could eat a moose," she said.

"Get some more sleep. That bear's not coming back. He's not an Elvis fan. If we're going to retrieve that canoe, we'll have to get that ax at the cabin, come back here and make good time doing it. The river's dropping fast, and we need every inch of water we can get to move that tree."

Cameron knew he was right, but she couldn't sleep. She lay awake until the sun rose, waiting for the bear to return and listening to Jack's measured breathing. It made her feel safer than she'd felt in a very long time.

THE NEXT DAY was the hardest of all. Cameron hurt all over and was so lame she could barely exit the tent. Jack had long since risen. She could smell coffee, and it was the only thing that got her moving. She crawled out on her hands and knees, and stifled a moan as she pushed to her feet.

"I feel like I've been run over by an 18-wheeler," she said, taking the cup of coffee he offered her.

"And dragged behind it, too, by the looks of you," Jack said.

"Thanks." She fished four mosquitoes out of her cup before taking the first sip. The whine of mosquitoes drove her back inside the tent, where she sat in misery, wishing she had some aspirin, good horse liniment or strong liquor, anything to help with the pain. She wondered how she'd ever be able to hike four hours to the trapper's cabin, then turn around and walk four hours back here with the ax.

"Maybe we could leave our gear here," she suggested through the tent door. "Haul it up in a tree so the bear can't get it. We'd make better time walking."

"I thought about that, but what if something happened and we needed it?"

Cameron sighed. He was right, and she knew it. Her father always told her that there was no room for mistakes in the wilderness. He'd promoted a belt and suspenders philosophy, and always had numerous contingency plans for when things went wrong, but in spite of all that, fate had doomed him in the end.

"We'll eat a big breakfast—that'll lighten your pack considerably," Jack said. "You packed ten pounds of food on your hike yesterday. Did you hear that wolf last night?"

"I was too busy listening to you snore. You must have just dreamed you heard a wolf."

"You're the one who was snoring, and I definitely heard a wolf howl downriver."

"I didn't sleep a wink after that bear came, so I know for a fact I didn't snore."

"You were sound asleep when I got up to make the coffee and snoring like a lumberjack."

She took another sip of the strong brew. It was true she didn't remember him leaving the tent, and he practically had to crawl over her to get out. "I was snoring?" The thought disturbed her almost as much as that great big bear returning to ravage their camp. Snoring wasn't sexy.

"Like a lumberjack," he repeated. She gazed at him over the rim of the cup. Had he been this handsome all along and she just hadn't noticed? Had she been too intent on finding him and then turning him over to his sister when she got him to the Mackenzie? Had she been focused only on the money, completely blinded by the five thousand dollars and a red Jeep?

She took another swallow of coffee. "Nobody's perfect," she said. "Sorry if I kept you awake."

"Nothing kept me awake. I slept like a rock. Why don't you stay here and rest. I'll go back to the cabin and get the ax. No point in both of us going."

Cameron shook her head. "You're not leaving me here with that monster bear," she said. "I don't know how to play a guitar, and I can't sing like Elvis."

THEY ATE A big breakfast. Huge. The bear had ripped a hole in Cameron's dry sack but hadn't made off with any of the chow. Jack cooked. He fried half a pound of bacon, cooked up the entire container of a dozen eggs and made toast, all on his tiny stove with one frying pan. He piled her plate into a tall pyramid and handed it to her through the tent door.

She devoured every morsel hungrily and felt warmth and strength flow back into her. She drank another cup of coffee.

"How was that?" he asked when he'd cleaned his own plate.

"Best breakfast ever," she told him with genuine gratitude. "I'll fix lunch when we reach the cabin."

"Sounds like a plan," he said.

Half an hour later they had broken camp and were on the march. It was another bright and shining day. The food had helped enormously to boost her morale, and Cameron felt better as moving warmed her muscles. But less than an hour into the hike she began to feel worse and worse. Was it possible that Jack Parker, the wounded warrior with only one good leg, was walking faster than her? That he was waiting for her to catch up? Was it possible that she was actually falling behind?

"You okay?" he asked in a patronizing way after one of his patient waits.

"I'm just a little lamed up, that's all. I'll be all right."

"If you think there's any possibility you have internal injuries, we should stop."

"I'm fine. I'm probably getting my monthly, that's all," she said.

That shut him right up, like she knew it would. Men usually avoided conversations about a woman's monthly. She wasn't sure that's what it was and hoped it wasn't. All her "monthly" gear was now in her emergency pack in the front of the canoe, which was submerged in the Wolf River, pinned beneath a giant spruce tree that they might not be able to shift even after they chopped through the trunk. She was suffering from bad stomach cramps, but she was like clockwork, and it was two weeks early for her period. The pain was probably due to the terrible struggle and bad bruising from yesterday.

Cameron stumbled after Jack, trying to keep up. Three more hours remained until they reached the cabin. She could make it. She had no choice. What she really wanted to do was fall to the ground and curl up in a whimpering ball, but she kept walking. She was sure there was a bottle of aspirin in the kitchen kit at the cabin, which was a strong incentive for her to push on.

Jack was always waiting for her just out of sight.

"Okay?" he asked as she came into view.

"Fine," she replied through an olive green veil of mosquito netting, which at the moment was thwarting a cloud of hungry black flies. Someday this would all be a very funny memory, but right now she was too miserable to manage a smile.

"How many days has it been?" she asked as she trudged along on his heels, struggling to keep up. "I've lost track. Seems like carrying a heavy pack and bushwhacking along this river is all I've ever done, when I wasn't busy capsizing canoes."

"This is day three…no, it's day four," Jack

said, half turning his head so she could hear. "Or maybe it's day five. Either way I have a few more days to make the Mackenzie River on schedule."

And to think she'd laughed when Walt had told her Jack's plans for an eight-day hike down the Wolf. She'd scoffed at the idea, and told Walt she'd have him waiting at the Mackenzie River in four days in her canoe. Four days, and she'd have him roped and tied, ready for his sister to pick up. Ready for the generous bounty that she'd be paid for his safe delivery.

Walt would get worried when she didn't call on the sat phone. He'd come looking for her on day five or six. He'd fly over, low and slow, searching the Wolf River for a wrecked canoe and floating bodies. She'd listen for the plane and signal him that they were alive but in trouble because she'd screwed up royally.

Jack was waiting for her again. She caught up. "You don't have to stop for me," she said. "I know the way."

His only response was to whistle again for a dog that was long dead. Which was why he had stopped. Not to wait for her, but to whistle for a dead dog. Then he kept walking.

"Do you really believe your dog could still be alive?" Cameron asked, overwhelmed with a kind of sick despair as the pain doubled her over. "I mean, do you honestly think she could have survived the bear attack and the winter?"

He didn't respond. Just kept walking. His limp was becoming less pronounced, no doubt about it. He was getting the hang of the prosthetic leg. He was getting stronger, she was getting weaker and he was leaving her behind.

Abandonment. She knew the feeling well. She'd grown up wondering why her mother had abandoned her. Why her mother never wrote, never called, never wondered what had become of her own daughter. Never cared enough to send a card at Christmas or remember her on her birthday. Her father had never said a bad word about her, even though she'd abandoned him, too, and run off with another man. "She loves you, Cam," he would tell her, "she just doesn't know how to show it. But she's your mother and she loves you, and she'll always love you."

It was easier for Cameron to believe her mother was dead than to think she just didn't care, that she was out there somewhere, dressed up in furs and jewels like a fashion model, living in a big city and drinking champagne every night, never ever telling anyone that she had a daughter named Cameron Johnson who lived in the Northwest Territories and worked as a bush pilot, guide and camp cook.

She was on the verge of collapse by the time they reached the cabin. She stood weaving with exhaustion while Jack went inside and came out with the ax in his hand a few moments later.

"Nice camp," he said. "You stay put and get some rest. Eat something. If I'm not back before dark, don't worry. I have everything I need with me to spend the night out. It might take me longer than I think to free the canoe. Okay?"

Cameron nodded. She wanted to argue that she should go back with him, but she couldn't. She couldn't even speak, much less walk all the way back to where she'd lost the canoe and help chop through the trunk of a giant spruce tree with an ax. She felt her eyes prickle with the shame of her weakness. Before he left, he carried her dry sack into the cabin, unlatched the bear shutters over the windows and opened the sash for a nice cross breeze through screened openings.

"No bear will bother you, not with my smelly socks hanging out there," he told her. "Climb into a bunk and get some sleep."

She watched him leave, and a peculiar feeling gripped her. He closed the cabin door behind him, and she heard his footsteps descending the cabin steps. She crossed to the door and opened it. He paused and looked back questioningly.

"Jack, why did you carry that guitar with you?"

"I used to play it every night when Ky was with me, back in Afghanistan. I thought if she heard me playing..." He shrugged. "So I brought it along. Haven't played it once, except to that bear, but it doesn't weigh much. It's no bother to carry."

"Maybe you could play it for me when you get back."

"I will, if you want," he said.

"What about some lunch before you go?"

"No time. I'll eat one of my energy bars."

"What if cutting the tree doesn't work?"

"I'll try to haul the canoe out from under the tree. I have a couple carabiners and some haul rope in my pack. If I'm not back by dark, it just means I'm waiting till tomorrow to head back."

"Be careful, Jack," she said in a voice that wavered.

He nodded and was gone, disappearing into the woods for the long hike back to the submerged canoe.

CAMERON WASN'T HUNGRY. She rummaged through the gear and found the bottle of aspirin, took four with a lot of water and hoped the awful pains would ebb. Her legs were like rubber. She sat on the edge of the lower bunk and gazed around the interior of the cabin. It was so neat and orderly she could almost imagine the personality of the trapper who wintered here. He was a craftsman for sure, laying the cabin logs up with dovetail notches, which was unusual and required far greater skill with an ax than the more common saddle notch.

The cabin dimensions were small, and all the furnishings handmade. The eaves were low and deep, and firewood was stacked beneath them on both sides. The only things he'd brought in were the woodstove and stovepipe, glass sash and roofing materials. Her father had built a cabin similar to this when he got out of the military. He'd built it on crown land, at the edge of a remote fly-in lake, and some of her earliest and best memories were of that camp and the times spent there with him.

She lay back on the bunk and closed her eyes. She never took afternoon naps and had no intention of doing so now. She was just going to rest until the aspirin took effect. The guilt of lying here motionless while Jack struggled back to the canoe weighed heavily on her, but she was so exhausted. If she'd gone back with him, she'd have held him up. The irony of this was not lost on her.

Cameron listened to the rush of the river, a soothing sound that eased her as she rested her palms on her lower belly, feeling their warmth through her flannel shirt. A hot-water bottle would be nice. A soak in a hot tub would be even nicer. She'd just lie here for a few minutes with her eyes closed, and rest.

CHAPTER NINE

JACK WAS GLAD Cameron had stayed behind at the cabin. His strength was returning by the moment, and he could travel much faster without her. Being out here in the wilderness was the best medicine in the world for him. The walking gave him time to reexamine his life, the choices he'd made, the paths he'd walked. He was starting to wonder if he wanted to continue in the direction he'd chosen, or if maybe there was something else out there. Something more than the Spartan life of a soldier.

It was that girl, of course. She'd been nothing but an annoyance at first, but after just three days—or was it four?—he was finding it more and more difficult to dislike her. She was unlike any female he'd ever known. Few women would have been tough enough to survive what she just had. She was covered with bruises, cuts and contusions, one eye almost swollen shut, but not a word of complaint from her. She just soldiered stoically along. She'd made a mistake, almost drowned and lost the canoe, but he doubted she'd ever tangle with a strainer again, no matter how much she cared about retrieving a sexy-looking hat.

Jack wanted to salvage the canoe for her, which was why he was pushing himself so hard. In his mind's eye he could envision himself chopping swiftly and effortlessly through the tree trunk. As soon as the tree was free, the force of the river pushing against it would pivot and swing the top downstream, rolling it just enough so that the canoe would be freed from the branches that pinned it to the rocky river bottom. He'd recover the canoe, bail it out, fashion a crude but serviceable pole if there wasn't a spare paddle lashed inside, and return to the cabin well before dark. When Cameron saw him approaching the trapper's cabin in the canoe, her smile would light up the Northwest Territories.

Jack paused for a breather. He found a rock beside the river and braced himself against it, pulled out his water bottle for a drink. He'd called his CO after leaving Water Reed and been granted his full sixteen-and-a-half days of medical "take and leave" to come up here and find his dog. It was more than enough time, but Cameron's appearance had complicated his plans, and her recent brush with death and the loss of the canoe had changed everything.

Now the roles were reversed. She was pretty banged up and afoot, and depending on him to sort things out. Would she still collect her bounty money if he was the one who got *her* to the Mackenzie?

It was the money part that bothered him the most, and that damned red Jeep, but she'd lived on the edge of poverty all her life. Why wouldn't she care about the money? Jack took another swallow of water. He tucked the bottle away, pushed off the rock and shouldered his pack. His mission was to retrieve Cameron's canoe and her gear. Once he'd accomplished that, maybe she'd start to regard him as more than just a five-thousand-dollar reward and a red Jeep.

CAMERON OPENED HER eyes with a start, not knowing for a few seconds where she was, what had woken her or why she was sleeping in broad daylight. Then the past few days all came back with a rush, and she sat up and let her sore feet dangle over the edge of the bunk. She glanced at her wristwatch: 8:00 p.m. She'd been sleeping since Jack left just after noon. That was one heck of a nap she'd taken. She felt much better. The sharp stomach pains were gone, and if she lay absolutely still and didn't breathe too deeply, her bruised muscles didn't hurt that bad. She wondered where he was, if he'd made it back to the canoe, if he'd chopped the big spruce trunk and freed the tree, and the canoe.

She wondered if he was all right.

And then she heard a sound that must have woke her. A long, lonely mournful howl filled the river valley. It was a heart-wrenching howl that raised the hair on her nape and at the same time made her feel so lonely that she wanted to cry.

Maybe it was the same wolf Jack had heard last night. Or maybe…

Maybe it wasn't a wolf.

The sudden thought sprang unbidden into her mind and galvanized her into action. She pushed off the bunk, moaning aloud as her sore muscles protested, wincing when her blistered feet touched the plank floor.

Maybe what she heard was Jack's dog. He'd said it was wild and looked like a coyote, and if it was still alive, maybe it howled like a wolf after a year of living in the wilderness. Jack's sister, Lori, had said that Afghanistan had wolves. Could be Jack's dog was really a wolf that looked like a coyote but howled like a wolf because it *was* a wolf, or part wolf, or had run with a pack of wolves all winter. She was crazy to be thinking like this. There was no way that

long-lost dog of his was alive. But what if…?
She pulled on her boots, rummaged through
her kit, took another handful of aspirin, then
opened the cooler. She'd cook something that
smelled good, just in case a miracle had happened and Jack's dog or wolf or coyote *was*
alive, and it was howling out there because it
had gotten a whiff of Jack's smelly old socks
and thought Jack had returned.

Maybe the smell of food and stinky socks
would keep it close until Jack got back.
Wouldn't it be something if she found his dog
for him. He'd treat her differently if she managed to pull that off. He wouldn't look at her
as if she were a giant mosquito buzzing around
his head. He might even start to like her if she
found his long-lost companion.

She selected a package of burger, still partially frozen in the bottom of the cooler, and
smiled. No self-respecting mutt would ever
pass up the chance for a piece of hamburger.
She'd build a little fire pit down beside the
river and cook the burgers there, where the
savory smell of meat juices dropping on the
coals could perfume the evening breeze. In
her mind's eye she could picture how it would
be, the dog creeping ever closer as she grilled
the burger. Timid but starving. Drooling for
the taste of meat. She'd be patient, mostly just

ignore it, avoid making eye contact, act like she didn't know or care it was there. Let the half-wild animal get used to being around her. Then, just as the shy animal took the first piece from her fingers, Jack would come around the river bend in the canoe to witness the miraculous moment.

Everyone loved a happy ending.

IT WAS A HOT, humid afternoon and the black flies were thick. By the time Jack had chopped almost all the way through the trunk of the downed spruce tree, he was wringing wet with sweat and being eaten alive by hordes of biting insects. A few more solid whacks and he'd be through. The trunk would drop into the river, the water would push the spruce downstream, and he'd move downriver himself to capture the canoe when it broke free and floated to the surface. Within the hour he'd be taking the easy route back to the cabin, letting the current carry him.

Three more good whacks of the ax and with a great splintering sound, the butt end dropped three feet from the embankment and crashed into the river, throwing up a big plume of water. The river pushed against the tree trunk, but the current wasn't strong enough and the water was no longer deep enough to move the tree downstream. The mighty spruce tree stayed right where it was, with the canoe no doubt trapped even more firmly beneath it.

Jack let the ax slip out of his sweaty hands. For a moment he stood transfixed and exhausted, waiting for something to happen, but nothing did. Disappointment and frustration roiled in his gut.

The only other option was to get a rope on the tree itself and try to shift it using a z-drag, but the size and weight of the tree was formidable. This had to be one of the biggest spruce trees along the river. He'd have to get the rope as close to the tip of the tree as possible, which would be difficult. He looked to where Cameron's hat still dangled from the tree branch near the very tip. It was completely clear of the water now and moving a little in the slight breeze. Back and forth, back and forth, almost like it was waving to him.

He decided to rest awhile. It was getting late. It had taken him much longer than he thought it would to make it back to the canoe. His pace had slowed as the miles stretched out, and now the perfect scenario he'd envisioned was vanishing into the waning daylight. He wouldn't be arriving at the cabin just in time for supper. He'd be spending every hour of daylight trying to shift the tree off the canoe, and spending the night here again, with that very large grizzly prowling through the dark.

This time, he didn't have his Martin classical backpacker's guitar.

Jack ate another protein bar along with a few black flies while he rested beside the river. He decided to put up his tent before he got too tired, then once the tent was up, which took longer than he thought because he was moving so slowly, he made the decision to try to shift the tree in the morning, after a good night's sleep. He was too exhausted to start the project now. His leg was bothering him, and he needed to tend to it, and he was having trouble forming clear thoughts. In the morning, the situation wouldn't look so dire.

He washed up at the river's edge, then stood there, studying the tree and noting how far the water level had dropped from the high levels after the torrential rains. Shifting that heavy tree was going to be a bear. Impossible, really. Retrieving the canoe had been a pipe dream. They were both going to have to walk out to the Mackenzie. He was just about to turn back toward the tent when a raven flew over, croaking. It broke flight, tucked its wings, executed a perfect barrel role, and as it flew downriver, Jack spotted something rippling in the water about twenty feet from shore and thirty feet in length, moving snake-like in the current down-river from the spruce. He moved along the water's edge, trying to get a better look.

When he recognized it as one of the snub lines from the canoe, a surge of relief washed through him. All he had to do now was retrieve the end of the floating snub line, attach his own rope to it, set up a simple z-drag and pull the canoe out from under the tree. Cameron would get her canoe back after all. He'd get a few hours of sleep and make an early start in the morning. With any luck, he'd be back at the cabin in time for breakfast.

As SOON AS dusk fell, the temperature began to drop. Cameron was cold. She wrapped her arms around herself and huddled as close as she could to the warmth of the campfire. She'd eaten one burger. The others rested on the edge of the grill. There was still time for Jack to arrive before dark, but with each passing moment, hope faded. It was almost dark. Jack would have pitched camp by now, even if he was on the river in the canoe. There were only so many hours in a day, and she knew his day had been long and difficult. Just the hike back to the canoe was a challenge, and then he had to chop through that big tree. She wouldn't worry about him. He was okay.

There had been no sign of the howling wolf that had woken her from her nap. She'd let her gaze wander upriver and down while she cooked and tended the fire. She'd just as casually scanned the woods along the river's edge and the clearing around the trapper's cabin, but she'd seen nothing remotely canine. Maybe she'd just imagined the howl. Maybe she'd dreamed it. She heaved a sigh. "I tell you what," she said aloud, "if anyone ever cared about me the way he cares about that damned dog, my life would be a whole lot less lonely."

Cameron's eyes stung, and it wasn't from the smoke. She was feeling sorry for herself, which she knew from past experience was very unproductive. She plucked a second hamburger from the grill and started to chew on it.

"I'm eating this delicious burger that *you* could be eating if you would just come out and keep me company," she narrated to Jack's imaginary dog. "You don't have to be so shy, Ky. I don't bite."

She finished the burger, set half of another on a fire stone as coyote bait and picked up the grill, using a stick to carry it to the river. She put it in the water and placed a couple of stones on top of it to keep it from washing downstream. Crouched beside the water's edge, she pulled her toothbrush out of her pocket and finished her routine as the first stars spangled the evening sky.

"I'm going to bed now, Ky," she said, the water bucket dangling from her fingers. "You can have that piece of burger. Better grab it before a bear does."

She walked up to the cabin, glad she would spend the night within four sturdy log walls. She closed the windows on the chill night air, pulled off her boots, wrapped herself in a wool blanket and within moments was asleep on the bottom bunk. If she'd been counting sheep, it would have been a flock of three.

FOUR HOURS LATER she opened her eyes to the sounds of gray jays and the muted rush of the river, and when she propped herself up on her elbows to look out the window she was startled to see that the ground was white. An unseasonable dusting of snow coated everything and brightened the forest. She moved tentatively, drew a deep breath. Her injuries were healing. Another week or two and she'd be back to normal.

She drank her first cup of coffee while walking down to the fire pit. The first thing she noticed was the piece of burger was gone. She came to an abrupt stop, and her heartbeat quickened at the site of fresh canid tracks lacing the snow along the river's edge and circling the pit. Would a wolf behave this way? She didn't think so. Wolves checked out campsites, but usually well after the humans had moved on. They were wary of humans, and with good reason. The tracks in the powdering of snow were too small to be a full-grown wolf, and they were already vanishing as the day warmed and summer returned.

"Well, I'll be damned," she said out loud. She hadn't imagined the howl. As impossible as it seemed, Jack's dog might still be alive.

She set her coffee cup on a flat spot beside the river and knelt to wash the sleep from her face. The water was ice-cold. She wondered if Jack was already on the river. She figured he'd retrieved the canoe by dark, camped at the same spot and would be back at camp in time for breakfast. At least, that's how she envisioned the morning.

She wiped her face on the tail of her flannel shirt and was reaching for her coffee cup when she caught a flash of movement out of the corner of her eye. She turned her head and was looking right into the eyes of an animal that was grayish colored, wolfish looking and very thin. Their eyes met for only a moment, and then it whirled and vanished back into the forest.

Cameron rose slowly to her feet, dumbfounded. "Ky?" she said. "Good girl, Ky. Don't be scared. Jack's here, he's coming."

She kindled a small fire in the pit, fished the grill out of the river and put it over the heat to burn off the remains of last night's hamburgers. She then walked up to the cabin to bring down the frying pan and bacon, and a container inside of which, cushioned by oatmeal, she'd nestled six eggs. Within minutes she was frying bacon in the pan and drinking her second cup of coffee. She moved the frying pan to the very edge of the fire, and while the bacon slowly cooked, she washed her laundry in the river and hung it over bushes to dry. Then she took a quick, chilly cat bath, put on clean underthings and donned her warm clothing. The bacon had rendered down to perfection, and she broke two eggs into the fat. She could've eaten all six, but she wanted to give Jack a good feed when he arrived.

After breakfast, she laid a piece of bacon in the same place she'd put the burger the night before. She left the bacon fat in the pan and returned it to the cabin, put out the fire in the pit, gathered more driftwood for the cook fire that night, swept and cleaned inside the camp and then began to wonder what was taking Jack so long. She occupied herself with domestic chores, wiping down shelves and washing the cabin windows, but she was worried. Jack should have arrived by now. Had everything gone smoothly, he would have arrived last night, so she knew he'd run into problems. By 11:00 a.m. she was really anxious. Having risen at dawn, she felt like she'd been waiting for him for ages.

The wolf dog hadn't reappeared, and the bacon had been stolen by a camp jay, something she should have anticipated in broad daylight. There were still four strips all cooked for Jack. At noon she took more aspirin, ate a quick sandwich, made four more sandwiches, packed them in her dry bag along with the bacon and more lightweight food, a thermos of tea and her water bottle. She left a note on the table telling Jack when she left and that if she missed him on the river, she'd be back before dark. And then, donning her orange whistle necklace and mosquito netting, she set off to hike the four hours upriver to the submerged canoe.

JACK WAS UP before dawn. His breakfast consisted of two protein bars and more water. Rigging the z-drag required two carabiners, a short section of rope to tie around the anchoring tree with one carabiner, another short section to at-

tach a second carabiner to the main line with
a prusik knot, and the fifty-foot-long piece of
rope, which, when spliced to the snub line from
the canoe, would barely be enough to do the
job. He found a long pole with a forked end and
figured he'd use it to snag the snub line. The
spruce trunk was branchless for at least ten
feet. If he straddled the trunk and scooted out
as far as he could, then used the pole to snag
the snub line, he'd avoid wading in the river
completely. If everything went according to
plan he'd barely get his feet wet.

But he also knew that sometimes the best
made plans went south really fast, so before he
tackled the job, he gathered dry kindling and
made a fire pit in the river gravel, using strips
of birch bark under the kindling and piling a
good-sized stack of dry driftwood nearby. He
laid his fire starter on top of his pack inside the
tent. It was cold, there was a dusting of snow
on the ground, and if he took an unexpected
swim, he'd need to warm up quickly.

He might have delayed longer, long enough
for the sun to work its way over the ridge line to
the east and warm the morning, but he wanted
to make it back to the cabin as quickly as possible. He was afraid that if he didn't show up
soon, Cameron would come looking for him,

and she was too beat-up and sore to make that arduous hike again.

So he made sure his prosthesis was securely socketed, took up the pole and used it to steady himself as he slid down the riverbank next to the big spruce and then hoisted himself onto the trunk, sliding the pole ahead of him.

He pulled himself along the trunk, securing the pole in the branches ahead of him. When he had gone as far as he could before running into tree branches, he was about eight feet from the floating snub line. His pole was eight feet long. By holding on to the first branch and leaning out over the water, he could just barely reach the line with the end of the pole. It took him several tries to get the tip of the pole underneath the floating line and raise it so the line slid back down the pole toward him. His free hand caught the line, and he laid the pole on the trunk until he'd pulled all the slack in and secured the end of the line around his waist.

He was about to start backing his way toward shore when he spied Cameron's hat caught in the tip of the tree, pivoting in the light breeze and still nodding back and forth as if giving him a jaunty wave. Maybe jaunty was the wrong word. Her hat was taunting him. Daring him to come get it. It occurred to him that he might score some points with her if he could somehow retrieve her hat *and* the canoe. He could use the pole to try to snag it, but he'd have to move farther along the tree trunk, and he'd have to stand up. Navigating the thick twine of spruce branches would make it pretty difficult, and it was just a hat. Not worth wasting time on.

He gave up on the idea.

Then, as he started pushing himself back toward shore, her Aussie hat gave him an especially flippant wave. He paused, reconsidering. He could untie the snub line from around his waist, leave it on the tree trunk, stand up, use the pole to balance himself, and thread his way very carefully between the branches along the trunk until he could reach the hat with the pole. Then he'd just have to snag the hat by the hurricane strap, let it slide down the pole and he'd have it. Easy.

He studied the trunk ahead of him and the placement of the branches. There were plenty of sturdy handholds to grab on to for balance if he should start to go over. It shouldn't be too difficult. He decided to try for the hat. He could abandon the attempt and turn around if it turned out to be too risky, but he didn't think it would. He'd get the hat first, then retrieve the canoe. When he returned to the cabin, she'd regard him as one of the most heroic men she'd ever met, certainly more heroic than her philandering ex-husband, Roy.

CHAPTER TEN

WALT WAS SLEEPING in his chair when the woman arrived. He often napped after lunch on slow days. It was only natural to give the body quiet time to digest a meal, and a nap midafternoon had become a ritual with him the past few days. With the forest fire out, Cameron gone and Mitch still ferrying smoke jumpers back to the airport in Fort Simpson, things had been real quiet at the office.

He was dreaming about Jeri. He dreamed about her often now that she was gone. In his dreams she was back again, and it was like she'd never left. She was making a pot of coffee like she did first thing every morning, and she was wearing those tight capri shorts, the purple Lycra ones, and the black Lycra top, the one that made her look like Dolly Parton. She smiled at him, and her smile made him feel young again. Jeri was a good-looking woman, so sexy she sizzled.

"I'm glad you're back, Jeri," he said. "I really missed you."

"I missed you too, Walt," she said with the most seductive smile over her shoulder before starting the coffeemaker. "I missed you so much I'm just going to have to show you." And then she proceeded to undress herself right in front of him, which didn't take long because she wasn't wearing all that much, and just as she started walking bare-assed naked toward him, the knock came at the door and Jeri, every sexy sizzling ounce of her, began to vanish into the ether.

"No!" Walt protested, struggling to keep hold of the dream.

"Walter?" a woman's voice said. "Walter Krantz?"

Another knock, and then the doorknob turned and the door swung inward. A woman's head poked around the edge of the door. Late twenties, dark hair, dark eyes, not bad looking but terrible timing. Couldn't be worse, matter of fact. She spotted him sitting in his chair and gave a tentative smile.

"I'm sorry if I woke you. I'm Lori Tedlow, Jack Parker's sister, the one who's been calling you daily and driving you crazy, I'm sure." As she spoke, she commenced the tricky job of entering the office, a maneuver undertaken carefully because the space was so small and she was so big. Her pregnant stomach thrust out in front of her and took up half the room.

Walt pushed out of his chair, which further shrank the space. His office at the float plane base was really nothing more than a small construction trailer. He couldn't understand why Lori Tedlow was here. It was very annoying, especially since he had nothing to tell her.

"I don't have any news, nothing to report since you called yesterday," he said. "Cameron said she'd call when she reached the Mackenzie River, so I guess she hasn't got there yet." He spread his hands. "I can't tell you anything else."

Lori Tedlow smiled again, apologetically. "I thought maybe you could try to contact her, find out where she is and what's going on. We don't even know that she's found my brother. Can't you call her? Doesn't a satellite phone work both ways?"

"Sure, but it has to be turned on. Cameron would keep it powered down and inside the waterproof case unless she was calling me. To conserve the batteries and keep it dry," he explained.

"Look, Mr. Krantz, I flew into Fort Simpson this morning because I can't sit home any longer waiting for news. I came fully prepared to hire you to fly me over the route they're taking. Please try to understand. I'm worried about my brother, and so is my mother. We're both worried he might be suicidal, and we both think that's why he came up here and went into the woods. We really, really need to know he's okay." She put both hands on the swell of her belly as she spoke, as if trying to keep it from expanding.

"But, you're pregnant," he said.

Lori Tedlow looked at him wearily. "I know that. Believe me, I do. I'm asking you to fly me over the route my brother's hiking, that's all. I'm not asking you to deliver my baby. He's not due for another three weeks."

"You might not fit in the plane."

"Don't worry, I'll fit."

Walt glanced down at his watch. It was 2:00 p.m. The weather was calm, sunny, perfect for flying. "I dunno. We're pretty busy around here, and there's nobody but me to man the phone with Jeri gone and Cameron out hunting for your brother. It's a three hour round-trip to get to the lake and back, then another hour to fly down the Wolf River to the Mackenzie."

"Then it's a good thing it stays light so long this time of year," Lori said. "We'd better get going. I trust you have an answering machine that will take calls while you're gone?"

"Even if I said yes, there's no reason for you

to go. Having a passenger along just adds to the paperwork."

"Having a passenger along gives you twice the search power," Lori Tedlow countered.

Walt pulled a foil-wrapped package of chewing tobacco out of his rear pocket and stuffed a generous pinch under his upper lip, stalling for time while he considered his options. "This is going to cost you," he said, tucking the tobacco back into his hip pocket. "I charge by the mile, aviation fuel is pricey and there's lots of paperwork involved, especially with a pregnant woman. Hours and hours."

"Don't worry." Lori Tedlow reached inside her purse for her wallet. "I'll make it well worth your while."

CHAPTER ELEVEN

AFTER THREE HOURS of hiking back upriver, Cameron made a vow to herself that she would never, ever walk along another river that didn't have an established footpath, or better yet a major highway running alongside it. In fact, after three hours she made a vow that she'd never walk anywhere ever again that she didn't absolutely have to. She'd fly a plane, paddle a canoe, ride a horse, drive a red Jeep, but she was giving up on walking. There was nothing whatsoever that she enjoyed about it. She had blisters on her feet, every muscle hurt, she was scratched and gouged from head to toe and covered with bug bites. She was so hungry that even after she was done eating her stomach growled, and it was all because of the endless struggle of bushwhacking along this damned river.

The harder she tried to move quickly, the slower she went. There was no way to make good time. Every step had to be calculated. A single misstep could result in a wrenched or broken limb, and out here that sort of accident could be fatal. The walking had been tough yesterday and hard the day before that, and it was even worse on day four—or was it five?—though the early-morning cold had kept the bugs down.

Every ten minutes, she would blow five long blasts on her whistle. There was the possibility she and Jack might miss each other completely if he were in the canoe and she was bushwhacking along the shore, and she didn't want to walk one extra step if she didn't have to. But there was no sign of Jack and no answering whistle.

Anxiety had twisted her stomach into a knot by the time she reached the downed spruce tree, and she was filled with dread as Jack's camp came into sight. She saw his tent, saw that the trunk of the spruce had been chopped through, but there was no sign of Jack. No activity. No sound. She drew closer and saw the ax lying against the base of the tree. Then she spotted the snub line coiled on the spruce trunk. Neatly. As if he'd left it there, ten feet from shore. But he would never have left it out there unless he'd fallen into the river.

Her blood froze in her veins when she realized what had happened.

"Jack!"

Her shout would have wakened the dead, but there was no response.

A wave of weakness nearly dropped her to her knees. Cameron's worst fears had come to pass. Jack had drowned trying to retrieve her canoe. She was sure of it. He was dead, and all because of her incredible stupidity. She stood for a few moments, numb with shock. Then she closed the distance to his tent at a stumbling run, shrugging out of her pack and letting it drop behind her as she ran. She fell to her knees at the tent door. She was struggling to breathe, trying to process what she was looking at in the dimness of the tent's interior as she reached for the zipper, but it was already open.

He was lying facedown, feet toward the door, as if he'd crawled in and collapsed. His arms were up around his head as if cradling a pillow. Was he breathing? She couldn't tell. She grabbed his ankle. The pant leg was wet. His boot was wet. She crawled inside, her hand on his leg, on his back, his shoulder. He was soaking wet, head to toe. He'd fallen in the river, and that water was like ice. He was like ice. Like death.

"Jack!" She shook his shoulder. He was unresponsive. Was he even alive? Had he already died of hypothermia? She rolled him over in the tight confines of the tent. She had to get him out of those wet clothes, get him warm. She worked swiftly on the buttons of his shirt and paused when his head moved and he moaned, then coughed. She let him roll onto his side as he succumbed to a fit of coughing. She pounded his back. "That's it, cough up that water," she said. "I know just how you feel. That river almost got me, too. Cough!"

She glanced around the inside of the tent and saw his sleeping bag, neatly rolled up next to his pack. She saw something else, too, and a jolt of disbelief made her gasp aloud. Her hat was resting on top of his pack. The hat she'd almost died for. The hat that had been caught in the very tip of the downed spruce tree. She reached out and touched the damp felt crown, stunned, then a flash of anger surged through her.

"How could you be so stupid? That hat nearly killed me, and now it's nearly killed you, too! I *hate* that hat, do you hear me, Jack Parker? I don't want it. You risked your life for *nothing*! Don't just lie there moaning and coughing. You'll get no sympathy from me. I won't let you die—you aren't going to get off that easy."

Fear and anger gave her strength. She rolled him on his side, got one arm out of his shirt, rolled him over and got the other arm out, stripped away the wet fabric and tossed it behind her. He wore a thermal top under the shirt, and she jerked it up, fed one arm through, then the other, then got it over his head. She unbuckled his belt and stripped it off. She was working in a blind frenzy, her movements strong and sure, fueled by anger and fear. He was hypothermic, seriously hypothermic, and she knew how dangerous that was.

"I should sue you for causing me such emotional trauma," she said as she struggled to remove his hiking boot. The other one and his prosthetic leg were missing, which was a good thing because she had no idea how to get it off. "I should get a good lawyer and sue you. You've taken years off my life. I'm practically an old woman now because of you. I bet my hair's turning gray." She managed to get his pants off and was unrolling his sleeping bag, unzipping it, wrapping it around him, rolling him in it. He was almost completely unresponsive. This was bad, really bad.

Her hands were trembling. She was shaking all over. "What am I supposed to tell your dog, Jack? She's waiting for you back at the trapper's cabin. That's right, Ky's alive. What am I supposed to tell her if you don't come back with me?" His skin was cold, ice-cold. She knew of only one way to warm up a hypothermic victim out in the wild, and she stripped down to her underthings, draped her wool blanket over her shoulders and plastered herself against him under the sleeping bag. "I found your dog, Jack, do you hear me? I found your dog. She's alive, so you can't die now. That would be the stupidest thing you could ever do!" Was he still breathing? She laid her hand flat against his chest. Felt the shallow rise and fall. She pressed her ear against it and heard the faintest of heartbeats.

"If only I'd set out first thing this morning, I'd have been here hours ago," Cameron said, shivering with remorse and cold. "I should have come first thing. I should never have let you come back here by yourself. Stupid of me, stupid! Everything I've done has been so stupid." She wrapped herself around him like a warm blanket, tucked the sleeping bag around them both. "I'm in good company, though, because you did a stupid thing, too, Jack. It was a sweet stupid, but it was a huge one. Going after my hat. We're both stupid."

For a long while she lay pressed against him, willing him to keep breathing. It was like cuddling with a corpse. She listened for his heartbeat, counting the beats silently. She was shivering with the cold of his body, with fear, with shock. She had no idea how much time had passed—minutes, hours—when she heard a faint sound that was very familiar. It was the drone of an approaching airplane. Walt's plane, the de Havilland Beaver, *her* plane. She knew the sound of that Wasp engine, the rattle of every loose rivet in that old workhorse. Walt was looking for her, flying slowly along the river just like she'd known he would.

Hallelujah! They were saved!

Cameron wriggled out from under the sleeping bag and crawled to the door of the tent. She had to signal Walt that they were in serious trouble and needed help. The zipper on the tent's door stuck, and she jerked at it frantically as the sound of the plane grew louder. At the last moment, she ripped the zipper up and crawled out, rising to her feet just as the big red-and-white plane came into view from downriver, flying low and slow down the broad river valley. She moved a few steps away from the tent and waved her arms over her head, back and forth. He'd spot her. There was no way Walt could miss this bright colored tent right on the shore and her standing there nearly naked in her black Victoria's Secret lingerie, waving her arms at him.

The Beaver passed overhead and began a long banking turn up the wide valley beyond the campsite, came back flying just as low and slow, while Walt had another long look. She waved her arms again and jumped up and down, and he dipped the wings back and forth in response.

"Oh thank you, Walt, thank you!" Cameron called up to him, throwing him kisses with both hands. "I'm sorry for all the times I was bitchy with you, and I'll never complain about being overworked and doing endless amounts of paperwork for you again, I promise!" she shouted after the plane. "Any time you want me to fly, I'll fly, just send help quick! We're in a bad way down here."

Walt made one final pass, gave her one more reassuring wing wag and then set course for home. He was probably already on the plane's radio, calling for a team to mount a speedy rescue mission by boat from the lake. He might even send in a helicopter that could lower a basket and haul them to safety.

"We're saved," an emotional Cameron told the unresponsive Jack as she crawled back into the tent and under the sleeping bag. "That was Walt. He spotted us and we're saved. Hang on, Jack, you can't die on me now. Help is on the way. Hallelujah!"

WALT HAD A hell of a time adjusting the seat belt to fit his pregnant passenger once he got her into the plane, which was no easy feat in and of itself. He was having second and third thoughts about the whole thing right up until the moment the plane was airborne, whereupon he figured he was doomed and submitted passively to his fate. She'd go into labor halfway to the lake. The bumpy flight would cause her water to break and bring on the contractions. He'd end up delivering a baby at Kawaydin Lake in the back of the plane. The paperwork would take him the rest of his life, but maybe she'd name her kid after him. Walter Tedlow. Had a nice ring to it.

He racked his brain for the entire flight, trying to dredge up his first-aid training, stuff he'd learned through the years. His ex-wife had given him a daughter, but he hadn't been in the hospital for the delivery. He'd been overseas. She'd sent him photos that made him squeamish and uneasy enough to question the health of the baby, which had seriously pissed her off. She named the baby Madeline, Maddy for short. Cranky Maddy. The first time he held her she did nothing but cry, and come to think of it, she'd been mad at him all her life. Maddy was a perfect name for her.

His daughter was married now with kids of her own, living in Calgary near her mother. She married a tall, skinny guy who monitored website security for a big insurance company and liked to golf and collect beer steins from Germany. Most boring person Walt had ever met, but Maddy wasn't exactly normal, so he supposed it was just lucky they'd met each other.

By the time Walt reached the lake, it was late afternoon. He started flying down the river, as low and slow as he could go. The Wolf was a twisty river and flying it was like tracing a snake. If he ran into trouble, it would be tough putting the plane down anywhere along this stretch. The river valley was fairly broad, which made flying easier, but the boreal forest grew right down to the river's edge, and that made searching for Cameron difficult. There were very few places to pitch a tent in the open. He figured she'd be pretty close to the Mackenzie by now, so when he navigated a corner and saw movement up ahead, a blue tent pitched in a tiny clearing beside the river and a small figure standing by it, he was surprised. Could that be Cameron? Day five and barely halfway to the Mackenzie?

"There! Look. *Look! Right down there! There they are!*" Lori shouted over the engine noise, pounding his arm and pointing with great excitement out her side window.

Walt slowed the plane to just above stalling speed. He tipped the plane up on one wing to see better out his own window. His jaw dropped. "Wow," he said as he got a brief eyeful of a very well-stacked woodland goddess dressed in nothing but skimpy black lace lingerie. Suddenly he understood why Cameron was behind schedule. She was indulging in romantic dallying with the Lone Ranger, and in broad daylight! All that fancy food and wine combined with Cameron's natural knockout beauty had worked a little too well. At this rate it would be another five days before they made the Mackenzie. Hell, another ten days.

"I guess she didn't need handcuffs or duct tape after all," Walt said to himself, and uttered a growling laugh. He looked over at Lori Tedlow and gave her a thumbs-up.

She was beaming. Everyone loved a happy ending.

CHAPTER TWELVE

WHEN JACK WAS a boy his mother used to task him with watching his baby sister when she went to work. He was ten years old, and Lori was six. His mother waitressed at a diner in town. She worked the night shift, so it fell to Jack to feed his sister supper and then put her to bed. Being afraid of the dark, Lori never wanted him to leave the room. She thought all bad things existed in darkness and would beg him to stay until she went to sleep. He obliged her because it was the only way to get her to go to bed, but he thought she was a sissy girl, that all girls were sissies and all boys were brave.

That was before he discovered his own fears.

"Don't leave me alone, Jack. Just lie here with me and I promise I'll go to sleep." She'd pillow her head on his chest and cling to him as if he had the power to slay her fire-breathing dragons, which made him feel brave and guilty at the same time.

Her arms tightened around him, but then all at once everything changed, and it wasn't his sister and he wasn't a boy anymore. He was in a dark place, fighting for his life in the Hindu Kush, hand-to-hand combat with an enemy who had surprised him in his sleep. He surged up, threw the struggling form over and away from him with one strong, convulsive movement. A woman screamed his name in the darkness as he straddled the struggling body.

"Jack!" the strangled scream came again, and he awakened in a cold sweat, still grappling with the enemy. When he came fully awake, the tent was half collapsed around him.

"Jack, wake up! *Jack!* It's me, it's Cameron!"

In a matter of seconds he'd traveled from his boyhood home to Afghanistan to this tent in the Canadian wilderness. It all came back to him—the past five days, and the spruce tree and the canoe and Cameron's hat, and the cold river sucking him under over and over again, and now somehow she was pinned beneath him in his tent and he'd been seconds away from killing her.

Cameron was gasping for breath, and when he rolled aside and sat up, she did, too, scrabbling backward, away from him. In the darkness of the collapsed tent he could hear her rapid breathing.

"Cameron," he said, sickened by what he'd just done. "What are you doing here? You were supposed to wait at the cabin."

"I did!" she finally managed in a voice that shook. "I waited and waited and waited, and then when you didn't come, I came after you because I knew you were in trouble. Jesus, Jack! A few hours ago I was worried you weren't going to make it, and now you're strong enough to throw me through the tent wall. I guess you're going to be okay."

"I'm sorry." He sank back beneath the billowing fabric of the tent. "I'm sorry. I didn't know you were here, and when I woke up I just thought... I have nightmares sometimes." He struggled to make her understand. "Flashbacks. Sometimes I—" He stopped abruptly and shook his head. How could he explain something he couldn't deal with himself? "You weren't supposed to be here. You were supposed to wait for me back at the cabin."

"It's a good thing I didn't. You were in the tent when I got here, soaking wet. It must've been four or five o'clock, and you were pretty far gone. Unresponsive. Hypothermic. You've been out of it for hours. You would have died if I hadn't come."

He didn't remember anything. Not one thing of her arrival. "I'm sorry," he repeated. He didn't know what else to say.

She'd been fumbling in her pack while he spoke, and her headlamp came on, illuminating the interior of the half-collapsed tent. She stared at him, a little wild-eyed. He stared back at her. She was wearing some of the sexiest black underwear he'd ever seen. He was wearing next to nothing, as well. And it was cold. Really cold. He had no idea why they were both undressed.

"I'm going to start the campfire," she said. "I need to dry your wet clothes."

"Forget my clothes," he said. "I have a dry set of long johns in my pack. Jesus, I'm sorry, Cameron. I really am. I might have killed you."

"I doubt it. I'm pretty tough, and I'm a good fighter." She was gathering up her pants, pulling on her T-shirt, dressing quickly in the glow of her headlamp. "I promise I'll be right back. I have to fix the tent. It wasn't built for circus stunts."

"I'd never hurt you. You have to believe that."

"I do. Really. It's okay, Jack. You woke up, and you didn't know who or what was in the tent with you. You didn't hurt me. You just scared the daylights out of me. I'll be right back after I fix the tent."

CAMERON'S THOUGHTS WHIRLED as she crawled out of the tent. She was shaking all over and needed to give herself time to calm down. Jack hadn't meant to hurt her, she knew that, but he was right. He could've killed her. And if it happened once, it could happen again. Every time he closed his eyes, he could go back to Afghanistan, back to a war zone where the enemy was out to kill him. Now she knew. Now she'd be more careful. No more sleeping all tangled up with Jack Parker.

The night air was cold, but not as cold as last night. After fixing the tent, she paced the perimeter of the camp, walked along the shore, walked back again, over and over until the shaking caused by her fear became the shivering of being cold. Jack wasn't dead and neither was she, Walt knew where they were and he'd be sending help, and she'd found Jack's lost dog. Everything was going to be all right. The stress of the past few days would soon be forgotten. Deep breaths.

After washing up she crouched by the river, letting the sound of the water soothe her. She'd had so much adrenaline running through her veins she felt sick from it. She imagined Jack felt the same, but maybe not. He was a career soldier—they probably lived on adrenaline. It was probably one of their major food groups. She went back to the tent, crawled inside and fumbled for her pack in the darkness. Jack had pulled on his dry long johns and was sitting in the murky darkness, almost exactly where he'd been kneeling when she left.

"I brought along some hot tea and a sandwich for you," she said. "You must be as hungry as I am." They looked at each other in the light of the headlamp, and she tried to smile but failed. "It's okay, Jack. Really. You didn't hurt me." He made no response. He just shook his head and lowered his eyes.

She poured him a cup of tea. Steam curled up from it. It was a good stainless-steel insulated thermos that kept things hot for nearly twenty-four hours. She handed him a sandwich and took one for herself, and they ate in silence. Jack made it through two sandwiches and all four slices of the cooked bacon. They shared the thermos of tea between them. When they'd finished the meal, Cameron screwed the cup back onto the top of the thermos and sat for a moment with it cradled in her lap.

"Jack," she said, "you remember that wolf you heard when we camped here the other night? Well, I heard a long howl right near the cabin in broad daylight so I cooked supper outside, right by the river, hamburgers so the smell would be tempting. I left half a burger near the fire pit last night and saw tracks, tracks too small to be wolf. They were in the snow this morning coming right up to that spot.

The burger was gone. While I was reading the tracks I caught sight of it, our eyes met for a split second and it bolted back into the woods. I don't think it was a wolf, Jack. I think it was your dog."

He didn't speak for a moment, just stared at her as if she hadn't spoken, his face expressionless. Finally he said, "What did it look like?"

"It looked more like a wolf than a dog," she admitted. "But it wasn't a wolf, it was too small. I've never spotted a wolf so close to camp. It was real skinny."

He looked away from her and stared out the tent door into the darkness. She heard him draw a long deep breath and expel it slowly. "We need to get back there as soon as possible."

"But Jack, your leg…"

"My leg's fine."

"No, it's not, it's missing. It's not in here, and it's not outside, either. I looked."

"I brought a spare."

"You have a spare leg?"

"In my pack. I lost the other one in the river. My foot got caught in some rocks. I had to release the leg to get free."

She stared at him, confounded. "Well, your real leg's a mess. It was bleeding. You can't possibly walk on it. Besides, you have no boot.

It's still on your other leg. If you can show me tomorrow where you got hung up, I can try to retrieve it. The river's gone way down. I could practically walk across it now."

"Okay, if you can rescue it that's great, then we'll try to get the canoe out from under the spruce tree first thing. The snub line is up on the tree trunk. I just have to tie my rope to it and rig a z-drag. We can haul it out from under the tree and use it to get back to the camp."

"Assuming it isn't completely squashed," Cameron said. "But even if it is, we won't have long to wait for help to come. Walt flew over late this afternoon. He made three flybys and answered my wave. He definitely saw me. He'll make sure someone comes to get us out of here. Your leg's not fine, it's a mess. You can't walk, and we need help."

If Cameron thought news of their impending rescue would be welcome, she was mistaken.

"If that's Ky back at the trapper's cabin, the worst thing of all would be a whole swarm of strangers showing up to rescue us," Jack said. "If you want to be rescued, that's up to you, but one way or the other, I'm getting back to the cabin. Eight days is when I told your boss I'd probably want to be picked up. I have a few more days to reach the Mackenzie."

"Well, the thing is, Walt probably came looking for us because I told him I'd have you out to the river in four days."

"What made you think you could do that?"

"I had lots of good food in the canoe and some great bottles of wine, and I was pretty sure after a few good meals you'd want to stick with the canoe," Cameron told him. "It's rough going, bushwhacking along the river afoot."

"Don't take this the wrong way," Jack said after a brief pause. "You're a great cook, an accomplished individual and a beautiful girl, but the reason I came up here was to find my lost dog. That said, I do appreciate your sexy black lingerie."

"Sexy black lingerie," Cameron echoed.

"Very sexy," he said. "I may be a one-legged soldier, but I'm still a man, and I know sexy lingerie when I see it."

"I'm sure you do," she said, but she was thinking about her Victoria's Secret lingerie and how, when she crawled out of the tent to wave at Walt, that was all she'd been wearing. She began to wonder what Walt must have thought. How it must have looked to him, her jumping around almost naked in broad daylight. "When I heard the plane, there was no time to get dressed."

"That's perfect," Jack said. "He probably thought you were signaling that you'd tamed the beast, caught your quarry, that the five-thousand-dollar bounty money was yours, in the bank, and a red Jeep and happiness were in your very near future. He probably thought you were really excited about how I'd changed your life for the better."

"If you're right, we could be in a world of trouble. What makes you think that canoe is salvageable?"

"Even if we can't retrieve the canoe, I've walked this far and I can make it to the cabin. One way or the other, we'll manage. If you really need to be rescued, I have my GPS unit. But it would have to be life or death before I pushed that button. Turn out that headlamp and get some sleep."

Cameron switched off the headlamp and tucked the thermos back inside her dry bag. She sat in the darkness, reluctant to lie back down in the same tent with him. She was amazed that he could suggest such a thing after what had just happened.

"You don't need to worry about a repeat performance," he said, as if reading her mind. "I know you're here now, and I won't go back to sleep. Get some rest. I'll take the wool blanket, you take the sleeping bag. It's another hour or so before dawn."

"No. You take the sleeping bag. You're the

one who was hypothermic. I'm fine with the wool blanket."

They arranged their bedding in the darkness of the tent. After he lay down, Cameron made sure she was arranged in the opposite configuration, with her head near the tent door. At least he couldn't reach out and grab her if he had another nightmare, and she could escape out the door. She was tired but couldn't sleep. Couldn't relax.

"Warm enough?" she asked.

"Yes. You?"

"I'm fine."

"I'm really sorry about what happened."

"I know."

"War changes a person."

"I know."

"I didn't ask you to come along on this journey."

"I know."

"But I'm glad you did."

That surprised her. "You are?"

"Everything happens for a reason."

"Do you really believe that? You think your dog got lost for some cosmic reason?"

"She was chasing a bear out of camp. She didn't get lost, she got hurt."

"So it wasn't some deep universal plan. It's just action and reaction?"

"I don't know. The older I get, the less I know," he said. "I don't know why some people live to grow old and some die young. I don't know why I'm still alive and some of my men aren't."

"I don't know why either one of us is alive, but I'm glad we are." Cameron spoke softly into the darkness. After lying in silence for a while, she said, "What happened yesterday?"

"I cut the tree, but that didn't free the canoe. The water levels had dropped too much. Then I saw the floating snub line. Maybe it was there the whole time, but I only noticed it after I cut the tree and a raven flew over. Maybe the light was just right. I started down the tree trunk and retrieved it, *then* saw that hat of yours and had this bright idea that I could hook it with the same pole I used to get the snub line. I had to get pretty close to the end of the tree, but I unhooked your hat from the branch. When I was turning around, I lost my balance and fell into the river, fortunately on the downstream side. I got your hat, though."

"That hat nearly drowned the both of us. It's brought nothing but bad luck." She wondered why he'd done something so foolish. It was just a hat, not even his, and not worth dying for. The conversation had helped. She was losing her wariness of him, relaxing, drifting closer to sleep. Jack was a victim of war. She couldn't hold his nightmares against him. She just had to be aware that he had them, and after tonight she'd never forget. She'd certainly never sleep next to him again, and she'd never be so foolish as to wake him up by leaning over and shaking his shoulder. She'd poke him with a stick from a safe distance. She rubbed her sore shoulder where she'd hit the ground when he'd flung her off him. PTSD was nothing to mess around with.

CHAPTER THIRTEEN

When Cameron woke, she was alone in the tent and the sun was well up. The rush of the river and the swell of northern birdsong filled the morning. It was cool, but she was warm wrapped up in the wool blanket. She could smell wood smoke and coffee boiling. She stretched and yawned and felt, suddenly, quite good. In spite of what had happened last night, and in the days before that, all her aches and pains, and there were many, were getting better. She felt *good*. She sat up, ruing once again that her kit was in the sunken canoe. She had no hairbrush, no decent mirror, just the toothbrush in her cargo pants pocket. She pushed her hair back out of her face, finger combed it as best she could and had just finished braiding it when Jack appeared at the door of the tent.

"Coffee's ready," he said. He unzipped the door and offered the insulated cup to her. "Listen, about what happened last night…"

She held out her hand for the coffee and when their eyes met, she felt the heat come into her face. She, who never blushed, was blushing. He was so close, so virile, and so very necessary to the morning and to this moment. In the light of day, her reaction to his behavior last night seemed foolish. Last night she'd behaved like a shrinking violet, and now she felt ashamed.

"No more talk about last night, Jack," she said. "I would've had the same reaction as you did if I woke up thinking I was alone in a tent, and felt something wrapped around me. I'd have done the same thing. Well, I wouldn't have been able to toss you through the air like that, but you get my drift. You didn't hurt me. Let's just put last night behind us and move on. I'm just glad you're alive."

He'd obviously rehearsed something to say to her, and her words caused him to pause. At length he nodded. "Okay. Hope you don't mind that I raided your dry bag to make breakfast."

"No," she said, and then noticed that he was wearing both his boots. "You found your leg!"

"Yup. River's so low it was sticking up out of the water. Hard to believe I almost drowned there yesterday. I rigged up the z-drag. It's all set to go. We can give it a try after breakfast. Oatmeal and toast coming right up."

The sun was so bright the inside of the tent was a kaleidoscope of colors, but of all the prisms that shined and danced, his eyes were the prize. They were clear and hazel. They were beautiful. And his eyelashes and his mouth and his strong jawline and the way several days' worth of beard shadowed it. And the strength of him, the raw strength of him, his shoulders, forearms, wrists and hands, so strong. She'd discovered just how strong last night. She'd seen his powerful torso bared to the universe and scarred with war wounds, and she'd seen his leg and the bloody battlefields written upon it, and could only feel gratitude and admiration for a man who would give everything he had in the name of freedom.

"That sounds fine," she said. He nodded, backed out of the tent and zipped the door, leaving her to her morning coffee when what she really needed was more Jack Parker. Much more. She felt her face with the fingertips of one hand. Her skin was covered with gouges and welts and scratches that were healing now, but she must look like Frankenstein. The swelling had mostly gone from around her eye, but she was sure it was still black. The cut on her lip was almost healed. In another month or so, she'd be back to her old self. She took a sip of strong hot coffee and let the caffeine percolate through her. In another month, where would her old self be? Where would Jack be?

Would they be walking different paths in different worlds after sharing this incredible journey together?

She pulled on her cargo pants and fleece pullover in stages while she finished her coffee, and then exited the tent to join Jack beside the cook fire. She'd packed a bag of dried fruit and nuts and was pleased to see he'd added half of it to the oatmeal.

"Almost done," he said. He was sitting on a smooth river rock beside the fire. While she'd been sleeping, he'd been working. She could see the z-drag rigged to a tree along the shore a little downriver from their campsite.

They ate breakfast in dedicated silence. They could have eaten twice what she'd packed. When they got back to the trapper's cabin, Cameron vowed to herself that she was going to cook a decent meal, one that would fill them both and stick to their ribs for a while, and when they were done eating that meal she'd start fixing another. Maybe she'd make something sweet. She'd noticed the raspberries were ripening. A raspberry cobbler would taste mighty fine. They could share a very domestic afternoon at a cozy log cabin in the Northwest Territories. Assuming Walt had summoned help, it would take the rescue crew a day to reach the trapper's cabin by boat. Maybe even two days. They'd have at least that much more time together.

She held that thought as she cleaned up the breakfast dishes at the river's edge. Jack was getting antsy, making adjustments to the ropes he'd connected to the canoe's snub line. Cameron didn't think it would be a successful morning and was more than willing to put off trying to retrieve the canoe, except that there loomed the very real and unpleasant specter of having to walk all the way back to the trapper's cabin. So she packed away the breakfast kit and washed her hands and face at the river, and then got down to business.

"I already tried doing it myself," Jack said as she took a grip on the line. "I couldn't budge it."

"Figured as much," Cameron said, getting into position. "You obviously need my muscle." Jack was behind her. They would both heave on the rope and hope the z-drag provided enough leverage to pull the sunken canoe from beneath the fallen tree.

"On the count of three," Jack said. "One.... two...three!"

They pulled mightily on the z-drag, gaining nothing.

"Again," Jack said. "One...two...three!"

Together they threw their combined weight

against the line in a mighty heave, and this time it gave so suddenly they both crashed backward to the ground. For a moment they lay stunned, then Cameron scrambled to her feet, hoping to see the canoe floating to the surface, buoyed by the flotation bags in stem and stern. There was no sign of the canoe, but as Jack regained his feet and pulled in the slack rope, he retrieved a splintered piece of wood, part of the thwart the snub line had been tied to.

"Well, I guess that's that," she said as Jack began to disassemble the ropes. "No more pistol, canoe, satellite phone, deluxe tent, emergency kit or sleeping bag." She unfastened the rope and carabiner from the tree and walked back to the tent. While he coiled the lines, she crammed his sleeping bag into the stuff sack and rolled her wool blanket and dropped it into the dry bag. Taking down the tent took moments. Within thirty minutes, they were ready to depart. Jack hoisted his pack and shrugged into it while she did the same with her dry bag.

"Where's your hat?" he asked. "Did you throw it in the river?"

Cameron shook her head. "I was afraid we'd encounter it again if I did." Jack cast around and spied it in the bushes where she'd flung it. He retrieved the hat and placed it on her head while she radiated silent disapproval.

"We're not leaving it here," he said. "Both of us almost died trying to retrieve the damned thing. Besides, it looks like it might rain later today. Ready?"

She nodded, and they started walking downriver.

WALT WAS JUST finishing breakfast when he heard the slam of the car door, glanced out the office window and groaned. The very pregnant Tedlow woman was waddling up the path toward the trailer, one hand holding her stomach, the other pressed into the small of her back. Now what did she want? She'd gotten her sightseeing flight, seen firsthand that Cameron and her brother were camped out together in her brother's tent, sharing some afternoon delight, and she'd paid him the hefty flying fee without quibbling. She should be on her way back to Montana, not slowly hauling herself up the three rickety steps to the construction trailer's little porch.

"Walter?" she said, tapping at the door. "Are you in there?"

He opened it and motioned her inside. "I thought you'd be halfway home by now."

"I was going to leave, but something just didn't set right about yesterday, when we spotted Cameron."

Walt poured himself a second cup of coffee and held up the pot. She shook her head. "I've had an acid stomach all morning," she explained. "Anyhow, what made me start thinking about it was that we never saw my brother, we only saw Cameron. I mean, it was broad daylight. Jack would've been up. And the way she was waving, don't you think that was a little overly enthusiastic? Desperate, even? I think she was signaling for help."

Lori Tedlow looked as if she hadn't slept all night. There were dark circles under her eyes. She stared intently at Walt, waiting for him to calmly explain away her fears. Walt sighed and took a sip of coffee. What could he say to her? How could he explain this so she wouldn't be embarrassed? She was pregnant. She must understand about sex.

"Cameron knows how to signal for help. She's a young woman," he began slowly, "and like all young women she has healthy…appetites. You saw what she was wearing, so you had to guess what they'd been doing inside that tent. Sure, we did three flybys, but if your brother was trying to get dressed, he still wouldn't have had time to make an appearance. And another thing. Cameron didn't know you were aboard. She was waving like that because I warned her before she started this trip that she might not be able to rope and tie your brother. That waving was just her way of telling me she'd bagged her man."

Lori was frowning. "So you think all that jumping up and down and arm waving was just pure showing off?"

"Sure, a victory wave. Well, part of it might have been her waving me off so she could get back to business. My guess is she'll be giving me a call in four more days, and I'll go pick the both of them up. Soon as she calls me, I'll call you. You can fly back up here and be waiting for your brother when we get back. How's that sound?"

"You think it's going to take four more days?"

Walt grinned broadly. "At the rate they're traveling, it could be more than that. They're having themselves a fine old time out in the beautiful wilderness. That's good therapy for your brother, and he couldn't be traveling with a more qualified guide, who also happens to be an excellent cook. I know they have plenty of food and some real nice bottles of wine because I helped Cameron load it all into the canoe."

"But I didn't see any canoe. Did you?"

Walt hesitated. "No, but I was kind of focused on Cameron. I wasn't looking for it. Besides, the canoe would've been real hard to spot pulled up along that shore."

Lori hesitated, shook her head. "Something just doesn't feel right," she said. "I didn't sleep at all last night thinking about it, and I have this churning in my stomach."

"That's called a baby," Walt said, pleased with his wit. He patted her awkwardly on the shoulder. "Trust me. Right now those two are having the time of their lives."

THREE HOURS INTO the walk back to the trapper's cabin, the rain Jack had predicted started to fall and the uneven ground became slippery. They were lucky that all the tributaries that fed into the Wolf River had been small and easily crossed, but even so, the miles passed slowly. Cameron was tired and getting careless, and she slipped several times before tripping over a blowdown and landing hard, facedown, the breath knocked out of her. Jack was up ahead, out of sight. He was leaving her behind yet again.

She pushed herself up, rolled over onto her side and drew one leg up to lever herself to her feet. A bolt of pain shot through her knee when she pushed off the ground and the leg straightened, causing her to gasp aloud and drop back. She'd never hurt one of her knees before. Never even twisted an ankle to the limping stage. She tried to get up again, and again the pain left her staring in disbelief at a leg that had betrayed her for no apparent reason.

Jack was probably already out of hearing. Rain spattered down, muting the sound of the river. She twisted her hips with a little hitch to sit up straighter and leaned down to check her leg. The kneecap felt out of place. A cold sweat chilled her brow. The pain was really bad, and she couldn't straighten her leg at all. This was crazy. She was in great shape. It hadn't been a bad fall. She'd taken far worse than this without any consequence. She couldn't have broken anything, but neither could she get back on her feet, and she was feeling more desperate by the moment.

This couldn't be happening to her. Nobody could encounter this much bad luck in one canoe trip. She was a competent guide, good at what she did. She shouldn't be having all these problems. Her entire self-reliant life was falling apart, and she was turning into a Calamity Jane. She'd jinxed herself when she'd bragged to Walt she'd have her quarry safely delivered to the banks of the Mackenzie River in four days. She'd been so arrogant, so sure he'd be an easy mark. And now her quarry, the wounded warrior with the prosthetic leg, who should have been so easy to bag, was leaving her behind. Walking away.

In the future, she'd stick to flying and leave the bounty hunting to someone else.

"Jack!" She shouted his name at the top of her lungs, then took out her whistle and blew it.

After what seemed like a long time, she heard him returning. He shrugged out of his pack, knelt beside her and asked, "What happened? You okay?"

"I fell climbing over that blowdown and now I can't straighten my leg."

He felt her knee gently through her wet pant leg. "Your kneecap's dislocated."

"But that's not possible," Cameron said, realizing as she spoke how foolish she sounded. "I didn't do anything bad enough to dislocate my knee."

"You must've twisted your body to catch yourself when you fell. That's usually how a kneecap goes out. Sharp twisting changes of direction. Basketball players are prone to this particular injury, and you've been through a lot lately." His hands were on her knee, palpating as he spoke, almost as if he knew what he was doing and had done it before. This was totally annoying, having him take care of her.

"I can't get up. It shouldn't hurt this bad, but it does."

"Knee injuries usually do. I'm going to roll up your pant leg to get a good look. Feels like it's already starting to swell."

She was wearing her baggy nylon cargo pants, and he peeled the cloth back easily, rolling it above her knee. She propped herself onto her elbows and stared. He was right. Her knee was already visibly swollen and definitely out of place. His warm, strong hands bracketed the injury as he studied the situation, then he glanced at her with a serious expression. "I'm going to straighten your leg and put the knee-cap back where it belongs."

Cameron lay back down and clenched her fists around whatever she could grab, roots and branches, and then she nodded. "Okay. Go ahead. Do it. Get it over with. I'm ready."

"This is going to hurt," he warned her.

"Dammit, Jack," she snapped. "Don't tell me how painful it's going to be, just do it and get it over with!"

He manipulated her knee back into position quickly, but the bolt of pain was so bad she almost cried out. She lay still afterward, bathed in a cold sweat, staring into the gray sky while rain flattened her mosquito netting onto her face and her stomach roiled with nausea.

"You did great," Jack reassured her. "Your kneecap's back where it should be, went right back in. Sometimes they don't, and it takes several tries. You were lucky. I'll put a wrap around it to give it some support. You okay?"

"Never better," she said faintly.

She lay there, a silent victim of her own self-pity, and let Jack wrap up her leg while the rain pattered down. His pack was an endless source of supplies. Along with a spare leg, he even had an Ace bandage that he produced like a rabbit out of a hat. Other than protein bars and packages of dried noodle soup, it seemed the only things he carried were first aid and emergency gear, all of which had proved very useful. Black flies and mosquitoes swarmed around them as he first rolled her pant leg down, then wrapped the bandage around her knee and over the wet pant leg. She knew she had to make it to the cabin. She couldn't lie there indefinitely, but she dreaded the rest of the journey. They still had a ways to go, at least another hour.

"That too tight?" he asked when he was done with the wrap.

"It feels fine."

"Good. You ready?"

He helped her to stand, and she leaned against him for several long moments while he steadied her. Her knee felt a little strange, but the intense pain was gone. She moved away until she was standing on her own, still clinging to his hand just in case. She shifted her weight onto the injured knee. Bent it slowly, cautiously. Straightened it again. She blew out her breath. "Fixed," she said. "Thanks, Doc."

Jack put on his own pack and then shouldered her duffel. He paused to rearrange the mosquito netting over her hat and gave the brim a tug to seat it properly on her head. They exchanged a long silent gaze through a haze of olive-drab insect netting, and a million words passed between them. Two million. Then Cameron took a deep breath and said, "Okay, I'm ready," and took her first step, then her second. She walked ten steps, then paused and looked behind. Jack nodded encouragement. She nodded back and kept walking.

CHAPTER FOURTEEN

IT WAS MIDAFTERNOON before they reached the trapper's cabin, and the rain was still coming down hard. That last hour of hiking had taken two hours at her slower pace. She was still limping along in the torrent, head down and miserable, when she heard Jack swear aloud.

She looked up and stopped. The cabin was in front of her, and the solid log wall was a welcome sight, but something looked different about it. Very different. With a sinking feeling, she saw that the screening hung down from the closest window. There were items strewed about the clearing—food items: the shredded remains of a loaf of bread; a bag of sugar ripped apart, the sugar spread on the ground beneath the window with the torn screen; the last one-pound bag of coffee, empty, the grounds blending into the dirt and mud.

"Oh, no," she said, her heart sinking as realization struck. "I forgot to close the bear shutters when I left yesterday." The loss of the coffee was catastrophic. She wouldn't be able to get up in the morning without coffee. She picked up the empty bag and began carefully scooping up the wet coffee grounds.

Jack checked the cabin to make sure the bear was gone. He came to the door. "All clear. Lucky that the window wasn't broken. The bear just pushed it open after he ripped the screen."

Cameron climbed up the cabin steps and paused inside the door, still clutching the bag of salvaged coffee grounds. The neat little cabin she'd left behind looked like it had been ransacked by thieves searching for money and drugs. For a moment she could only stare. The mattresses were still on the bunk beds, but everything else had been dragged around or knocked over, including the cast-iron woodstove. Jack's guitar case was next to the cooler, and it was shredded. Mauled. While she watched, he pulled the crushed remnants of his instrument out of the case. Broken strings dangled from the neck, and several pieces of wood dropped to the floor. He tossed the guitar and case out the door. "Guess the bear won that round," he said. "No more Elvis."

"Oh, Jack," Cameron said, filled with remorse. "I'm so sorry. It's all my fault that bear got in."

"It's nobody's fault, and it's just a guitar. In the grand scheme of things, it doesn't matter much." He looked back at the ransacked room. "It's not as bad as it looks. I'll clean this up. You change into some dry clothes and lay down. Get off that knee and get some rest."

Cameron shook her head, pulled off her mosquito netting and ball cap and flung them onto the top bunk. "I'll clean up. You have more important things to do." When he gave her a questioning look, she added, "You're looking for Ky, remember? Whistle, call her name. She's here, Jack, I know she is. You have to let her know you've arrived. I'll take care of this mess, and then fix us something to eat, assuming there's anything left."

Jack righted the woodstove and dragged it back into position, hooking up the stovepipe, which dangled in midair. "We'll both clean up," he said, "then I'll look for Ky. If she's really here and got a whiff of my socks, she won't be too far away."

Cameron was too tired to argue. It took half an hour for the two of them to tidy up the worst of the mess, after which Jack fixed the window screen while she prepared a very simple meal of thickly sliced sharp cheddar cheese topped with equally thick rounds of summer sausage, both items rescued from the ransacked cooler, and served up with two bottles of water. They ate silently, both too tired to attempt conversation, then Jack departed to have a look around and she unwrapped her knee and changed out of her wet clothes and into a dry T-shirt, socks and long johns. It took all her strength to climb into the top bunk, where she collapsed, exhausted, pulling her wool blanket around her. She heard Jack whistle once, downriver from the cabin. He might have whistled nonstop for hours after that, but she didn't hear a thing because in the next breath she was sound asleep.

JACK WOKE TO the rumble of distant thunder. It was dark enough to be night, but light enough to be close to dawn. Cameron had been sleeping when he returned to the cabin after two hours of an unsuccessful search, not finding any sign of the wolf dog she'd spotted. The rain had stopped earlier in the evening, but now he heard it pattering gently on the cabin roof as he lay in the lower bunk. It was a soothing sound until he heard Cameron whimper in her sleep.

The whimper nudged him wide awake. Was she dreaming, or was she wide awake, lying in her bunk, crying? Should he say something to let her know he was awake? He didn't want to wake her if she was sleeping. She needed the rest. But what if she was in pain?

He lay quietly for a few moments to see if the whimpering stopped. It did. Thunder rumbled again, closer. He started to drift back to sleep, then heard her shift in the upper bunk. There was a solid "thump!" as she bumped her head on the cabin ceiling, followed by a soft curse. Her stocking feet swung over the side of the bunk, followed by a pair of long shapely legs clad in black thermal tights and a lithe, slender body covered in a dark T-shirt. She lowered herself to the floor like a monkey. There was just enough murky light to make out the figure that crept to the door of the cabin and opened it. Lightning flashed and illuminated her in brilliant white, like a flashbulb going off. Cameron stood in the open doorway and he could hear her murmuring softly, measuring the time between the flash of lightning and the thunder.

"…four, one thousand five, one thousand six…"

The thunder crashed and boomed, closer still. Now she was looking for her boots. Feeling for them in the shadows.

"You're going outside now?" Jack asked. "That's bad timing."

"I have to pee," she muttered, pulling on her boots.

"Why don't you use your headlamp?"

"I didn't want to wake you." A few moments

later, she recovered her headlamp from the table, switched it on and pulled it over her head.

"Hold on a minute, and I'll go out with you. That bear could still be around."

"If the bear were still around, we'd know it by now," she said. "He'd have come back through the window for the rest of the food. I'll be fine." And just like that she was gone.

The outhouse was a good fifty feet or better behind the cabin. He listened for her footsteps, but the drum of rain on the cabin roof covered all sound. Most girls wouldn't have dared go out there alone knowing there might be a bear in the vicinity, lightning flashing and thunder rumbling, but Cameron wasn't like most girls. She just pulled on her boots, grabbed her headlamp and went. If the bear got in her way, she'd probably kick it aside.

Jack reached for his prosthesis. He'd get the bear spray out of his pack and go out and meet her, make sure she got back okay. But in spite of his efficiency, she wasn't gone long enough for him to get his boot tied. When she returned, it was at a much greater speed than when she'd gone out.

"Jack!" she said urgently as she burst through the door. "You won't believe what I just saw!"

"Bear?"

"When I was coming back from the out-house, I saw a pair of eyes looking out from under the cabin! I think Ky's under the camp! I think she's right here, right under our feet!" She was carrying the headlamp in one hand, gesturing as she spoke, sending beams of light everywhere. Her hair and clothing were dripping wet. "I was afraid my headlamp might spook her, so I took it off, held it under my shirt. You should talk some more, let her listen to your voice. She's here, right here, Jack, right underneath you. Sing some Elvis to her!"

"Maybe it was a bear's eyes you saw," Jack said.

"No, it wasn't. The eyes reflected green, and a bear's eyes reflect red, just like human eyes. Sometimes a dog with blue pigment in their eyes reflects red in a flashlight beam, but you said Ky had yellow eyes, right?"

"How do you know all this eye color stuff?"

"Back when I was living in Yukon, I was a volunteer pilot for the Yukon Quest, that's a thousand-mile sled dog race run between Whitehorse and Fairbanks, and while I was volunteering I met another pilot whose wife, Rebecca, was running the race. Mac was flying support like I was, ferrying veterinarians and supplies and dropped dogs. Mac and I became friends, and afterward he invited me out to their place near Dawson. I spent a whole week there with them. They took me dogsledding. We camped out at thirty below, watched the northern lights at 2:00 a.m., sipped Talisker whisky from a silver flask and howled with the huskies. Anyhow, that's how I learned about eye shine. Going out into their dog yard wearing a headlamp, knowing which dogs had blue eyes, which had brown eyes, which had both colors in each eye. It was like an informal study in nocturnal reflections."

"What color does a wolf's or coyote's eyes reflect?"

"I don't know, I've only studied huskies and shined bears at the dump, but whatever's under the cabin isn't a bear no matter what the eye color is. The eyes were too small and too close together, and besides, a bear couldn't fit under the cabin unless it dug a noticeable hole. When you were looking for Ky this afternoon, did you see any sign of her?"

"No."

"That's because she was right here, right under the cabin, trying to get as close to you as she could!"

Jack didn't want to get his hopes up, but maybe she was right. "I did hear some whimpering noises earlier. I thought it was you, but I guess they could have been coming from under the cabin."

"I don't whimper. We should put some food out for her. I'm already wet. You stay inside and keep talking. She knows you're in here. Talk to her. Sing her a song. I'll bring out those pawed-over scraps of bread the bear was chewing on." Cameron already had the remains of the bread bag in her hand and was out the door before she finished the sentence. Rain was pounding on the cabin roof, and within seconds she was back, thoroughly drenched.

"Mission accomplished!" she said with an elated smile, flinging her wet hair out of her eyes, kicking off her boots. "Jack, I have to admit I didn't believe your dog could be alive after a whole year in the wilderness, but she is. It's a miracle. You've found your friend again. Somehow you knew she was alive, and you didn't give up on her, and I think you're pretty damn wonderful."

Lightning flashed, thunder shook the ground. The storm was almost on top of them. Cameron switched off the headlamp, left it on the table and crossed to the bunks, but instead of crawling up into her bunk she stripped out of her wet T-shirt, flung it behind her, peeled off her long johns and socks and, without a moment's hesitation, slipped nimbly onto his bunk. Startled,

Jack felt her strong, trembling body wrap itself around him. There was no mistaking her intentions. He thought he should say something, but couldn't think what it should be, and then her mouth found his and started a wild electrical storm all its own, and in the end, words weren't necessary.

THE STORM MOVED through before dawn, and Cameron lay awake, listening to the thunder recede into the distance, listening to the slow drip of rainwater off the cabin eaves and the strong, steady beat of Jack's heart. She was warm, sleepy and very content. There hadn't been another man since Roy, and none before him, either, so her ex-husband was the only measure she had for the three hours she'd just spent in Jack's arms, and she was still trying to process everything she'd been missing for the past three years. She was blown away by the experience. With sex that good, how did two people ever get anything accomplished? What was their motivation to get out of bed?

As if on cue, her stomach growled an answer. Hunger was the motivation to get out of bed. It was light enough to see the inside of the cabin. The birds were awakening, morning had arrived and another day had begun. But today, everything was different because last night she and Jack had crossed an intimate line. Intimate not just because of the sex, but because of how she felt when she was around him. Frightening because she realized how vulnerable those feelings made her.

She pushed away the vulnerable feelings and fears and very carefully, so as not to awaken him and invite another possible episode of PTSD, she slipped from Jack's bunk bed. Stark naked in the early light, she crossed to her duffel and pulled out dry, clean clothing and a towel. Carrying the bundle in her arms, she left the cabin barefoot and made her way to the river's edge.

She bathed in a back eddy, washed her hair, scrubbed herself clean. The water was high and stingingly cold, and she was shivering when she was through. She dried herself briskly with the towel and donned dry clothing. Then she rinsed out the bandage and hung it over a bush to dry. Her knee felt so good she doubted she'd need it again. From the way the day was shaping up, it was going to be cool, bright and sunny with a good breeze. She'd wash out all her dirty clothes and Jack's, too. They'd share a domestic day of much-needed rest and recovery.

But first, breakfast. A big breakfast. Huge. And then there was Ky to tame after her year alone in the wilderness. And there was last night to think about, to process. Her sexual hunger. Her impulsiveness. Her fears and vulnerabilities. Her growing attachment to a man she vowed two nights ago not to get too close to. But after last night, things had changed, and for right now, in this very moment, she was going to take everything he offered and give as much of herself as she could in return. She'd be crazy not to.

Her stomach growled again, and she walked into the cabin, surprised to see that Jack was up and dressed. Just the sight of him standing there made her blood warm. He was so rugged. So male. So sexy. She wanted to push him back down on the bunk bed, remove his clothing piece by piece. Forget about breakfast. They'd have each other for breakfast. Forget about Ky. The dog had waited this long to see him, she could wait a few more minutes. She wondered if Jack could read her mind, if he knew why she was tongue-tied, blushing. They regarded each other across the small room in awkward silence.

"I heard more noises under the cabin," he said, grabbing her headlamp from the table. "I'm going out to have a look."

Cameron nodded. "There's one last piece of bread in that torn bag and a piece of cheese inside the cooler. Maybe a hot dog or two. I'll get breakfast started."

While he was gone to reunite with his dog, she cooked the last of the bacon, measured some of the salvaged ground coffee into the coffeepot after picking out the biggest twigs, and by the time he returned, the coffee was well boiled. The cabin was warm from the wood fire in the cookstove and smelled of fresh brewed coffee, woodsmoke and bacon fat. She handed a mug of coffee to Jack with a smile that slowly faded as she read his expression.

"What is it?" she asked. "What's wrong? Wasn't she under there? Didn't you see her? Didn't she recognize you?"

He took the mug, returned to the open doorway and stood for a moment, gazing out across the river. "You know, it's the damnedest thing," he said quietly. "There *is* a dog under the cabin, just like you thought, but it's not her. It's not Ky." He shook his head. "I don't know how there could be another dog way out here in the middle of nowhere, but there is, and it's not Ky."

Cameron was stunned by his words. She shook her head, unable to process what he'd said. How could that be? How could the dog under the cabin not be Ky? She watched him, wanting to cross the distance and wrap her arms around him because he was being so stoic, and she knew how much finding that dog had meant to him. She knew how much every mile he'd walked had cost him. She didn't ask him if he was sure it wasn't her. Of course he was sure. He knew the dog, he'd loved the dog. The dog had saved his life twice, and he'd just gone through tremendous hardships to find her. But the dog that was under the cabin wasn't Ky, and the cruelty of that disappointment had to be tearing him apart.

Cameron turned back to the cookstove, dividing the salvaged bacon beside two mounds of oatmeal. She poured maple syrup over both servings, set the plates on the small table beneath the east window and then crossed to where Jack stood staring out the doorway, and gave his shoulders a gentle squeeze.

"Come eat," she said. "It's not fancy. The bear didn't leave us much."

They ate in silence. Cameron didn't try to fill that silence with empty words. When he'd cleaned his plate, he raised his eyes to her and she said, "I'm sorry, Jack."

He shook his head again. "I swore I wouldn't get my hopes up, but I did. My fault, not yours. By some freak twist of fate, there's another dog under the cabin, maybe more than one. I think she has a puppy under there."

"A *puppy*?" Cameron leaned across the table, galvanized by his words.

"That was the whimpering I heard last night."

"There's a *puppy* under the cabin?"

"The mother ate what you left her last night, and she came right out and nabbed what I offered this morning."

"One puppy? Are you sure? Just *one*?"

"Not sure. I had your headlamp, but couldn't see that well. I'm way too big to fit through that little hole under the cabin, and she made it pretty plain she didn't like me looking under there. Anyhow, she's hungry and she's nursing and she's not totally wild but pretty damn close. How much food's left?"

Cameron frowned, calculating their provisions. "Not much. Two sticks of butter, a block of cheese, some sausage, a plastic bag of biscuit mix, a few more hot dogs. But there's a big can of oatmeal and another of rice in the trapper's stash. I'll catch some char right after I clean up from breakfast. She'll live on fish just fine, and we can, too." She shook her head. "We'll have to bring her with us, and the pup. We can't leave them here."

"No. We won't leave them behind."

"I'm sorry she wasn't your dog, Jack. Really sorry."

She pushed to her feet and gathered the

empty plates, then paused, shored up her courage and looked at him. "About last night. I just want you to know I don't jump into bed with just any guy in the middle of a thunderstorm." He met her gaze but remained silent, so she forged onward, not really knowing where she was going with the conversation but knowing they had to have one. "I swore after Roy I was done with men, but you're different. You're not like Roy, and don't get me wrong, I'm glad you're not, I really am. But in a way it would be easier if you were, because it would make things so much simpler. I just want you to know that I'm not going to cause any messy problems for you down the road. There won't be any complications or emotional entanglements. I'm all about keeping things simple."

Jack stared. "Okay," he said.

Cameron's heart was pounding, and she felt a little dizzy. She could tell by his expression that he hadn't grasped what she'd been trying to tell him. She stood with her hands full of breakfast dishes and waited for more. "That's *it*?" she finally prompted. "That's all you're going to say?"

He blew out his breath. "I don't know what you want me to say. Money was your motivation for chasing after me, and except for the fact that you've had a run of bad luck, it probably still is. Maybe last night your motivation was different, but if you're regretting it this morning, then I'm sorry it happened. And I'm especially sorry that you wish I was like your ex-husband, because I think he was a real jerk. I won't stand in the way of you getting your five thousand dollars and that red Jeep, if that's the sort of emotional entanglement you're afraid of. I wouldn't dream of it."

Cameron felt a sudden flash of anger that he'd twisted what she'd said. "That's not what I meant at all. I just meant that I don't want you to think I'm going to turn all clingy and needy or anything like that just because of what happened between us last night, because I'm not like that. I just didn't want you to read too much into it, that's all, or feel threatened by it."

"Okay. How about this. We'll just forget about it. Move on. Just like the other night when I threw you across the tent, right? We'll forget about both nights, pretend they didn't happen."

"I didn't mean that. You're twisting my words!"

"I get it, Cameron," he said. "You're a beautiful girl. You could have the pick of the crop, but your first pick was Roy. Big mistake. Your second pick sure as hell isn't going to be a disabled soldier suffering from PTSD, and I don't blame you. We'll keep things simple, say our painless goodbyes on the banks of the Mackenzie River, and you'll have your money and your red Jeep and life will be good."

"That's not what I meant, and you know it!" Cameron shot back. "You're going back to your army career. You said that's what you were going to do, and I just thought you should know that I wouldn't stand in your way, even if I do think that you wanting to go back to Afghanistan to get shot up again is really, incredibly stupid."

She spun on her heel and marched to the sink, stacking the dishes in the dishpan. "I can't believe I'm even saying these things to you. If you want to go back there because you think you have to prove something, then go back and do what you have to do, but it makes me madder than hell when you keep talking about the money because I don't give a damn about the money anymore or the red Jeep. I can't think straight right now, so I'm going to do these dishes, and then I'll go catch that poor starving dog some fish, and I'm sorry she's not your dog, Jack, I really am. It's not fair, but nothing in life ever is, and I'm sure you know that better than most."

The lump in her throat squeezed her endless babbling sentence into an embarrassing squeak. She kept her back to him, poured hot water from a kettle heating on the woodstove into the dish pan, added a dollop of dish soap, then stirred the water with the greasy spatula. She started washing the dishes even though everything was a blur. She heard Jack push out of his chair and walk toward the door. He paused to give her shoulder a gentle pat on his way past, and she barely held it together long enough for him to leave the cabin.

CHAPTER FIFTEEN

JACK PACED TO the river, brooding. Cameron's outburst had shaken him. He didn't begin to understand what she'd meant by it all, except that she regretted her behavior last night and didn't want him to read too much into it. She knew damn well that if he got sweet on her and stuck around, she'd end up looking at him over her coffee one morning, wondering how she could have made another poor choice. He shouldn't have gotten angry with her. She was just protecting herself.

He walked along the edge of the river, far enough to find a private place to sit and think. The sound of the river mesmerized him. Mist rose from the back eddies. He leaned back against a smooth rock and let the sun warm his sore muscles. He thought about love and loyalty. He thought about Ky and how she would sleep on his narrow army cot, climbing so carefully onto it, curling around once and lying down so her back pressed against his thigh. She would close her eyes and heave a contented sigh, a sound of pure bliss. He'd lay his hand on her head and stroke her until all the stress and ugliness of war left him and sleep came. A dog had the power to chase the nightmares away. Ky had that power.

But Ky wasn't the dog under the cabin. Cameron was right. Life wasn't fair. Life was beautiful and awful and filled with tragedy and triumph and brief moments of sublime happiness, but it was never fair. There were no rules, no promises. Jack didn't know why things happened the way they did. They just happened. Life just happened, and you dealt with it day by day and tried to make the best of it.

The river made a soothing sound, rushing past. Jack thought he should go back to the cabin and see if Cameron was okay, because it really mattered to him that she was okay, but for a few more moments he'd just sit here by the river and watch life flow past.

WALT OVERSLEPT. HE'D never have overslept when Jeri was here. Jeri woke him with the smell of coffee brewing on the tiny office stove. Sometimes she'd sit on the couch and rub his knee. "Coffee's ready, Walt," she'd say in her raspy smoker's voice, and when he opened his eyes, she'd be holding his mug out to him. "Rise and shine, flyboy."

She always called him flyboy, referring to his years of being an air force jet jock. He'd been young then, and wild. Now he could barely roll out of bed without groaning like an old man. Hell, he *was* an old man. Sixty-three in a few short weeks. How had that happened? Time had gone supersonic on him.

"Hello? Walter?" Tap tap tap on the trailer door. "Walter? Are you in there?"

He groaned again and sat up. It was that woman again. Lori Tedlow. She kept reappearing just when he thought she'd gone back home. She opened the door and poked her head around, saw him lying on the couch and smiled apologetically.

"I'm sorry to bother you again, but it's almost nine o'clock and I've been waiting out here for an hour."

"Why?" Walt growled, out of sorts. He rubbed his face. His jaw was covered with stubble because he hadn't shaved yesterday. What was the point of shaving when Jeri was gone? "You should be waiting back home with your husband. That baby could come anytime."

"I really needed to talk to you." Lori opened the door wider and began the awkward process of entering his cramped office. It was almost impossible. She seemed even bigger than before.

Walt had slept in his clothes, blue jeans

and a chamois shirt. He needed a shower. He needed hot coffee even more. He pushed to his stocking feet and padded to the tiny kitchenette, putting together a pot of coffee with the fewest movements possible. He lit the burner under the percolator and rummaged through the dirty dishes piled in the miniature sink for two chipped mugs, rinsing them out with cold water. He was out of dish soap. Jeri had always kept things in stock, and he was out of just about everything, including toilet paper. Life just plain sucked without Jeri.

"I haven't heard anything since yesterday," he said, placing the mugs on the little table.

"Actually, I was hoping you'd be agreeable to flying me out there again just to see how close they've gotten to the Mackenzie River."

Walt sat on one of the folding metal chairs and motioned to the couch. "Have a seat. Coffee'll be ready soon."

"I'm afraid if I sit down on something soft I won't be able to get up again," Lori said. "And I can't drink coffee. My stomach won't tolerate it right now."

Walt gave her a bleary-eyed stare. "I don't see how your stomach tolerates what's in it now. Is it twins?"

Lori shook her head and laughed. "One baby, believe me. I've asked that same question of my doctor several times. Walter, I'm really worried. You should've had a phone call from Cameron by now. She'd report in, wouldn't she? Even if it was just to tell you everything was okay."

The coffee had started to perk, and Walt felt better, smelling it. He rubbed his face again, making a silent vow never again to play pool into the early hours with Hank and Slouch. Late nights didn't set well with him anymore.

"Look, I'll pay you, the same amount I did before," Lori said.

Walt poured a slug out of the coffeepot before it was ready because he really needed a swallow or two to tide him over and help him think. He carried the mug back to the chair and sat, contemplating her offer while the coffee continued to perk. He'd lost a good chunk of change last night playing pool. He could use the money. He could always use the money. He took a swallow of the strong brew and nodded.

"Okay, I'll go have another look to see where they're at, but you're not going. There's too much paperwork to fill out every time we fly a client anywhere, and I hate paperwork, and besides that, flying's too risky in your condition. That safety harness isn't big enough to fit around you. If we hit any turbulence, it's apt to squeeze the baby right out. I'll go right after

I finish this pot of coffee. You come back at four this afternoon, and I'll have some answers about your brother."

Lori's expression was almost worth the trouble. "Thank you, Walter. I knew you'd come through for me. You're a good man."

CAMERON WAS GLAD Jack was gone when she came out of the cabin. She needed time alone to compose herself, and fishing was good therapy. She caught four good-sized char one right after the other and killed and cleaned them promptly. Four char would feed all of them for a couple of days. She set aside two for her and Jack in the cooler and boiled the other two at the fire pit to make a fish stew for the dog. She added two cups of rice to the pot after the stew had started to boil. While it cooked, she brought all her laundry down to the river and washed it, strung a line between two black spruce and hung it to dry.

This should have been a pleasant day of doing nothing but tending the fire, stirring the fish stew once in a while and watching the river flow. No walking endless miles on blistered feet. No paddling a canoe. No making conversation. No thinking. Just the mindless occupation of simple chores. But the negative thoughts kept creeping back in, and she couldn't build walls thick enough to protect herself. It had been a big mistake crawling into bed with Jack. A huge mistake. It wouldn't happen again. It couldn't. She'd made herself far too vulnerable. Caring about someone was dangerous. She'd learned that much and then some from Roy.

She crouched on her heels beside the river and tossed small stones into the blur of water. The river was really high, almost overflowing its banks. The heavy downpours last night had flooded the entire watershed. She felt dizzy, watching it rush past on its way to the Mackenzie. She rose to her feet and turned back toward the cook fire. The fish stew was done. She lifted the pot off the fire and carried it up to the cabin, where she scooped some into a shallow pan to cool more quickly.

"Smells delicious, Mama Dog," she announced to the dog she knew was lying right beneath the floorboards. "I'll bring you a dish just as soon as it's cooled off."

She set the pan on the cabin table, then walked back outside. Jack had returned and was standing near the cook fire, poking at the bed of coals with a stick. She drew a breath to steady herself, approached with as much resolve as she could muster and looked him straight in the eye.

"I'm sorry I got so worked up this morning," she said. "It won't happen again."

"No need to apologize," Jack said. "You were right."

She frowned. "About what?"

"Everything."

"Perhaps you could enlighten me."

Jack's expression remained carefully neutral. "Well…"

"You didn't understand a thing I was trying to tell you. I could tell by your expression."

"You were a little emotional."

"I never get emotional"

"No, I'm sure you don't."

"And I don't think it's fair that you should trivialize this discussion as being all about me being emotional because I'm a female when it isn't. It's about what happened between us last night."

"Right," Jack said.

"And I can assure you that what happened last night has nothing to do with what you think it did."

"Of course it didn't," Jack said, but he was wearing that same baffled expression.

"And there's something else," Cameron continued, and was about to explain exactly why it was so important that he understood exactly why she'd been so upset, when she spotted something lodged against the riverbank not fifty yards upriver of the cabin and on the same bank. Something long and low, floating in the water, caught up among the alders because the river was so high it was almost over its banks. Something that looked like a log, only it wasn't a log because it was the wrong shape. It had an upswept bow and stern. And it had a color. Red.

"My God!" she said, raising her hand and pointing. "Jack, turn around, *look*!"

JACK WHIRLED, FULLY expecting to see a large angry grizzly charging toward them along the riverbank, but there was no bear. Then he looked upriver where she was pointing and stared in disbelief when he spotted the nearly submerged canoe lodged against the riverbank. Only the gunnels, bow and stern were above water. The canoe was kept afloat solely by the flotation bags in both ends, and the bow had wedged itself into the overhanging alders. There was no telling how long it had been there, but even as they watched, they could see the stern of the canoe begin drifting farther out into the river. Once the canoe got crosswise of the strong current, it would be pushed downriver and the front end would work free of the overhanging alders that were temporarily anchoring it to shore.

"Look! *Look!* It's our canoe!" Cameron was overcome with excitement. "The high water must have shifted the tree off it last night and floated it down here. My God, what are the odds? I can't believe it. It's right here, on our side of the river, but it's going to pull free any moment. We've got to get it before it gets away. Hurry. Let's go!"

"Run up to the cabin and get that piece of rope that's hanging on the wall behind the woodstove," he said, and while she sprinted toward the cabin, he started up the riverbank. The canoe was only fifty yards upstream, but it was rough going. He heard Cameron bounding back down the cabin steps, and she quickly caught up with him. They plowed through the thick tangle of alders that lined the river, not daring to cut inland where the going was easier because they didn't want to lose sight of the canoe. Within minutes they were out of breath from the brutal struggle. Jack paused for a breather, and Cameron stopped behind him. "Can you still see it?" she asked, gasping.

"Yes, it's still moving. The current's pulling it out of the alders."

"We can't lose it again," she said. "Hurry!"

They plowed forward desperately, but they

weren't moving fast enough. Moments later, the canoe worked free and began to move down-river, slowly at first, but it would soon pick up momentum. Jack cursed aloud when he saw that the current was taking it away from the riverbank. "By the time it gets to us, it'll be too far from shore to reach."

Cameron spun, and before he could question her, she was plowing full blast back through the alders, racing the river. He followed. What-ever plan she had was better than just standing and watching the canoe move past them. By the time he broke free of the alders, she was already racing back down the cabin steps to the river, rope in one hand, the handle of a big cast-iron Dutch oven in the other. She knelt at the river's edge and quickly lashed the rope to the Dutch oven's handle.

"This piece of cast iron weighs about eight pounds, and if I can swing it into the canoe and it fills with water and sinks, it might be heavy enough to catch on a thwart and let me pull the canoe ashore," she said, rising to her feet, eyes fixed on the submerged canoe as it approached. "Get ready, Jack. She's coming pretty quick."

Cameron swung the Dutch oven back and forth, back and forth, waiting for just the right moment, leaning her upper body over the edge of the riverbank. She made a perfect toss as the canoe drifted past. The Dutch oven landed just ahead of the rear thwart and sank out of sight as she reeled in the slack. The rope grew taut as the pot dragged along the bottom of the canoe. She pulled gently, then not so gently as the river carried the canoe past. The Dutch oven shifted as the pressure on the rope increased, and the stern of the canoe began to angle toward the bank.

"You've got her," Jack said, moving along the riverbank with her. "Just a little more. She's coming in." Jack crouched, reaching and ready. The current swung the stern a little closer but not close enough. She pulled a little harder, leaning her weight into it.

"Nooooo!" she wailed when the iron pot flipped over the gunnel and out of the canoe, but her final tug had moved the canoe just enough for him to reach.

"I've got it!" Jack said, gripping the gunnel near the stern. He had both of his hands on it now and was pulling the battered craft against the riverbank.

"Don't fall in and don't let go!" Cameron retrieved and tossed the iron pot onto the ground behind her before threading the free end of the rope through the middle thwart, knotting it off and then handing it to Jack while she searched stem and stern for the other snub line and found it. She pulled the rope into view and began flinging the slack behind her until she reached the free end and stood with it in her hand. She snubbed securely to the nearest thing she could reach with the length of line, a small black spruce near the fire pit. Then she untied the Dutch oven from the other section of rope and tied that line to the same tree.

"Okay, you can let go. I've tied it off."

The canoe was captured, pulled up against the riverbank, and full of water right up to the gunnels. They stood side by side, looking at it, dazed with disbelief. After all their struggle trying to free the canoe from the sweeper upriver, it had floated right into their hands. They looked at each other and broke into wide, elated grins.

Life was *good*!

CHAPTER SIXTEEN

By MIDMORNING, THE canoe was bailed out enough that they could haul it up on shore near the fire pit. There was a large irregular eighteen-inch tear in the fiberglass just forward of the middle thwart, no doubt caused when it was pinned beneath the fallen spruce. While Jack examined the damage, Cameron unlashed the spare paddle and retrieved her gear from the bow and unpacked it. She laid her pistol aside and focused on the satellite phone. She wanted to call Walt right away and let him know they were okay, but when she opened the waterproof case, her heart dropped. The case was waterlogged. The gasket had sprung a leak.

She held up the case and let the water pour out. "Looks like the canoe wasn't the only thing that got crushed by that tree."

"Take the battery out, wipe everything down and let it dry. If you have any rice to spare, seal the phone up with it for a day or two. Maybe it'll come back to life. If your boss flies over again, we'll signal to him we're okay. We can fix the canoe and make it to the Mackenzie under our own steam. We don't need rescuing. Not that kind, anyway."

"What about the dog?"

"She'll be tame after a couple of days of good eating, and we'll bring her and whatever's under the cabin with her along with us. They'll fit in the canoe."

"I was letting the stew cool down when all this happened. I'll go feed her now." Cameron carried the dead satellite phone and the rest of her gear up to the cabin. She took the battery out of the phone to dry and offered the dog under the cabin her first bowl of fish stew, cooled now to an edible temperature. She set the bowl near the shallow depression the dog was using to crawl beneath the cabin, then drew back and waited. Less than a minute passed before she saw a pair of wary eyes watching her intently.

"It's okay, Mama Dog, come eat," she said. "This is really good stew. You're going to like it. I'm a good cook." But the dog wouldn't come out while she was there, so she went back down to the fire pit to help Jack with the canoe. "She's probably finishing off that fish stew right now," she told him. "She was watching me from under the cabin, waiting for me to leave."

"It won't be long before she's eating out of your hand. Meanwhile we have a repair job to do," he said, eyeing the tear in the fiberglass. "It's a big hole in a bad spot."

"I've got a whole roll of duct tape in my throw bag."

"That might not be enough, but we'll figure something out."

"We'll need another paddle, too. I should've lashed the bow paddle beside the spare paddle, then we'd be all set."

"I can make a pole out of a small spruce. One paddle and a pole should do us. You can sit in the bow and nap as we drift downriver," Jack said. "When we reach town, we're going to have to find whoever owns this cabin and pay our debts. I'm just glad the door wasn't locked."

"We never lock cabins up here. They're too important to survival. And by the way, it's considered an insult to pay someone for the use of their cabin. The code of the north country is when you stay at someone's camp, you leave the place as neat as you found it, and if you use firewood and provisions, replace them. I didn't see a logbook inside, but we can leave a thank-you note for the owner, and some money, if you want. You Americans are peculiar that way. Fixated on money."

"We're not the only ones."

Cameron flushed. "There's half a pot of coffee left, and enough in the bag to last us till we reach the Mackenzie, maybe, if we can fix the canoe. I'll bring you another mug and all the duct tape I can find."

"Bring two mugs. Might as well live it up while we still can."

Cameron retrieved two mugs of coffee and rejoined Jack at the fire pit. She sank into her camp chair and wrapped her hands around her mug. "What are the odds that canoe would get hung up in those alders long enough for us to spot it," she mused. "It could just as easily have drifted past the cabin in the middle of the night or while we were eating breakfast. Proof positive that miracles do happen, Jack."

Jack tasted his coffee. "It wasn't a miracle. It was the line of thunderstorms and heavy downpours that shifted that tree off the canoe."

"It was a miracle," she repeated. "This trip's not over yet, Jack. There's still time for another miracle. You could still find your dog."

They both heard the deep drone of the approaching plane at the same time and glanced skyward. "And by the way? Walt flying by for another look-see doesn't count as a miracle,"

Cameron added, rising to her feet. "He just wants me to get back to work, but I think we deserve a day of rest after all we've been through."

"That being the case," Jack said, setting down his mug of coffee and pushing to his feet, "we better signal your boss that we're okay."

LORI TEDLOW WAS waiting at the floatplane base when Walt returned from his four-hour flight. She met him at the dock.

"They're fine," he said after popping his door open, climbing down and securing the plane. "They're both fine. I saw your brother, I saw the canoe, I saw Cameron. They're at the trapper's cabin about a day's hard paddle from the Mackenzie River. I made four flybys. They signaled they were okay. They had their arms around each other on the fourth flyby and gave me friendly waves and big smiles. It's just like I said—they're romancing their way to the Mackenzie, and proper romancing can't be rushed. Feel better now?"

Lori Tedlow stared for a moment, blinking her eyes as she processed the information. "Yes. No. I don't know. I mean, I'm glad Jack's okay, but why isn't that girl hustling him along? She stands to make a good bonus if she can get him to the Mackenzie River quickly. Why hasn't she called on the satellite phone to let us know what's going on?"

Walt shrugged. "My guess is the phone isn't working, for some reason or other. Shit happens. Doesn't matter. They're fine, I saw them, they signaled they were fine and they looked fine. If the phone doesn't work, they can make a call from Norman Wells when they reach the Mackenzie, and your brother has a GPS unit if they get in trouble. I'll go back in three days if we haven't heard from them by then, but my guess is, we will. They'll be running out of all that fancy food. You should feel better because they're fine, but I'm hungry, and when I'm hungry I get grumpy. I need something to eat."

Lori held up a paper bag. "I brought you some Chinese food from the Panda. I figured you'd need something to eat. I hope you like Chinese. I can get you something else if you don't."

Walt brightened. "Chinese suits me right down to the ground. What'd you get?"

Lori shrugged with an apologetic smile. "I'm not sure. I took too long to order, so the server told me I'd be getting Combo Number One."

Walt grinned broadly and took the paper bag from her. "Sounds like the Panda. Let's eat."

JACK DID THE best he could to patch up the damaged canoe using the roll of duct tape in Cameron's throw bag. It was a long gash and an irregular one. He waited for the sun to dry the interior of the canoe, then flipped it over and let it dry the bottom. It was a fine afternoon for canoe repair, bright sunshine, low humidity, a nice breeze and no bugs. It was pleasant to sit in the sun by the fire pit and work on the canoe. It felt good to rest his leg and to watch Cameron cleaning up around the camp yard, hanging her wet sleeping bag to dry, doing laundry, making lunch.

"Tell me more about this set of camps that's for sale in Yukon," he said when she brought out another round of sliced cheese and summer sausage and mugs of tea for lunch.

She sank into the other chair with a contented sigh. "That place is beautiful," she said, nesting a slice of cheese between two slices of sausage and eating half in one bite. "The main lodge is built of spruce logs, all dovetailed at the corners, just like this cabin. It has a commercial kitchen and a large dining and living area combined with a fieldstone fireplace. Big windows looking out at the lake and mountains. There are six guest cabins with private baths, all built of logs along the edge of the lake. You have to fly in or come by boat up the river, or by snowmobile in winter. My dad and I flew fishermen in there for years, and I came to love the place. It always felt like coming home when I was there. The owners lived there year-round and the fishing's legendary. Huge lake trout. When Marlborough Parker died of a heart attack last year, his wife Minnie put the place on the market."

"Marlborough?"

"Nicest guy you'd ever want to meet. Built dog sleds and snowshoes and canoes and was the reigning pistol-shooting champion in Canada for many years. Marl didn't smoke, either, in case you were wondering. Maybe you're related?"

"Maybe," Jack said, eating another slice of summer sausage and cheese. "It sounds like a nice place."

"I'd like to see Minnie again. She was like a grandmother to me when my dad first started flying for them and he had to drag me along on all his flights. She'd take me into the kitchen, set me down at the table and give me a glass of milk and some cookies right out of the oven. I can still smell those warm gingersnap cookies. She must be in her midseventies now. Wonderful woman. I didn't go to Marl's potlatch last fall. I'd just started flying for Walt and didn't dare ask for the time off. I feel bad that I wasn't there. I should've gone. They were always so nice to me."

"It's not too late to go see her."

Cameron nodded thoughtfully. "You're right. When I get back to Walt's, I'll just tell him I need another week off and I'll go pay my respects. If I had the money, I'd buy that place and ask Minnie to stay on as my adopted grandmother. I know she doesn't want to leave there. She and Marl always said they'd never leave. They'd both like to be buried there."

"Must be a big job, running a place like that."

"Just the maintenance of the cabins and lodge is a big job. Marl had a full-time helper for that. Minnie did all the cooking. She had two gals who helped with serving and cleaning. I'm not sure who stayed on when Marl died, but I heard the lodge didn't open this year."

"Maybe she'd hire you on to help out."

"I'd like to help her, but I like the flying. I don't want to give that up. If I were rich enough to buy that place, I'd hire a few good people and I'd fly all the clients in and out, and maybe do some guiding. I like to cook, so I'd keep a hand in the kitchen, but not be tied to it the way Minnie was. I grew up at sporting camps. I know what they're about and how much work they are to keep running. The women do most of the work. They're the slaves of the operation."

"What about kids?"

Cameron looked at him. "What about them?"

"Are they part of your plan?"

"I wouldn't have any issues with raising kids out in the bush, if that's what you're asking. It's a good life, living out in the wilderness, and they can learn about hard work and all that practical survival stuff that can't be found in books. But as far as me having kids, I hadn't given much thought to it. Roy never talked about wanting kids, and the way things turned out I'm sure glad we didn't have any."

"But if you found the right partner, you'd live out in the wilds and raise some kids, do some flying and cooking and adventuring and call it a good life?"

"You bet. What more could anyone want?"

"No red Jeep?"

She laughed. "Maybe I'd keep a red Jeep at the floatplane base in town, for those civilized long distance shopping trips to Whitehorse." She took a sip of her tea and finished off her last piece of stacked sausage and cheese. "What about you, Jack? What's your measure of a good life?"

Jack drew a breath and released it slowly. He gazed at the river, the mountains, the cabin, the girl beside him. "Right now? This," he said, and he meant it. If he could stop time, he'd never move beyond this moment.

She laughed again. "You'll get sick of 'this' real quick after a few more days of eating nothing but fish and oatmeal," she said.

"Maybe not."

"Oh, that's right. I almost forgot about your Kootenai connections. Maybe you'd settle right in. You probably have a passel of famous backwoods skeletons hiding in your closet, trappers and war chiefs and mountain men like Jeremiah Johnson."

Jack thought for a moment. "There's only one skeleton in my past that made his way into the history books. His name was Coyote Walking, and he lived back in the 1800s. They said he had the crazies, that he was always searching for something but he didn't know what. He wandered around a lot. He left the Flathead valley and his own village and headed north to hang out with the Blackfeet up near the Canadian border.

"After a while he took a Blackfoot wife, and they thought maybe he'd found what he'd been looking for. Then one day he went on a buffalo hunt with the Blackfeet and afterward noticed five or six calves wandering among the Indian ponies, searching for their dead mothers. This was back in the 1870s and the bison were heading toward extinction, and he knew it, so he came up with the idea that he was going to save this handful of orphan calves because it was important. He blew his breath on their faces, and they followed him back to the Blackfoot village like he was their mother. He was homesick for the Flathead valley and his own people, so he took his Blackfoot wife and started walking back home with the buffalo calves."

Cameron was watching him, waiting for him to continue. He took a swallow of tea and threw a chunk of wood on the fire.

"Well, what happened?" she prodded. "Did they make it? What happened to the buffalo calves?"

"They made it back to the Flathead valley and spent the rest of their lives there, and those orphans he rescued became the foundation for the herd of bison that wanders around Yellowstone today."

She was studying him. "That's an interesting skeleton."

Jack met her gaze and shook his head. "I don't know why I told you that story. It doesn't have anything to do with anything."

"But it does," Cameron said. "Coyote Walking went searching for something, he didn't know what, and he ended up saving the buffalo from being wiped out. He didn't know where he belonged or what his life was about until he found those orphaned calves.

"You came here searching for something that meant a lot to you, but didn't find it," she continued. "I came here hoping to make a lot of money so I could buy a red Jeep, and now I realize that Johnny Allen's red Jeep wasn't really what I wanted. Seems to me we're just two lost and lonely people looking for something and trying to find where we belong, just like Coyote Walking. But right now we belong right here, and the here and now is all that matters.

"You were right about me, Jack. I invited myself along on this trip. Right from the very beginning, I targeted you for my own gain. First for the money, and then for…" She paused and looked out across the river, searching for words that were just out of reach. Just beyond that big rock that split the current in two. Just over on the opposite shore. Just around the river bend. She blew out her breath when she couldn't find them. "Coyote Walking may have had the crazies, and it may have taken him a while to realize where home was, but he ended up saving those buffalo calves. He did good.

"We have two days to tame that wild dog under the cabin. If we can manage that and fix the canoe and get out to the Mackenzie safe and sound, all of us, we'll have done good. That's my mission in the here and now, and I'm going to get started." She pushed out of her chair and started to walk away, then paused and looked back at him. "And when I said you hadn't found what you came here for, I didn't mean you wouldn't. We still have time for one more miracle, Jack. You could still find your lost dog."

JACK WATCHED CAMERON return to the cabin, wishing she'd finished what she really started to say. She said she'd targeted him first for the money, and then for…what? One night of recreational sex? He'd never know the answer. Not that it mattered. In another few days they'd be back in civilization. She'd go her way, he'd go his. She'd made it pretty plain she wasn't interested in messy entanglements, which was sensible, for both of them. They lived in two vastly different worlds. As for finding Ky, he had to face the fact that he might not. She could be dead. The bear might have killed her. But not to have come here and searched for her would have been the ultimate betrayal of an extraordinary fidelity. And even though the odds were stacked against her being alive, he still felt like she was out there somewhere, waiting for him. Was he just avoiding reality?

With a defeated sigh, he directed his attention to the canoe. He'd grafted a small piece of sheet metal he'd found under the woodstove in the cabin over the outside of the gash in the canoe's side and glued it in place with a skim of roofing tar taken from a half-empty gallon can in the cabin. Once that was smoothed to his liking, he began placing strips of duct tape over the sheet metal, overlapping onto the dry fiberglass canoe by six inches on each side and overlapping each strip by half. He was halfway through the job and wasn't sure he'd have enough duct tape to finish. A little while ago that thought had bothered him.

Now he didn't care if the canoe got mended. He didn't want to go back to soldiering. He didn't want to go back to Afghanistan. He didn't care if he ever proved his worth in another firefight. He didn't want to reach the Mackenzie River and watch his sister hand over five grand in bounty money to Cameron for getting him there. He wanted to stay right here and let the river run past and leave the two of them behind.

But even as those thoughts clouded his mind, he kept working steadily, patiently, and there was enough tape to finish the job. There was even enough left on the roll to smooth some strips inside the canoe to secure the sheet metal patch even better. By the time he was finished with the patch job, he'd sunk into a manic mood. He and Cameron had two more days together, just two more days, and for him, at least, the next two nights were going to be pure hell.

CHAPTER SEVENTEEN

CAMERON USED THE ax leaning against the wood box inside the camp to enlarge the hole under the cabin just enough so she could get her shoulders through. She needed to squeeze inside far enough to see what was under there. There was a pup. They'd both heard it whining and whimpering, and she was pretty sure there might be more than one. There might be a whole litter. She chopped at the dirt on both sides of the opening, glad nobody was there to witness her mistreatment of such an important and obviously well cared for woodsman's tool. It didn't take long to accomplish the task, and she dropped the ax and knelt in front of the opening. She pulled her headlamp out of her jacket pocket and put it on.

"Mama Dog," she said as she adjusted the headband, "this might scare you and I'm sorry for that, but I have to look under there to see what's what." Cameron kept her tone calm and conversational. "I have two days to convince you that Jack and I are the good guys, and you'll be safe with us. We'll take care of you and make sure you get fed, and if you have a pup or two under there with you, we'll take care of your whole family. Okay? So be a good girl and let me have a quick look. No growling or biting."

She lay down on her stomach and proceeded to wriggle into the narrow opening beneath the cabin. Even with the digging she'd done, it was a tight fit. She used her elbows to propel herself into the dirt tunnel that curved under the bottom log. When she'd gotten her entire upper body firmly wedged into the opening, she craned her head to scan the underside of the cabin. The usable area of the den wasn't very large, maybe five-by-eight feet, and the first thing she saw were the glowing eyes reflected in the light of her headlamp. Four of them. And then she saw the very white teeth of Mama Dog, which were bared in a very menacing way, and heard an accompanying and distinctly unfriendly growl.

But she barely heeded the warning because the smaller pair of eyes had instantly captivated her. Milky blue with that just-opened mixture of curiosity and bewilderment, and belonging to the most adorable pup she'd ever seen. She forgot all about the snarling dog that was crouched menacingly a mere eight feet from her face.

"Oh my," Cameron breathed softly. "Mama Dog, you have a very beautiful pup. What a good mother you've been, what a good girl you are. I brought you something." She reached slowly in the cramped space and produced the last hot dog from her jacket pocket. "Here you go, girl, the last of the natural casing all beef Oscar Mayer. Share with your pup. It looks old enough to be starting on solid food pretty quick. I bet it's got those little needle-sharp teeth, and I bet they're starting to hurt when it nurses. That's a good Mama Dog. No more snarling. I won't hurt you or your pup, I promise."

She placed the hot dog at arm's reach in front of her, then used her hands and elbows to back out of the tunnel. Or tried to. Her jacket snagged on something, and she managed to move only a few inches back before being brought to a halt. Her partial retreat was enough to stop the defensive growling and teeth baring of the bitch and to trigger the curiosity of the pup, who was now advancing toward her on unsteady legs. Cameron guessed it was maybe three weeks old.

"Hey," she said softly. "Hey, puppy." Much to the mother's alarm, the pup came right up to her, fearless in the way of the very young. She let it sniff her, blew her breath in its face, breathed puppy breath in return and felt herself melt when the little tongue licked her hand and sharp needle teeth gnawed on her finger. *If I can catch this pup*, she thought, *I can tame the mother. She'll come to her pup. She might not get in the canoe, but she'll follow us along the shore to stay with her pup. She won't abandon it.*

She stroked the puppy very gently with one finger. Then two. Then with her entire hand. The pup liked the stroking and moved closer. Mama Dog growled again, a low, threatening warning. "It's okay, Mama Dog. I'm not hurting your little one. I won't hurt either of you."

Cameron ran her palm over the pup, let it get her scent and listen to her voice. She blew her breath over it again. "You're a boy pup," she said. "I'm going to call you Lobo, after the wild Wolf River, because it didn't drown us and because it gave us back our canoe, and because you're the only pup, and you're going to be the handsomest dog that ever roamed this wild land. You're not going to leave me like Roy did and like Jack's going to. You're going to be my friend and stay with me no matter what, because dogs are loyal and they never run out on you. Isn't that so?"

Cameron realized she couldn't take the pup away from its mother. For one thing, her jacket was caught on something and she couldn't make a quick escape. For another, it wouldn't be right to separate them. She had another day to work her magic on both. She'd leave the hot dog and the pup behind, and by doing so Mama Dog would come to trust her. By tomorrow, like Jack said, Mama Dog would be eating out of her hand. And then maybe she would have helped save something beautiful. She wouldn't be written into the history books like Coyote Walking, but she just might walk her way into Jack's heart, and that was something. Hell, who was she kidding? That was everything.

Yet she'd just as much as told him that last night hadn't meant anything to her, that she wasn't interested in a relationship, that she wanted to keep things simple. Uncomplicated. Why? What was the point of telling him that when it wasn't true? If they just had two more days together, shouldn't they make the most of them? What if two days was all she'd ever have of that good man's heart? Why was she running away?

She knew the answer. She was a coward. She was afraid of being hurt. Of being abandoned. Of being alone again when for the past week she'd been happier than she'd ever been in spite of the miserable conditions she'd endured. She'd been happy because she was with Jack, but he was going back to army life. And now she was trying to tame this wild dog so they could climb into the canoe, leave this place, return to civilization and never see each other again.

Cameron eyed the hot dog. It was within arm's reach. She inched forward and repossessed it. "I changed my mind, Mama Dog," she said. "Maybe wanting something really bad is better than having it." She broke off a small piece and extended it to the pup, who took it from her fingers and dropped it in the dirt, then picked it up and chewed it with sharp little puppy teeth. She gave it a second piece, and this time the pup consumed it without hesitating. "Good, isn't it? It's all those unhealthy nitrates. Go tell your mama what she's missing."

She stroked the pup again and then tried to wriggle backward out of the hole. Again her jacket caught and held fast to the lower log. "Damn it!" she said. She tried to peel out of her jacket, but the tunnel was too cramped to move her arms. If she squirmed forward, she might gain enough room. Mama Dog had dug quite a deep depression for her den, but she'd also made it plain she wouldn't like it much if

Cameron came any closer, and those teeth of hers were very sharp and strong looking.

Dilemma. What to do? It seemed she had no recourse but to wait for Jack, and it could be a long wait given the fact he was mending the canoe and it was a big job. Her one consolation was she was wearing her headlamp. At least she didn't have to wait in the dark. To appease the growling bitch, she tossed the last of the hot dog toward the back of the den. It seemed prudent to try to make friends.

JACK SAT FOR a long time after finishing the canoe, just watching the river and letting his thoughts flow like the water. He sat and thought about his life, about the paths he'd chosen, the things he'd done, the things he hadn't done and regretted not doing, the things he would do if he could and the things he could never do even if he wanted. Every thought came back around to Cameron.

She'd as much as told him they had no future, and he could see where she was coming from. Her life was here in the north country, flying planes, and he'd been in the army for so long he didn't know anything else.

That didn't mean he couldn't learn something else. He'd just never given it all that much thought. He was career army, on track to climb through the ranks until he lost his leg, but even then, the thought of leaving the army had never occurred to him. He was going to learn to use the prosthetic leg, and he was going to go back to his unit and do what he'd been trained to do. And up until a week ago, that had been his plan.

Now he felt all adrift, the same way Cameron had felt that morning at breakfast when she said, "I don't know what I think anymore." Neither did he, but one thing was certain. If he was feeling so blue about parting with her when they reached the Mackenzie, maybe he ought to talk to her about how he felt. But nothing he said would change the fact that he only had one leg, and she could just as easily fall for a man who had two. Didn't every beautiful girl dream of walking on a beach hand in hand with her man? Did that dream ever include a prosthetic leg attached to a soldier suffering from PTSD?

Jack rode an emotional roller coaster as he watched the river flow past. He brooded until he couldn't stand it any longer. He had to go talk to her or go crazy. He stood, picked up his plate and mug and returned to the cabin, surprised to find that Cameron wasn't inside. He set his tea mug on the table and then heard her muffled voice coming from beneath the floor.

"Jack? Can you hear me? I'm stuck under the cabin and I can't get out!"

IT SEEMED AS if she'd been trapped for hours in the near darkness, listening to the rumbling growls of Mama Dog and being chewed on by the curious pup. When she heard Jack's voice and felt his hands close around her ankles, Cameron felt a rush of relief. The darkness had become suffocating.

"You okay?" he said.

"Never better," she replied. "I've got a wild dog snarling in my face, a puppy with very sharp teeth chewing on my nose, my headlamp's dead and my jacket is caught on something. I'm stuck and in the dark."

"You sure there's just one puppy?"

"Just one, and I only have one nose, so please hurry."

She felt his hand sliding along her back. "Your jacket's caught on a nail," he said. "Make that two nails…bet this was set up for a porcupine snare, but I don't feel any wire, so the snare wasn't set. I'm going to try to drag you out, but I might end up ripping your jacket. I can't reach the nails to bend them."

"Rip away. I'm getting claustrophobic. I just want out of here."

She felt him jerk hard once on her jacket,

heard a loud ripping noise, and then he was grasping the waistband of her pants. He dragged her out of the hole facedown. Dirt slid up under her T-shirt. She didn't care. She wriggled free as soon as Jack had pulled her far enough out, rose to her feet and pulled her T-shirt back down and stripped out of her jacket.

"Thank you," she said, brushing dirt off her and examining the ripped jacket.

"No problem. I'm getting used to rescuing you. Makes me feel useful. If we were going to be traveling together much longer, I'd suggest walkie-talkies. That way I could respond sooner the next time you got into trouble."

Cameron scowled, bent and picked up the empty dog dish. "The pup's old enough to be chewing on things. He ate the pieces of hot dog I gave him."

"He?"

She nodded. "He's very cute. Did you fix the canoe?"

"I did. It should get us out to the Mackenzie without sinking. All that's left to do here is tame the wild dog, cut some firewood to replace what we've used and clean the camp."

"Right. On that note, I'll feed Mama Dog again." She started to step around him, and he blocked her.

"Cameron, we need to talk." He took the dog dish out of her hand.

She took the dog dish back and shook her head. "I can't talk about last night, Jack, I just can't."

He regarded her steadily, then nodded. "All right, you don't have to talk, but you need to listen to what I have to say. We need to talk about the future. We can't pretend we don't have one, not after all we've been through together. I saw one last bottle of wine in your gourmet food stash. Let's take it down to the fire pit and polish it off. We need to work things out between us if we're going to survive the next couple of days together."

AN HOUR LATER, Jack raised his glass of wine in a salute. "You really know your wines, Cameron Johnson."

Two glasses of wine had relaxed her. The late-afternoon sunlight had illuminated the most beautiful wilderness setting Cameron had ever seen. The sound of the river was soothing, the smell of woodsmoke from the fire pit was comforting, the breeze kept the bugs away. The trepidation she'd felt when Jack announced that he needed to talk to her had faded. The dreaded conversation about their future hadn't happened. In fact, Jack hadn't said much of anything. He'd just sat there enjoying an afternoon of doing nothing, same as she was doing. Well, that wasn't exactly true. He'd been working on the canoe pole, shaving it down with the freshly sharpened ax. She smiled at him as she raised her own glass in response to his salute.

"Hap's Place only carries the best," Cameron said. "It's actually the only wine he sells because his wife drinks it, and she told him if he didn't keep it in stock she'd divorce him and head back to Whitehorse."

"Smart woman."

"Smart man." Cameron regarded him over the rim of her glass, then took the plunge. "What was it you wanted to talk about?"

"I wanted to talk about what's going to happen when we reach the Mackenzie."

Cameron's fingers tightened on the wineglass. "Do we really have to talk about that?"

"You don't, but I do, because it's been bothering me. You're going to collect your money from my sister and buy that red Jeep. Fair enough. That's what you signed up for. But we've been through a lot together, and wherever I end up, I'd like for us to keep in touch. If you want to, that is."

"You mean, like writing letters to each other? Talking on the phone?" Cameron stared at him.

"That's what you wanted to talk about? Exchanging addresses and phone numbers?"

"I think that'd be better than just saying goodbye and going our own ways. I know you don't want things to get too complicated, but a letter or a phone call is uncomplicated and simple, isn't it?"

Cameron stiffened. She set down her glass very carefully on a flat rock beside her chair and stood. "I'll go get a pad of paper and a pen. I think I have both in my duffel. We'll exchange information, including birthdays, because I sure wouldn't want you to miss sending me a birthday card from Afghanistan. I bet the postage stamp would be really different. Maybe even collectible."

"Look, I'm not trying to upset you. I'm just trying to figure things out. After what happened between us last night… I know we have different lives. I don't blame you for wanting to stay up here, and I know you love flying. I'd never expect you to give it up, and I don't know what's going to happen in my future. I'm saying just because we go our separate ways when we reach the big river doesn't mean we can't stay in touch."

Cameron's heart rate surged off the charts in spite of the relaxing wine. "You know what your problem is, Jack Parker? You can't see that maybe I care about you, and that's what last night was about. How could I not care about you? I saved your life, so now it belongs to me. Isn't that how it goes? There's nothing simple about that. It's as tangled up as anything could ever get between two people. And last night? You want to talk about last night? I'll talk about last night. Last night was incredible. It was the most incredible night of my life, and now you want to exchange addresses and telephone numbers? You want to be my *pen pal*? Call me up once in a while?"

Jack stared at her, wearing the same confounded expression he'd worn that very morning. "What do you want, Cameron?"

She flushed. "I don't know."

"You said you cared about me."

"I do."

"Okay, we care about each other. At least that's out in the open. Then let's move on." He set down his glass as carefully as she had. He unzipped his pant leg, released the socket, removed his prosthetic and stripped the lower pant leg off the artificial limb. He held it up as an object of interest. "This is another one of the things I wanted to talk to you about."

"Your leg?" Cameron said.

"My *prosthesis*," Jack corrected. "If you care about me, you need to understand everything about it because it's a part of me now, a part of my life, and you need to visualize certain things. Like how romantic a walk on the beach would be with a man wearing an artificial limb. That's the physical reality, and that's just part of it. Then there's the psychological reality. Like lying in bed and wondering if you're going to be tackled if you move the wrong way. You've already experienced that. Like dealing with moods that turn black without warning. Phantom pain. Flashbacks. Nightmares. I've seen the worst side of humanity. I've seen things nobody should have to see, and I've done things I can never talk about. I was changed by it, physically and mentally, and somehow I have to learn to live with it, and it isn't easy."

Cameron felt herself twisting up inside. She'd been chastising him when she didn't have a clue what he'd been through. All the horrors he'd seen and experienced. "I'm sorry," she said, humbled.

"Don't be. I'm glad you don't know what I've experienced. Nobody should. This is a temporary prosthesis," he said, brandishing the artificial limb to refocus the conversation. "It weighs about four pounds. I was fitted with it after the surgeries when I got stateside, and I'll be using it for about six months, until I heal up completely. My residual limb, that's what they call what's left of an arm or leg, a 'residual limb,' my residual limb will gradually reduce in size as the swelling goes down, which was starting to happen until I checked myself out of the hospital. That meant the stump was healing. That was good.

"A prosthetic sock goes over the neoprene sleeve that fits over the end of my residual limb, just like this." He set the limb aside and pulled off the sock to expose the neoprene sleeve. "As the swelling continues to go down, more socks can be added so the socket on the prosthesis fits snugly over my residual limb. The air valve on the prosthetic socket creates a vacuum that holds the leg on securely. That's why it doesn't fall off when I'm walking. Are you following me?"

"Jack, if the point you're trying to make is that one of your flesh and blood legs is always going to be shorter than the other, I get it, I really do. But right now what I'm most afraid of is that when I get to the end of my life I might regret the things I never did, so I just wanted you to know that I care about you and I don't regret last night. If these next two days together are all we ever have, I'm going to make the most of them. Whatever happens in our future, so be it. At least I'll have no regrets about what happened in the here and now."

To prove her point, she bent over him and kissed him. Her kiss was passionate, hungry, high voltage. She wanted to tear his clothes off, devour him, and his reaction was equally voracious. She ended up in his lap and things might have gone a whole lot further, but when they came up for air she gasped out, between breaths, "There's just one problem, and it's a big one. Tell me you brought protection, Jack, please tell me you did, because last night was a little risky."

After a moment of stunned silence, Jack laughed. "You really think I hiked into the wilderness all by myself, carrying condoms, just in case?"

She slumped against him with a frustrated moan.

"If what we feel for each other is real, we can wait a few more days," Jack said.

"But what if these next two days are all we ever have?"

"They won't be. Life doesn't work like that. You can't just turn your feelings on and off like the radio."

"Roy did."

"I'm not Roy."

Cameron smothered a laugh against his

chest. "No, you sure aren't," she said. "Roy never said no to sex, just so long as the one proposing it was female." She sighed and pushed out of his lap. "There's no sense torturing ourselves. I'm going to go pick some raspberries in that patch behind the cabin. They're just coming ripe. I can make a cobbler, maybe, with what's left of the sugar I scraped off the ground and the biscuit mix. If we can't have sex, we can at least eat good. I'll fix char steaks and raspberry cobbler for supper."

Jack watched her straighten her clothes and his head dropped back with a groan.

CHAPTER EIGHTEEN

JACK WAS CUTTING firewood with a vengeance when Cameron took a one quart saucepan and went out to the small clearing with the raspberry bushes, located behind the outhouse. She was between the cabin and the outhouse, following the path, when she noticed a metallic gleam between the path and the river, and paused. She scuffed the earth with her toe and revealed a section of rusted chain, then bent and pulled on the chain, lifting another longer section. That section had a small eighteen-inch length of chain fastened to it, with a steel swivel snap on the end. She continued unearthing the chain from its covering of woodruff until she had exposed the entire length, which was a good twenty feet long and tethered between two black spruce. There were eight shorter and lighter lengths of chain attached to the main cable, each with a swivel snap on the end.

She'd seen similar setups at the musher's kennels and at checkpoints during the Yukon

Quest sled dog race. They were called picket lines, and sled dogs were tethered to them during rest stops. Perhaps the trapper who built this cabin had used a dog team to get in and out in winter, and perhaps the dog under the cabin was an escaped member of that team. She almost turned around to tell Jack about her discovery, then realized it was getting late and continued toward the raspberry patch instead.

She could smell the raspberries in the warmth of the late-afternoon sun. The patch in the clearing wasn't very big, maybe twenty feet square, but she'd easily get enough for a cobbler. The raspberries plinked as she dropped the first ones into the pan, then the sound grew muted as the pan quickly filled. She moved around the nearest edge of the patch and thought about the conversation she'd just shared with Jack. They hadn't actually talked about the future, but in a way they had. Only… nothing had really changed. He didn't say he was getting out of the military because he didn't want to say goodbye. He was perfectly willing to share the night with her, but as far as sharing anything more than that, he'd been very noncommittal.

As she picked, she became aware there were quite a few yellow jackets moving around in the middle of the patch, and she paused to watch

them. There was a ground nest in there, somewhere, and she wasn't going to stumble into it.
She'd done enough stumbling into catastrophes
lately, and the last thing she needed was to get
stung by a colony of wasps. She had enough
berries to make a cobbler. Time to go.

She started to turn around and noticed that
the patch beyond the moving wasps had been
crushed flat. She studied it for a moment. A
bear had been in here, and not too long ago,
judging by the way the wasps were still flying
around. She was lucky she hadn't been stung.
It wasn't an unusual thing to see signs of a bear
in a berry patch. The smell of the raspberries
would draw them like a magnet, but this little
patch wasn't all that far from the cabin. Which
meant the bear that broke into the cabin might
still be in the vicinity.

Cameron returned to the cabin, to the welcome sound of Jack chopping firewood. He
straightened from the task when she reached
the clearing, ax dangling in one hand.

"Got enough for a cobbler," she said, holding up the pan. "But I wasn't the only one ber-
rying. A bear was in there not too long ago,
got some wasps all stirred up. Jack, we should
think about catching Mama Dog as soon as
possible. If that's the same bear that broke into
the camp and had such a good feast, sooner or

later it'll be back. We have to get Mama Dog and the pup, and get back on the river as soon as possible. She's not totally wild, and I think I know how she got there. The trapper who built this cabin comes here during the winter and must travel in by dog team. I found a picket line for his team out back of the cabin. That dog must've been part of his team last winter, and she got loose and he couldn't catch her again. Some of those village dogs can be pretty spooky if they aren't socialized well, but I bet if we could just get our hands on her, get a collar on her, she'd be okay."

"If the trapper who owned her couldn't catch her, I don't see how we'll be able to do it. If she's got a pup, she was running with the wolves. She's turned wild."

"Maybe, but we have a big advantage that he didn't have," Cameron said. "Right now she's denned under the camp, and she's not going to leave her pup. When I was stuck in the hole, she was trapped in there and couldn't get past me. I could crawl under there again, only I'd go in all the way this time. You could block the hole while I try to get a collar on her."

Jack shook his head. "She'll tear you to shreds. Take a look at yourself in the mirror by the cabin sink. Do you really want to add bite marks to those injuries?"

"I don't think she'll bite me. She's been a sled dog. She knows what a collar and a harness is. She might snap a little, but I don't think she'll bite. How else will we be able to get our hands on her in a short amount of time?"

Jack rubbed the beard on his jaw. "You're not going back under there."

"But I've already been under the cabin with her, and she didn't attack me. She just growled and bared her teeth, but she was backed into a corner and I was messing with her pup."

Jack thought for a moment. "Okay, here's what we'll do. It's getting late, and I have to finish chopping this wood. Tonight I'll make a collar for her out of my belt and rig up a way to secure her in the canoe. You said there's some chain out back? I might need to use some of that. She could chew through rope really quick. Add some chain to the list of what we have to replace. First thing in the morning, when we know she's in there with the pup, I'll dig the hole under the cabin deep enough so I can crawl in there with her. You'll block the hole behind me with your body, and I'll put the collar on her."

"But Jack, if we caught her now, we could bring her and the pup inside for the night. That would give us time to handle them a little before loading them into the canoe. I'll put another pan of stew under there for her and then work on making the hole bigger while you finish up with this firewood. I just wish we had a shovel."

"There's a shovel under the bunk. The trapper stashed lots of useful tools under there. I'll dig the hole out tomorrow morning."

Cameron brightened. "I'll do it. It won't take long to make that hole big enough for you to fit through, and then I'll fix you some supper, and maybe we can catch Mama Dog before it gets dark."

AFTER SHE FINISHED enlarging the entry hole beneath the cabin, Cameron started fixing supper. Late-afternoon sunlight streamed through the window facing the river. From beneath the cabin Cameron heard scuffling movements, the sound of Mama Dog eating the food she'd just put under there, and Lobo making happy puppy sounds. At least once they were caught, they'd have a better future to look forward to, one with regular meals. Mama Dog might not like the whole capture scenario that they'd planned for her, but in the end she'd be better off.

Jack was still outside, chopping wood. He'd made a big stack, far bigger than what they'd used. He was good with an ax. He'd obviously split wood before, and lots of it. She wondered about his boyhood in Montana. About how he'd grown up. About his time in Afghanistan and all the awful things he'd seen and done, all the awful things that had happened to him, and how in spite of it all, he still wanted to go back. She thought about his dog, Ky, and how she couldn't possibly be alive. About his relationship with his sister. About his sick mother. And then she brooded for a long time about his sister's statement that twenty-two veterans committed suicide every day.

She thought about all this while she dumped the last of the biscuit mix into a bowl, then added enough water to make a batter. She buttered the Dutch oven she'd used to rescue the canoe. Put a few more blobs of butter in the bottom, and then, after a brief hesitation, she added all of it, the entire stick, the last of their butter because they were both so hungry, so starved for fat. She poured the raspberries on top of the butter, dumped the last of the salvaged sugar onto the berries and spooned the batter on top of it all. It might be an unappetizing blob to city folk, but she and Jack would eat it and think it was manna from heaven. And it would be.

The fire in the pit was burning down to a nice bed of coals, perfect for grilling the char steaks and baking raspberry cobbler. She nestled the Dutch oven into a bed of coals, shoveled more coals atop the lid and prepared another bed of coals for the grill. Jack was stacking the last of the wood he'd cut and split beneath the roof's eaves, where the trapper had stashed the bulk of his firewood.

"Twenty-two," she said when he came over to the fire pit. He had his leather belt and jackknife in hand and was preparing to make the collar for Mama Dog.

He gave her a questioning look.

"That's how many veterans commit suicide every day," Cameron explained. "Your sister told me that to try to explain why she was so worried about you, why she wanted me to come out here and find you." She laid the char steaks on the grill and they began to sizzle. Char was a nice fatty fish. Delicious.

Jack divided the last of the wine between their two glasses and set down the bottle, handing her glass to her before claiming his chair. He remained silent, just sat and watched the steaks cook, holding the belt and his knife in motionless hands.

"I just hope when you see her again, you'll remember she's family and she loves you, and I hope you don't hold what happened to your dog against her because that wasn't her fault." Cameron remained crouched beside the fire, where she could keep a close eye on the thick, deep red char steaks. Overcooking a piece of fish this beautiful would be a terrible thing. She gazed into the glowing bed of coals. "Family is important. When my dad was killed in that plane crash, my world came crashing down around me. I was wrecked by his death. I never realized how big a part of my life he was. Roy said my dad was lucky because he died doing something he loved, but I didn't see it that way."

She looked at him across the campfire. "I lost someone I really cared about when that plane's engine quit, and there was nothing lucky about it. What happened to my father happened to me. That's what it feels like when you lose someone you really love. A part of you dies right along with them. At least, that's how it was with me."

She turned her attention back to the steaks. Fat hissed, and wisps of fragrant smoke curled upward. She shifted the Dutch oven, settling it deeper into the bed of coals. Thought about what she was trying to say. Somehow she needed to make Jack understand. She met his gaze again over the smoke of the cook fire and shored up her resolve.

"The thing is, I can't leave here, Jack. I love this land, and I love flying. I don't want to leave this life behind, and I don't want to be your pen pal, either. So I guess what I'm trying to say is, I really care about you, and this has been one hell of a journey, but when we reach the Mackenzie River, I think a clean break would be the best thing for both of us."

Jack regarded her silently for a long moment before nodding. "If that's how you want it to be."

"I do." Cameron rose to her feet. "I'll get the plates. The steaks are almost done."

THE STEAKS WERE cooked to perfection. The raspberry cobbler had come out great. Smelled wonderful. Tasted amazing. Cameron had to force every bite down. Jack remained quiet. He ate everything she put in front of him, cleaned his plate, told her how excellent it was and thanked her, but that was all. There was no small talk. Nothing but awkward silence. After supper, while she was cleaning up, he concentrated on finishing the dog collar, using the awl on his knife to make holes to adjust it to the right size once they got it on Mama Dog. He used two drop lines off the picket line to make a tether they could use to tie her in the canoe. Then he cleverly split a small section of the remainder of his belt to make a tiny collar for the pup. All of this he did in brooding silence. Or maybe he wasn't brooding. Maybe he just didn't feel like talking, which annoyed her because she wanted him to say something. Something more than just, "If that's how you want it to be."

But he wasn't going to. He'd already moved on from the subject of a clean break when they reached the Mackenzie. He certainly wasn't going to declare that he couldn't live without her, that he was going to quit the army just so he could stay in the north land. He'd probably be relieved to see the last of her. He'd go back to Afghanistan and tell his army buddies stories about his endless trek down a wild river with "Calamity Jane," and they'd all laugh. Meanwhile, she'd be back here in Northwest Territories, lonely and alone, flying wealthy, overweight sports into hunting camps so they could drink a lot and shoot something they could brag about. She'd fend off unwanted advances and wonder why she'd told Jack that she loved what she did when the truth was, she only loved parts of it, and those parts weren't enough anymore. This life used to be all she ever wanted. Now, thanks to him, she was truly miserable.

After the camp was cleaned and tidied and the dishes put away on the shelf, she walked back out to the canoe where Jack was rigging the tether to the middle thwart.

"We should try to catch Mama Dog before dark," she said. "I made the hole big enough for you to fit under the cabin."

He glanced up at her. "It's nearly dark now. I'm going to finish this job, and then I'm turning in. If I'm going to get torn to shreds by a wild dog, I'd rather get a good night's sleep first. We'll make an early start in the morning. We'll catch the dog and pup first thing, and if all goes well we could be on the river before noon."

"But if we caught her now, she could spend the night inside with us, getting used to us. I think we should try. What if that bear comes back?"

Jack shook his head. "That bear won't come back as long as we're here." He paused to look at her. "Tomorrow's going to be a long, hard day. Get some sleep. I'll be up when I'm done here."

His voice was clipped and curt, a stern dismissal. Cameron wheeled around and returned to the cabin. She thought she was too worked up to fall asleep, and wanted to stay awake to continue this conversation, but after she'd climbed into the top bunk and lay down, her body betrayed her.

CHAPTER NINETEEN

TWO HOURS LATER Cameron awoke with a start and lay still, wondering what had disturbed her. She listened intently but heard nothing other than the muted sound of the river flowing past.

"You awake?" Jack's voice came out of the darkness. It was as if he'd touched her across the distance, stroked her with his hand. His voice filled the empty ache inside her and made her feel like crying.

"Yes."

"Did you hear that?"

"No." She listened again and heard nothing. The silence stretched out. All she could hear was the rush of the river and the beating of her heart. Her badly damaged heart. She was in such misery she was about to climb uninvited into Jack's bunk when Mama Dog growled beneath the cabin floor. It was a long, threatening growl that raised the hair on Cameron's nape. Shortly afterward, she heard something moving out behind the camp. Something big. Mama Dog growled again, louder. Her heart rate accelerated, and she swung her legs over the edge of the bunk, wondering where she'd put her headlamp.

"Something's out there," Jack said. "Could be that bear, looking for more of our food."

"You said it wouldn't come back." Cameron slid from the top bunk, felt her way to the table and fumbled for her headlamp. She found it, then remembered that she hadn't changed the dead batteries. "Where's your headlamp? The batteries are dead in mine."

"Should be right there on the table." She could hear him moving, getting up.

She fumbled in the dark until she found it, then switched it on. Light illuminated the cabin's interior. Jack was sitting up, pulling on his prosthesis.

"Don't worry, I've got this," she said, reaching for her .44 Magnum pistol. "If it's a bear, I'll fire a few shots in the air. The noise will scare it off."

"Scare it off or piss it off," he said. "Get the bear spray out of my pack."

"This pistol will do the job." She checked the pistol and pulled on Jack's headlamp. As she reached for the door, they heard a loud burst of ferocious sounds behind the cabin. A fight had begun and was rapidly escalating between the dog and the intruder.

"Wait for me!" Jack ordered, but Cameron was already descending the cabin steps. From the sound of the commotion, there was no time to waste. First thing she did when she reached the bottom step was fire a shot into the air. The .44 Magnum pistol had a deafening report. Ears ringing, she rounded the corner of the cabin, the sounds of the fight undiminished. Whatever was happening was life or death, and Cameron walked right into the middle of it.

The darkness was thick, and the headlamp cast a bright but narrow beam into a whirlwind of dark motion as Mama Dog fiercely defended her den against a bear that had invaded her territory and threatened her pup. Cameron had made the hole under the cabin larger with the shovel. Was the pup still alive or had the bear already reached in and killed it?

Cameron fired the pistol in the air again, then fired a third shot, but Jack was right. The noise had no effect. The bear was completely focused on killing the dog that was attacking it. Mama Dog darted in and sprang back out of reach, snapping at the bear, then retreating as the bear lashed out. Again she sprang in, again the bear drove her back. When the bear turned toward Cameron, Mama Dog lunged forward and seized onto the bear's flank. The bruin bawled, whirled and with one great powerful swat sent Mama Dog tumbling through the air.

"No!" Cameron was raising the pistol to shoot the bear when Jack's hand came out of nowhere. With one quick move, he wrested the pistol out of her hands and pushed her behind him. He took two steps forward, pistol in one hand, bear spray in the other, and the moment the bear's head turned from the fallen dog to look toward Jack, he sprayed it point-blank in the face from a distance of less than ten feet. The bear let out another furious bawl and stumbled backward, then turned and lumbered blindly into the thick spruce forest behind the camp.

Mama Dog lay on her side. Her eyes were open, but blank and unfocused. Was she dead? Cameron dropped to her knees beside her, then felt Jack's hand grip her shoulder.

"Get inside *now*! That bear could come back," he ordered. "I'll carry her in and then check for the puppy."

The puppy! On hands and knees Cameron scrambled toward the hole. She stuck her head through the opening and felt a rush of relief when she saw the small pair of eyes reflected in the light of the headlamp. She wriggled forward until she was under the cabin, and seized hold of the frightened pup. There was no time for gentleness. Jack was right. That pissed-off bear could return at any moment. She gripped the yipping struggling pup firmly by the scruff of its neck and wriggled backward until she was free of the den. As she rose to her feet, Jack scooped Mama Dog into his arms, and together they beat a hasty retreat into the cabin.

Once inside, Jack laid the dog on the floor beside the lower bunk, lit the oil lamp, then took the headlamp from Cameron and went back outside to close the bear shutters. Cameron cradled the frightened pup against her and crouched beside Mama Dog, who lay motionless. Jack came back inside and closed and barred the door behind him. He knelt beside Cameron to examine the injured dog.

"I don't see any blood, but that bear really clobbered her," he said. "She might have internal injuries. Let her see and smell the pup. That might help."

Cameron placed the pup on the floor beside Mama Dog. Lobo crowded up against his mother, pushing between her head and chest and hiding his face against her warm fur, but she made no response. Her breathing was labored and her eyes still half-open with a fixed stare. Cameron sat beside them and leaned against the bottom bunk. She was shaking now. Shaking all over. She couldn't have stood if she tried. She wanted to touch Mama Dog. Stroke her gently. Let her know she was okay. Instead, she looked up at Jack.

"If we'd caught her last night, this wouldn't have happened," she said.

Jack blew out his breath and glanced at his watch. "It's a little after three. It'll be getting light soon. I'll put on a pot of coffee."

They drank coffee and waited for the dawn, and the silence between them became an unbridgeable abyss. When the first bird song alerted them to morning, Jack went outside and opened the bear shutters. Mama Dog's eyes had closed, but she was still breathing and the pup was still cuddled up to her. Cameron was sick with remorse. She should have insisted that they catch Mama Dog last night. She should have done it herself when Jack wouldn't help. So far she'd done everything wrong on this trip. Every. Single. Thing.

"All's clear outside," he said when he came back in. "We can carry the dog down to the canoe in my sleeping bag after I get everything packed up. We should make the Mackenzie River by early evening, camp there, then go on to the town in the morning. They must have a veterinarian there, right?"

Cameron sat in silence, not responding. What point was there in telling him that veterinarians were a southern luxury? The pup roused, rooted hungrily down its mother's side and began to nurse. Mama Dog's eyes flickered, and she tried to arrange herself to allow the pup better access.

"That's a good sign," Jack said. "If she hasn't died yet, she'll probably make it."

"I'll take care of them both if she lives," Cameron said, keeping her eyes on Mama Dog. "They'll have a home with me."

"Who's going to look after two dogs while you're flying hunters all over the territory?"

"I'll manage. They'll be well cared for, which is more than you'd be able to do, soldiering in Afghanistan."

Jack thought for a moment. "The trapper who built this camp probably owns the dog. He might have something to say about it."

Cameron shook her head. "He left her behind, and in my book, that's abandonment. When he did that, he forfeited any ownership he might have had. If we hadn't come along, she'd have starved to death and the pup, too, or been eaten by that bear. She's mine now. They both are."

"So, by your reasoning, if Ky were still alive and someone else came down this river and found her and took her in, she'd belong to them now, even if I showed up a year later, searching for her? Finders, keepers? Possession is nine-tenths of the law?"

Cameron met his gaze. "You're going back to Afghanistan, Jack. Back to the army. What would you have done if you *had* found Ky? Would you have loved her up and then left her behind again with your sister? Was that your plan? I don't see how you can possibly explain abandonment to a dog. Twice."

Jack ran his fingers through his hair. "I don't know where you're taking this conversation, but I don't want to talk about Ky anymore, or all the things I've done wrong. I'm going to fix breakfast, and then we're going to pack up our stuff, load the canoe and head downriver. You can sit there and blame me for every bad thing that's happened on this trip, but like I said before, I never asked you to come along."

"Believe me, I wish I hadn't. And don't fix breakfast on my account. I'm not hungry."

She brooded in silence while he cooked oatmeal on the cookstove. When the pup was done nursing, she picked him up. His belly was round with milk. He was relaxed now and not the least bit afraid of her. He chewed her fingers, licked her chin and then fell promptly asleep in the cradle of her arms. Mama Dog gave a long sigh and her eyes closed halfway. Cameron wondered what she'd do if she stroked her. Would she growl, or would she trust them now? Would she realize they'd saved her life and the life of her pup, and were only trying to help her?

Cameron reached slowly and stroked Mama Dog's head, ready to draw her hand away quickly if she should snap, but she remained motionless. Not so much as a twitch of an ear or the flicker of an eyelid. Still as death. She bent closer, listening, waiting to see Mama Dog breathe, waiting to see her rib cage move up and down, holding her own breath because she didn't want to take another until she was certain. She watched for what seemed like a long time.

"Jack," she said, her voice faint. "Mama Dog's not breathing. She's not breathing! I think she's dead. I think she just died. I think she fed her puppy one last time, and then she just died!"

Jack crossed from the stove, crouched and rested one hand on Mama Dog's rib cage for a long moment, then checked for a pulse in her femoral artery. He stroked Mama Dog's head very gently several times, then looked up at Cameron and shook his head.

Cameron pushed to her feet and sat on the edge of the bunk, the pup cradled in her lap. She struggled to process what had just happened.

"I don't understand," she said. "All this time she's been out here trying to survive. She had this pup, and somehow managed to keep herself and her puppy alive. Then we show up out of the blue and feed her fish stew and plan to rescue her, and now she's dead. What's the point of it all? What's the point of any of this?"

Jack rose to his feet and went back to the stove, stirring the oatmeal. She heard the clank of the spoon against the side of the pan. She wanted to cry but couldn't. She was too numb. Jack shut off the stove, divided the oatmeal and brought the bowls to the table.

"Come eat," he told her. "It's going to be a long day."

"She fed her pup one last time, and then she just died," Cameron repeated, stroking the sleeping pup as tears trembled on her eyelashes. She looked again at Mama Dog, hoping to see that Jack was wrong, that she wasn't really dead after all, but nothing had changed. "I don't understand anything," she said.

"Come eat," Jack repeated.

"We should have caught her last night."

"I'm sorry, Cameron," Jack said. "If I could change things, I would. But if we hadn't showed up when we did, that pup wouldn't be sleeping in your lap right now. The bear would've dug under the cabin, killed the mother when she tried to drive it off, killed the pup and eaten them both. That's how it works in nature. You of all people know that. Bears don't kill because they're evil. They're just trying to survive. I'm sorry about the dog, I really am, but right now I'm just damned glad that bear didn't kill you because it just as easily could have if the dog hadn't been distracting it. A pistol's no match for a grizzly. It would take a twelve-gauge shotgun, rifled slugs and a lot of luck to kill one. Now come eat."

He spoke to her as if she were a child, and, like a child, Cameron moved to the table, picked up her spoon and forced herself to eat. Jack was right. This sort of stuff went on all the time in the wild. Life was hazardous, even for top of the food chain predators. There were no guarantees. She and Jack had almost drowned on this trip and were both lucky to be alive. And he was right. She'd been foolish to think she could take on a full-size grizzly with a pistol. That bear could easily have killed her with one swat, just like it killed Mama Dog. Jack could've been killed trying to keep her from being mauled to death, and this little fat-bellied pup that slept in her lap might have become a hungry bear's next meal.

Bad things had happened to all of them, but good things had happened, too. Maybe there didn't need to be a reason for why things happened. Maybe there just needed to be the promise that each new day brought, and the hope that something good might come their way. Because sometimes, it did.

After a glum and silent breakfast, Cameron set about the task of cleaning the cabin for the last time and packing up gear while Jack dug a grave for Mama Dog out behind the camp. The digging was hard, and it took awhile because he wanted the hole to be deep. Afterward he carried rocks up from the riverbank, and they built a cairn over the grave. When all was finished, they stood over the grave for a few moments. Cameron held Lobo in her arms. "I promise I'll take good care of your puppy, Mama Dog," she said.

They finished packing in silence. Cameron ached all over, and her heart was heavy. It seemed like forever ago that she started out on this journey, this easy little trip that would net her so much money, enough to buy Johnny Allen's red Jeep that she thought would change her life. It seemed a lifetime ago that she'd had such shallow aspirations.

They lugged their gear down to the river, and before they loaded the canoe, Cameron wrote a note and left it on the table for the cabin owner, thanking him for the use of his cabin, telling him about the grizzly bear and Mama Dog, and where she was buried. She was torn about mentioning the pup, but in the end wrote that Mama Dog had died bravely defending a very young pup she'd birthed in a den she'd dug under the cabin. She listed the items they'd taken: the oatmeal, half the rice and some tea; the piece of sheet metal and roofing tar to patch the canoe; the two drop chains from the picket line. She left her name and contact information. Even if it violated the unwritten code of the north, she wanted to leave money in gratitude, to replace the items they'd used, but the irony was she had none. No money in her pockets. No money in her bank account. None.

She had a job that included a moldy old house trailer with a leaky roof, and a boss who paid slave wages because he himself made so little that Jeri, who'd been with Walt forever, had finally up and quit. Well, it wasn't just the pay. Another reason she'd left was because she was in love with Walt, and Walt took her completely for granted. Jeri was worth something to Walt. She was worth a lot, and her coffee was priceless, but Walt never told her any of that. Jeri would have stayed and worked forever for slave wages if he'd just told her how much she meant to him, but now she was gone.

Men were fools.

"Ready?"

Jack's voice from the doorway made her jump. She met his eyes, nodded. Not all men were fools, she amended silently as Jack placed a wad of bills on top of the note and set the oil lamp over it. They secured the door, the bear shutters, left the camp clean and shut up tight, then slid the canoe into the back eddy and loaded it.

Cameron worried about the pup. "I'll have to keep Lobo tucked inside my jacket," she told Jack when it was time to get into the canoe. "I don't want him loose in the canoe."

"Sounds like a plan," Jack said.

"I don't know how to keep him safe other than to stuff him under my jacket. If he falls overboard, he's done for."

"You'll figure it out. Mothers are good at that."

His words had a calming effect. Her anxiety eased. She tucked the pup inside her jacket and climbed into the bow of the canoe. Everything would be okay. Lobo would be okay. She and Jack would work things out.

CHAPTER TWENTY

THUNDER RUMBLED. A long dark skein of rain hung from the belly of dark clouds gathering in the mountains and darkened the pink glow of sunset. Jack guided the canoe ashore toward the back eddy of a stubby spruce-clad peninsula that jutted into the river. The point of land would make a good campsite. Cameron was tired. They hadn't spoken a word since noon hour, when he'd put ashore for lunch. That had been shortly after the rapids, which they'd had to portage, unloading all their gear, carrying it down below the rapids, then lining the canoe down with ropes and reloading it. Exhausting work that had taken several hours out of their travel time.

"Looks like we aren't making the Mackenzie River today," she said wearily when Jack headed for shore. She climbed out into the shallow water, carefully cradling the pup, and hauled the bow of the canoe ashore.

"The Mackenzie might be around the next

bend," Jack said, "but it's going to rain. We need to get camp set up and get settled in."

She gathered driftwood with Lobo still tucked inside her jacket, then made a small cook fire on the rocky shore near their gear while Jack pitched the big tent. He loaded their sleeping bags inside while Cameron fixed a simple supper of panfried char and hot tea. The pup ate fish stew, a good-sized portion, and worried their bootlaces while they sat beside the fire and ate their own meal in silence.

Thunder rumbled closer. Jack scooped the pup off the ground to save his laces and plopped him in his lap. "He's a cute bugger," he said, offering him a tiny piece of fish, which Lobo enthusiastically accepted. Cameron remained silent, and her silence was far worse than her angry words had been. Jack would rather she shouted at him than sit there quietly, brooding about Mama Dog and how they should have saved her, and would have, if he'd listened to Cameron. The wind began to pick up. Lightning flashed against the backdrop of the thunderheads. "Bed time," he said, pushing to his feet with the pup tucked under one arm.

They made it inside the tent just before the storm hit and the torrential rains came down. The pup wandered loose within the confines of the tent while Cameron pulled off her hiking boots and shed her outerwear, leaving her long johns on. Jack did the same. The darkness brought on early by the storm was welcome. The pup burrowed inside Cameron's sleeping bag. She and Jack lay side by side, listening to the rain pound the tent fly like buckshot, listening to the deafening cracks of thunder that followed the brilliant flashes of lightning. They were close together but had never been farther apart, and even if they'd wanted to make conversation, they couldn't have, which Jack figured was probably just as well.

THE NEXT DAY dawned overcast and cool, and they packed the canoe in silence, weary and lame and tired before they even got started. Breakfast was the last of their coffee and oatmeal while the pup ate what remained of the fish stew. The morning was overcast, windy, too cold for bugs. While they sat by the small fire Cameron had kindled to heat the water for coffee, they heard geese flying high above and spotted a ragged v heading south.

Winter came early in the north. They were paddling their way through the last two weeks of August. The colors of autumn would stain the taiga with reds and yellows. Frost would come on every morn, and soon after, the snows that never melted until the following spring.

There was a somber feel to the day, as gray and troubled as the weather. Cameron tucked the pup inside her jacket, climbed into the canoe and left Jack to the paddling. They headed downriver toward a fate neither could guess at or talk about, traveling in a silence that felt almost funereal.

It took most of the morning to reach the Mackenzie River, and there was no feeling of triumph in either of them when they did. It was simply an unheralded arrival at the confluence of the two rivers, where the clear black water of the Wolf pushed into the gray silted water of the broad, powerful Mackenzie, and both flowed north toward the Arctic Ocean. It was a moment that brought them closer to the end of their journey together, a moment neither felt like celebrating.

Lunch was made on the south bank of the Wolf near where the rivers met. Cameron boiled a pot of strong tea and cooked the last of the char. The pup ate a slurry of mashed char and water. Cameron took the satellite phone out of her dry sack, replaced the battery and tried to power it up, but it was just as dead as it had been when she pulled it out of the waterlogged canoe. No matter. They'd be in town by nightfall, and she could call Walt from there and arrange for their pickup.

Cameron repacked the satellite phone and choked down her lunch without tasting it. She held the pup on her lap and watched the swift dark water of the Wolf River push aside the silted water of the Mackenzie, and wondered how many miles it would take before the clearly defined boundaries between the two rivers blurred and then disappeared. Out of the corner of her eye she watched Jack finish his meal, take a swallow of hot tea. He'd lost so much weight his face was gaunt. Not even a week's growth of beard could hide the struggles of his journey. She knew she looked even worse, her face badly bruised and abraded, her clothing shredded from miles of rugged bushwhacking. She didn't realize her sigh was audible until Jack turned his head toward her.

"Home stretch," he said.

"Is that what you'd call it?"

"According to the map, the town's only five miles down river, and it's on this side, so we don't have to cross. Would be twice as far otherwise, and damned dangerous on a windy day like this with a leaky canoe. Look at the waves out there."

Cameron looked. They were big enough to easily swamp their canoe, strip the duct tape, roofing tar and sheet-metal patch right off and sink them before they'd covered a quarter of the distance to the far shore. She heaved another sigh. Right now being swamped in the middle of the cold Mackenzie River seemed preferable to the way she felt.

She was about to voice that sentiment when the sound of an approaching jet engine turned their heads. A small passenger jet flew over very low, heading north and descending rapidly. They stared. The sight of the red-and-white jet with the Canadian Air logo was so incongruous that it took a few moments to process.

"Guess we aren't the only two people in the world after all," Jack said.

"Landing gear was down," Cameron observed. "We might be closer to town than you thought."

"I'll buy you supper tonight at the best restaurant in town, assuming there's more than one."

She managed a laugh. "It's not as hick as you think. It's a really nice town, and there are a couple good places to eat. Norman Wells is where the Canol pipeline project was kicked into high gear by your government during World War II, to help build the Alaskan Highway. The pipeline to Whitehorse wasn't much of a success. In fact from what I've read, it was a colossal waste of money and was used for only one year, but they're still producing oil up here, and it's no small village, not like you're thinking. It's a real town. They even have a couple of hotels with hot showers."

"Like I said, I'll buy you supper at the best place in town."

"I'll take you up on that offer, since I don't have any money on me," Cameron said. "The best place to eat is the Big Bear Tavern at the Tulita Hotel. I just hope they allow puppies."

THE PADDLE DOWN the Mackenzie River was a miserable one. It began to rain, there was no convenient place to put ashore to don their rain gear, the wind was bad and there was no way to escape the waves that built up. The patch began to leak, and Cameron's bailing couldn't keep up. In the end Jack put ashore on a sandbar barely two miles downriver, and Cameron hauled the canoe into the shallows. She was cramped, wet and miserably cold and glad he'd opted not to push on. There was six inches of water in the bottom of the canoe. They were starting to rummage through their packs for their rain gear when a shallow-bottomed skiff coming up the river spotted them and headed toward the sandbar.

"Heyho!" the man sitting in the stern greeted as he drove the aluminum skiff ashore, cutting the engine and hauling up the outboard motor in a perfectly executed maneuver. "Need a lift to town? I can tow your canoe, and you can ride with me. Fifty bucks. It's getting rough on the river and it's supposed to rain all day. Bad weather, lots of wind."

Cameron and Jack exchanged glances.

"We'd appreciate it," Jack said.

He started to pull out his wallet when the man said, "You can pay when I get you there safe," and laughed as if he'd made a joke. He had a hand-rolled cigarette in his mouth, which the rain had put out long ago, and he talked and smiled around it and didn't seem to care it wasn't lit. His skin was dark and weathered, his eyes dark slits in a stoic face that somehow managed to reflect great humor at their situation. It was hard to tell his age. He could have been fifty or eighty. He was lean and dressed poorly for the weather—worn-out blue jeans, patched jacket and tattered ball cap—but he seemed perfectly comfortable with the elements.

They were quick to load their gear into the skiff, lash the canoe behind and climb aboard. "I'm Jack Parker, and this is Cameron Johnson," Jack said as Cameron boarded, one hand cradling the pup inside her jacket, the other clutching the gunnel to keep her balance.

"Fred Andrew" came the reply from the man in the stern, who nodded and smiled with his eyes.

"Thank you, Fred," Cameron said. She sat up front and took a quick peek inside her zipped-up jacket at the pup, who lifted milky blue eyes and seemed as content as the captain of their little boat. Jack pushed the boat off the sandbar and sat behind her in the middle seat to converse with Fred Andrew.

"We would have spent the night on that sandbar if you hadn't come along," Jack said.

"I figured," Fred replied, letting the bow of the boat swing downstream and starting the motor with one pull. "Your canoe was full of water and your woman was cold. I could see that from a distance."

"You live in town?"

He shook his head. "About a mile downriver from here," Fred replied. "Don't like towns much, except for the food. The food is good."

When he opened the throttle, the boat surged forward and all conversation ceased. The motor made too much noise. The ride was rough but fast in the swift current with the 60 horsepower Johnson at half throttle. Cameron cursed her stupidity for not donning her rain gear before they set out. She was freezing. Soon roof lines of the town came into view, the little houses on the outskirts, the airfield, the town dock and bigger buildings between the river and the airstrip. She was shivering uncontrollably as Jack climbed out to tie the skiff to the pier. He helped her out, then took their gear as Fred handed it up to him.

"We canoed down the Wolf River and stayed at a trapper's cabin about twenty miles from the Mackenzie when our canoe got wrecked," Jack explained to Fred as they unloaded the skiff. "We'd like to find whoever owns that cabin and thank him."

"No need to do that," Fred said. "You get in trouble up here, you need to get inside a cabin, so nobody locks their doors." Fred smiled around his soggy cigarette. His eyes crinkled almost shut. "What will you do about your canoe? You can't keep paddling unless you fix it. I could fix it for you."

"We'll haul it out onto the pier for now, before it sinks completely." Jack handed Fred the promised money for bringing them to town. "Come have supper with us, Fred. I'm told there's a good restaurant in town, and Cameron needs to warm up."

Fred nodded, climbing out without further prodding. "I like eating food I don't have to cook," he said. "You buying?"

"I'm buying," Jack said.

"Big Bear at the Tulita Hotel has the best food. Easy walk from here."

Fred helped Jack haul the canoe onto the pier and tip it over so it covered their pile of sodden gear. Jack shouldered his pack. Cameron didn't care if every last shred of their moldering gear fell into the river and floated to the Arctic Ocean, she was so cold. She just wanted to get someplace warm. When Jack put an arm around her and rubbed her arm up and down to warm her, she leaned gratefully against him, and they followed the spry and cheerful Fred Andrew up the pier and onto the street. The Tulita Hotel wasn't far at all, maybe a hundred yards. Enough distance to get the blood flowing in her legs.

The foyer was warm. Suffocatingly, wonderfully warm. The Big Bear Tavern was to the right of the entry, and the place was half full. Jack helped her strip out of her soaking wet jacket and hung it next to his on hooks just inside the tavern door, and they hung their dripping hats atop their jackets, where they made puddles on the worn linoleum. Fred walked in like he owned the place and led them to a booth Cameron assumed was the one he always laid claim to. He tossed his wet jacket beside him as he slid onto the bench seat and left on his dripping ball cap. They hadn't been seated ten seconds before a middle-aged matronly server deposited a big thermal carafe of hot coffee on the table and three big mugs to go with it.

"Same as usual, Fred?" she asked, no pen or notepad in sight. Fred grinned around his sodden cigarette and nodded happily. She looked at Cameron and Jack while handing them plastic-covered menus. "Sweeties, you look like you could both use something a little stronger than just plain joe," she said, then crossed to the counter and reached behind it for a bottle of brandy, which she deposited on their table. "Fred must've rescued you just in time. He's good at that. On days like this he cruises the river looking for boaters in trouble. I'd recommend you both order our Antifreeze Special. You could use it."

"Thank you," Cameron managed through chattering teeth, closing her hands around the heat of the mug that Jack had already filled.

"Is this the best hotel in town?" Jack asked. "We need to get dried out, have a hot shower."

"Town's full of engineers," the waitress said. "Hotels are all full. They're doing oil exploration stuff, and I guess they've made some new discoveries. Fred rents a room, though. His place isn't too far from here. He might have something for you."

Fred nodded. "I do. Seventy bucks, and that includes the round-trip boat ride."

"Is there a shower?" Jack asked.

Fred shook his head. "Plenty of water, though, a whole river of it, and I have a sweat lodge. A sweat lodge is better than a shower—cures whatever ails you."

"We'll take it," Jack said.

"That's good." Fred looked happy and took another swallow of coffee. "My wife died last fall, before the snows," he said. "It's been lonely with her gone. So now I rent rooms to boaters like you. There are a lot of boaters who canoe the Mackenzie every summer."

"I'm sorry about your wife," Cameron said.

Cameron wanted a hot shower almost more than she wanted food. She needed to change into some dry clothes, assuming there were any left in her pack. She took a small sip of her coffee after Jack put a generous dollop of the brandy into it. Alcohol fumes wafted up on the steam. She breathed them in while scanning the menu for the description of the Antifreeze Special. Lobo slept curled beneath her fleece pullover like he'd been born and belonged there. He was either the most highly adaptable pup on the planet, or weak and dying. She reached a finger beneath her pullover and tickled his fat warm little belly until he heaved a contented moan and she felt him curl into a tighter ball. She relaxed. He was the most highly adaptable pup on the planet.

The waitress returned, setting a heaping platter in front of Fred, stacked with what looked like two very fat and greasy burgers bracketing a mountain of golden fries. Cameron eyed Fred's platter and felt her mouth start to water. Fred carefully laid the remains of his soggy cigarette on his paper napkin when the platter was delivered, picked up one of the burgers topped with sautéed onions and bacon and bit into it with obvious enjoyment.

"I'll have what Fred's having," Jack said. "Cameron?"

"Me too," she quickly responded.

"That's our Antifreeze Special," the waitress replied, gathering their menus. "So much fat, it can't freeze no matter how cold it gets."

"Sounds perfect," Cameron said, and when the waitress left to place their order, she pushed out of the booth to follow her. "I have to wash up," she explained, pulling the pup from under her fleece and handing him to Jack. "I'll be right back."

The hot water in the ladies' room felt so good she wanted to crawl into the sink. She soaped her hands several times, washed her battered face carefully, then finger combed her hair. There was a pay phone in the lobby, and she used it to call Walt before returning to the tavern.

He answered on the third ring—he was probably asleep in his chair—and he accepted the charges. When he heard her voice he bellowed, "Jesus Mary and Joseph, where in the hell have you been? What's taking you so long? I've been right out straight trying to run this place single-handed!"

"Nice to hear you were worried sick about me, Walt. We're in Normal Wells. Made it into town about an hour ago, and we're about to head for our lodgings. We're staying with a Dene by the name of Fred Andrew. He lives upriver a ways. Hotels are full of engineers. I knew you'd want to know we were okay. We'll be here tomorrow morning at the town pier if you could pick us up."

"Hell, yes. I'll be there by 10:00 a.m.," he said, then lowered his voice. "That woman's been here the whole time, Lori Tedlow, the Lone Ranger's sister. She's outside right now. Hasn't left since she got here a week ago. She's been driving me crazy, and she's about to have a baby. The thing could come any second now."

"It'll be over soon, Walt. Bring money. I don't have a loonie on me."

On her way back to the booth, she stopped at the counter where the waitress was filling ketchup bottles. "Where do people bring stray dogs when they show up in town?" she asked. "We're looking for a female dog that looks like a coyote and got lost along the Wolf River last summer. We think she might have found her way here."

"Oh, boy," the waitress said, shaking her head with a dubious expression. "Stray dogs don't last long up here. Sometimes they'll hang out at the dump for a while looking for food, but mostly they just disappear. Nobody has the money to feed stray dogs, not like down in the big cities. I don't like to say it, but there are always a few dead dogs at the dump."

This wasn't what she wanted to hear. She returned to the booth, where Fred was working on his second burger. A few moments later the waitress arrived and plunked two more huge platters of food on their table. Cameron stared at the greasy bounty and was reaching for the first burger when the waitress returned.

"Couldn't help but notice that cute puppy," she said, offering Cameron a small stainless-steel bowl full of chopped meat, chicken scraps and scrambled egg with milk poured over it. "Leftovers, but he won't mind."

CHAPTER TWENTY-ONE

BETWEEN THE SPIKED coffee and the enormous fatty meal, Cameron could barely move. She put her head down on the table for a moment to rest her eyes while Fred spun some weird endless thread about extinct Hare Indian dogs and how they'd looked like a coyote crossed with a fox, and the radium mine at Great Bear and a village of widows where the men who worked in the mine had all died of cancer. He went on about the Manhattan Project, and how some of the Sahtu Dene had gone to Hiroshima and Nagasaki to apologize for the bomb because they had helped mine the uranium that made the bombs, and then Jack was nudging her with his arm, taking the pup and the empty bowl out of her lap and saying, "Time to go. Fred's taking us to his place."

Fred went ahead of them to the boat while they donned their wet, clammy jackets and hats. Cameron tucked the pup back inside her jacket, and they trudged out into the cold rain. She wanted a long hot shower and a soft bed, and she wasn't looking forward to the boat ride back upriver and into the wind, but at least her stomach was full and, according to Fred, the ride wouldn't last too long.

They loaded their essential overnight gear into the skiff, left the rest on the dock beneath the overturned canoe, and Fred ferried them back upriver into the river chop. An endless half hour later, plowing into headwind and waves, he veered into a little tributary and docked at a crude log, stone and board pier that jutted from the bank. Above the creek, on a high piece of land, was a cabin built of black spruce logs that looked like a much larger replica of the one on the Wolf River. It had a steel roof, a narrow porch that looked over the trees toward the river and two metal chimneys, one on either end. The front end of the cabin was taller than the back end. There was a large woodshed, a generator shed and what looked like a large machinery graveyard way out behind the cabin, before the field darkened into woods. In the rain, everything looked dreary and bleak.

They carried their gear up the steep path to the cabin. Cameron was so stiff and cold she could barely drag herself up the steps. She could only imagine how Jack felt. Fred took them inside, showed them around the small kitchen and living room area, which was as neat as a pin, showed them the stairs to the loft above the kitchen, then took them down a hall. He showed them a bathroom with a toilet and a bucket of river water for flushing, another bucket of water for washing in the sink, then moved to the back of the cabin where he opened the door on another big room with a woodstove and a table and two chairs and a bed. There was one window over the bed, and a door that went directly outside.

"This is the guest room," he said proudly after he'd lit the fire laid in the woodstove. "It was the original cabin. When the kids came, we built onto the cabin and used this as our bedroom. The kids slept in the loft over the kitchen. That's where I sleep now. It's warmer in winter. I keep this shut up and just rent it out to boaters."

"It's perfect," Cameron said, dropping her dry bag at her feet. "Thank you, Fred."

"Okay." He nodded. "I'll start the fire in the sweat lodge. It takes time to heat up. You need a good sweat to warm up. You can play cards if you like, or I can start the generator if you want to watch TV. I have a satellite dish. Or I can play the fiddle for you. I like to play the fiddle."

Clearly, Fred was looking forward to a long evening of socializing. Cameron was looking forward to getting some sleep. She was fading fast. She wasn't excited about the idea of a sweat lodge or card game. "Jack, why don't you play some cards with Fred while I take Lobo outside?"

She ignored Jack's look as she slipped past them and went out the back door. The pup wasn't happy about the rain, but when he did his thing she praised him lavishly, scooped him off the wet ground and stuffed him back under her jacket.

Cameron listened at the back door, heard no voices and opened it. The men had gone back into the kitchen. The heat radiating from the fire in the woodstove felt wonderful. She let Lobo wander around the guest room while she unpacked her sleeping bag and kit from her dry sack. There was a bureau against the wall with a mirror above it. She put her kit on the bureau and met her reflection in the mirror. For a moment she didn't recognize herself; the deep scabbed-over gouges and bruises on her thin face, the one black eye that had turned yellowish green, her straggly wet hair. She raised a hand to her mouth and uttered a laugh. No wonder she'd gotten all those sympa-

thetic stares from the staff at the Tulita Hotel.
They must have thought Jack was an abusive
monster, except for the fact that he looked almost as bad.

She fluffed out her damp sleeping bag and
laid it atop the double bed in the hopes it would
dry out in the next five minutes. She did the
same with Jack's. She took her hair out of the
ponytail and brushed the tangles from it, leaving it loose to hide as much of her face as possible. Lobo was still exploring the room. She
closed the door to keep him confined and went
to use the bathroom and wash up. Then, to be
polite, she went back into the kitchen. Fred had
kindled a roaring fire in the big woodstove, lit
an oil lamp and put it in the center of the table,
where he and Jack were sitting with a cribbage
board and a deck of cards. Jack motioned for
her to sit, but she shook her head.

"I'm beat," she said. "I'm going to lie down
for a while."

Fred sent his squinting smile her way. "It'll
be awhile before the sweat lodge is ready."

Cameron had no intentions of staying up for
a sweat lodge. She gave Jack a "don't you dare
wake me up" look before turning around and
retreating back down the hall. It didn't take her
two shakes to skinny out of her damp clothes
and into a set of dry long johns, then slip into

the damp sleeping bag with Lobo. She lay on her back and listened to the rumbling undertones of the river, the croak of a raven flying over, the cold rain drumming on the cabin roof. A sudden gust of wind rattled rain against the window.

Lobo fell instantly to sleep and whimpered and twitched in his dreams. Was he remembering his mother? The night when the bear came? Did he feel all alone and afraid in his dreams now that his mother was gone?

She felt tears sting her eyes. They came out of nowhere. She rolled onto her side and cradled the little pup and cried herself to sleep.

BY THE TIME Jack made his way to the bedroom he was half-convinced Fred was right. The ghost dog of the Sahtu Dene had been real, the Sahtu Dene and the Navajo were of the same people, and the clear black waters of the Wolf River had made him crazy for a woman he could never have. He sat on the bed, felt for Cameron and patted her hip through the sleeping bag. She was lying on her side, facing away from him.

"You awake?" he said.

"I am now" came the sleep muffled reply. "What time is it?"

"Time for a sweat lodge. Fred says it's ready.

It's close to midnight. I lost the last card game and all the other games, too."

"I'm so sorry for you."

"Fred had some stories to tell."

"And some whisky to go with them, eh?"

"Homemade wine. Elderberry. Very good." He patted her hip again, overwhelmed with affection for her. He shrugged out of his flannel shirt and dropped it over the chair, then sat back on the bed in his river driver top, pants still on. "Damn, I'm drunk. C'mon, get up. We have to take a sweat bath."

"I don't want a sweat bath. I want to sleep."

"Cameron, it was Fred's cabin we stayed at on the Wolf River. I thought it might have been when I saw how similar the two cabins were. They looked like they were built by the same person. All the corners were notched the same."

"What?" Cameron rolled over and propped herself up on an elbow. "Does he have a dog team? Did you tell him about Mama Dog?"

Jack nodded. "He does, and I did."

"Did you ask him why he left her there?"

"She slipped her collar, just like you guessed, and he couldn't catch her. Too shy. When it was time to pack up and head back here, he hadn't seen her in two weeks. Figured a wolf might've gotten her, and if she was still alive she knew the way home. He said fifty miles is an easy day's travel for a sled dog."

"You mean, he never went back to look for her?"

"Couldn't get his boat past those rapids, and like he said, she knew the way home. There was no point in looking. She wasn't lost, and he figured if she was alive she'd come home when she was ready."

Cameron slumped back with a sharp sigh. "So he knows where Lobo came from."

"He guessed as much."

"Did he say anything?"

"Like what?"

"Like he wanted the pup back?"

"Nope."

"Because I'm not giving up Lobo."

"I know that." Jack patted her again. "You're a finders, keepers kind of girl. Get up. It's sweat bath time."

"I mean it, Jack. I'm not parting with this puppy, no matter how bad Fred wants him, and no matter how bad a person that makes me."

"Hell, when my sister pays you for bringing me in, you'll be rich. You can buy that red Jeep and all Fred's dogs too. I'm sure he'll sell them. He has a price for everything. He's got this big army bulldozer out back that he said he'd sell me for a thousand bucks."

"Why would anyone have an army bulldozer way out here?"

"He told me there's a small fortune of abandoned 1940s army construction equipment he inherited from his father. It's out behind his cabin, just left there when they finished the Canol pipeline and pulled out. A clever mechanic could buy all those machines cheap, restore them and then haul them over the winter road and sell them for a small fortune."

"Or just haul 'em out over the winter road to a garage, where he could restore them in comfort and get the parts he needs without paying a fortune to have them flown in. Then sell them. Did you ask him if he'd seen any sign of Ky?"

The good humor left him. "I told him why we were on the river, and he never said anything. When we get back to town tomorrow, I'll ask around there, too. Maybe we can post a reward outside the grocery store before we leave. They must have one."

"That's a good idea," Cameron said.

He pulled out of his brooding mood and patted her again. "Come on. Get up. Fred's put four buckets of water and some soap in the sweat lodge. You hear that, woman? We can have a steam bath that cures all ills. That's worth getting out of bed for."

JACK WOKE WITH a strong headache, a weak stomach and a dry mouth. He moaned and covered his eyes with his forearm to shut out the morning light. He felt like he'd gone nine rounds with a prize fighter, but all he'd done was drink Fred's homemade elderberry wine. One bottle? Two? Jesus. Strong stuff.

"Cameron?" he muttered.

There was no reply. He lowered his arm, turned his head. Her side of the iron-framed bed was empty. No Cameron. No clothes draped over the back of the chair. She'd gotten up and gone out. Abandoned him to his misery. Long yellow fingers of sunlight stretched through the east window, laying bright bands across the foot of the bed. The pup was sound asleep, curled in a ball between the pillows. The room smelled faintly of woodsmoke and the oakum that had been used to chink the peeled logs. He thought about getting up but decided he could wait a little longer. It was still early for a man with a bad hangover.

The sweat lodge hadn't cured him of that, but it had driven the cold out of his bones in more ways than one. Cameron, sitting on the bench beside him in the gloom, poured water on the hot stones, ladling a tin dipper into a five-gallon bucket and dribbling it over the rocks until steam rose up so thick it was hard to breathe. They had three buckets of water to pour over themselves when the heat became too much, and a bar of soap to scrub with. He had a vague recollection of Fred carrying the last of the hot rocks into the lodge in a metal bucket, piling them atop the other heated rocks in the circle, saying, "That's all of them. The heat will last a long while now. In the morning I'll show you my dogs."

Cameron, bathing herself first in the dim light cast by the small oil lamp, washing her hair, lathering her body, rinsing off, then scrubbing his shoulders with the soap, pouring dippers full of water over him. Washing his hair, her fingertips firm, massaging his scalp. Cameron, pouring another dipper of water on the hot stones, making more steam, kissing him on the mouth in the steamy darkness, her body slippery with soap.

Steam and soapy lather and passionate sex and dippers full of cool water when meltdown seemed imminent, followed by more sex and clouds of steam. Jack was glad the sweat lodge was a long walk from Fred's cabin because their sex was wild and uninhibited, and by the time the stones had cooled they had melted together in the steamy dark of the sweat lodge, and it was only by the greatest of efforts they were able to make it back to the cabin.

Or had he just imagined it all?

The door to the hallway swung silently inward and Cameron slipped in, two mugs of coffee in hand. She crossed to the bed, waiting while he propped himself into a sitting position before handing him a mug. "Coffee. Good and strong. Fred put something in yours. Said it would help you get over all the hooch you drank last night."

Jack took a sip and tasted whisky. "Hair of the dog," he said. He looked at her. "About that sweat lodge," he began.

"I'm surprised you remember any of it, you were so drunk. I practically had to carry you back here." She took a sip of her coffee and gazed at him, cradling her mug in her palms. "It was nice, though."

"Nice?"

"Saunas are very good for you," she said primly. "They flush out toxins and boost the immune system."

"Huh." Jack took another swallow of coffee and eyed her closely. Her small mysterious smile had a slightly naughty look.

Cameron lowered her eyes and took another sip of her coffee. "I talked to Fred about Lobo. I told him I really wanted to keep him."

"What did he say?"

"He said Lobo was a good-looking pup, and

that his mother had been an excellent sled dog. He told me she was one of his lead dogs." She dropped her eyes from his with a discouraged sigh. "So I asked him how much he thought Lobo was worth."

"What did he say?"

She shrugged. "He didn't give me an answer. He told me a strange story about a ghost dog on the Wolf River near a place called Red Dog Mountain. I'm not sure I understood what he was talking about, but I think it's an extinct dog of the Sahtu Dene. He thinks maybe Mama Dog got bred by the ghost dog, and that Lobo could be a very special pup."

"Sounds like he's angling for a high price."

Cameron took another taste of her coffee. She watched the pup, who had woken when she entered the room and was chewing with grave determination on a strap of old boot leather Fred had given him the night before. "He's gone out on the river to check his traps for whitefish," she said. "He told me he'd be back soon, and he'd feed us breakfast before taking us back to town. He's boiling fish and rice outside on a fire pit, in half an old fifty-gallon steel drum he calls the Temple of the Dog. I'm tending it for him, so I better go give it a stir. He says rice burns easy if you don't stir it."

"Don't look so gloomy," Jack said as she

started for the door with the pup tucked under her arm. "Fred likes money. Lobo will be coming with us. The only question is how much of that five grand you're going to have to part with."

BUT CAMERON WASN'T so sure Fred would sell the pup for any price. By the time Fred drove his aluminum skiff up to the pier below the cabin, she was sure he was going to ask for the pup back, tell her he couldn't part with it. She went down to meet him. He handed eight whitefish to her, and she laid them on the pier. "The stew's done and the rice didn't burn," she said. "It's cooling now."

"Good," Fred said. He climbed onto the pier and secured his boat. "If the fish don't start coming in better, it'll be a bad winter." He left the fish on the pier to clean and walked up the path with her toward the cabin.

"Fred, did Jack talk to you last night about his missing dog? The dog he came here hoping to find?"

Fred paused to contemplate her question. "We played cards a long time, drank a lot. He might have mentioned it."

"She looked like a coyote, and she was lost on the river near your cabin a year ago. His sister was taking a canoe trip down the river. She camped near your cabin, and the dog chased a bear away from the camp and never came back."

Fred nodded thoughtfully.

"Did you trap in there last winter?"

Fred nodded again.

Cameron sighed when he remained silent. "I just thought I'd ask. I figured all along she was dead, the bear killed her, but Jack was set on finding her. He was sure she was still alive."

Fred was still nodding with that same expression on his face. "Get your man, and I'll show you my dogs."

"Jack's not up yet. That wine of yours did him in. But I'd like to see them."

When they reached the top of the knoll, she followed Fred down a well-worn path that led behind the cabin, past several sheds and outhouses and a big pole tepee much larger than the sweat lodge with no covering. The path went through a stand of black spruce and emerged on the edge of a field full of fireweed and old machinery. She saw a big Cat bulldozer, several trucks in rusting army olive drab, and other construction equipment she couldn't identify.

As they walked into this military junkyard, she noticed movement among the machinery. Each piece of equipment had a section of chain attached to it, and a dog was tethered to the end of each chain. The dogs peeked out warily at the stranger that came into their midst. They had erect ears, thick coats, long legs, dark alert eyes, and they were wild-looking, just like Mama Dog had been. Most of them dove out of sight when they spotted her.

"My grandfather had some of the best dogs on the Mackenzie," Fred said. "He was one of the Sahtu who guided the surveyors laying out the Canol pipeline trail to Whitehorse. That trail runs on the other side of this field. You can walk it now, but it's a tough hike. Used to be, you could drive a truck down it, but now it's grown back in and washed out in lots of places.

"He lived off the land, fished and hunted and trapped, and his dogs were the old river dogs. When the snow machine came, most of the Dene got rid of their dogs but my grandfather kept his, and my father. He tried to keep them going, but when times got hard he had to get rid of most of them. By the time I was old enough to trap, there weren't many village dogs left and they were all mixed up with other dogs that the whites brought in when the oil pipeline was put in. This is all that's left of the breed."

"They look strong and tough."

Fred nodded. "Mackenzie, that dog over by

the truck, he's my main leader. His father was the same ghost dog that fathered your pup."

Cameron looked at him. "How do you know that?"

"I heard him," Fred said. "Same as I heard him every winter for the past six winters. He has a different kind of howl, and he comes in close when I'm at the cabin. Closer than a wolf should. His territory is the Wolf River valley around Red Dog Mountain. I try to trap him every winter, but he's too smart."

Cameron remembered the wolf both she and Jack had heard and wondered if it was the same. If so, Fred's ghost dog was a wolf that apparently had a thing for female sled dogs in heat. Maybe he didn't have his own pack. Maybe he was a lobo wolf, an outcast. Maybe Fred's sled dogs were the best he could do.

"What would you do if you did catch him in your trap?" Cameron asked.

Fred's eyes squinted with humor. "Shoot him and put his skin on my cabin wall."

"Maybe you could train him to pull a sled, like his son does."

Fred shook his head. "You can't tell a wolf what to do. It's a funny thing. You get a half wolf, they're good, the way Mackenzie's good. That pup Lobo will be good. A full-blood? No good. So this winter, I lost a good dog because that ghost dog lured her away. I trapped for two months at the cabin on the Wolf this past winter. She got loose at the end of the season, slipped her collar and ran off. I set traps to catch her with food she knows. Wolves won't eat human food, they don't trust it, but she would eat my leftovers so I baited the traps with them. But I didn't catch her because she was running with the ghost dog, and he wouldn't let her come near the traps.

"Funny thing happened though. I set those traps to catch the leader I lost, and I caught another dog instead." Fred shook his head, remembering. "I thought it was the ghost dog when I saw it in the trap, but it was too small. Good-looking dog, like an Indian village dog or a Sahtu dog with a lot of wolf in it. Had yellow eyes."

Cameron felt her heart skip a few beats. She reached out and gripped Fred's arm. "What happened to that dog? Where is it now?"

"It had big scars and it was skinny, nothing but bones," he said. "It was starved almost to death. So I got my rifle off the sled to put it out of its misery, but when I got closer I saw it had a red collar around its neck. Strange, a wolf dog way out there wearing a red collar. So I didn't shoot. I took her out of the trap and brought her back to the cabin, and when I came back here, I brought her with me. I thought maybe she belonged to Paul Henry. He traps out of Tulita and runs a string of dogs, but he said it wasn't his."

Cameron felt light-headed, stunned by what Fred was saying. "Where is she now? *What happened to her?*"

"I thought maybe when she healed up and put some weight on I could teach her to pull a sled, so I kept her. She's got a good build and she's smart, and I need another leader to take the place of the dog I lost. I harness broke her this spring. She did good. She's tough and strong." Fred pointed toward the Caterpillar D7 bulldozer. "She sleeps in an empty oil barrel behind the dozer."

"Show me."

Fred walked around the dozer and pointed at a rusted oil barrel tipped onto its side. "I put grass hay in the barrels—they make good houses in winter," he said as they walked over to the barrel. Cameron saw a dog's head peer out warily at their approach. Sharply pointed face, gray fur, golden eyes, faded red collar. She caught only a quick glimpse before the dog ducked back inside the barrel and hid.

Cameron's heart was pounding and her mouth was dry. "Fred," she said, "this has to be Jack's dog. This is the dog he was looking

NADIA NICHOLS   331

for. This is Ky, I'm sure of it. She was lost last year right near your cabin. He's been looking for her for a long time. He's just about given up on her. I have to go get Jack!"

She whirled and raced back toward the cabin. Jack was up, standing on the porch watching Lobo sniff hungrily around the cooling pot of fish stew and still working on his mug of coffee. When she rounded the corner and spotted him, she skidded to a stop, breathless with pent up excitement.

"Jack!" she managed to gasp, pointing behind her. "Come quick! Fred caught a dog in one of his traps five miles above the cabin on the Wolf River this past winter. She's in a barrel in the field out back, she looks like a coyote and has yellow eyes. It's Ky. It has to be her. Come see! *Hurry!*"

CHAPTER TWENTY-TWO

WHEN CAMERON REJOINED Fred behind the massive D7, Jack wasn't far behind. She pointed, cradling Lobo in her other arm.

"There! She's inside that barrel."

He took a few steps beyond where she and Fred stood, then stopped and studied the barrel lying on its side for a few moments before walking toward it, angling so he could look within without crowding the dog. He saw movement in the darkness of the barrel's interior. Alert, upright ears. Familiar profile. He knelt. His hands had begun to shake.

"Ky?" His voice was rough. He cleared his throat and tried again. "Ky?"

Was it really her? It had been over a year since she'd last seen him. Would she recognize his voice? Would she recognize his scent? Would she remember him at all?

The morning sun was lifting fog off the meadow grasses and the old machinery. A raven flew over with a loud swish of wings. He heard the rattle of a chain from another tethered dog and the distant sigh of the river. He let his breath out slowly, slowly. His heart was pounding in his ears.

"Ky? Come on out, girl."

He heard Fred suggest that he just pull her out of the barrel using the chain, and he heard Cameron reply in a low, urgent voice, "No, let Jack talk to her. Let her come to him. He's been searching for her for so long. We need to give them some time."

He waited. There was more movement within, and the dog approached the mouth of the barrel cautiously. He watched the morning light illuminate her features. He saw the familiar face; the ears, the golden eyes that mirrored her untamed spirit. The feeling that swept over him made him weak. It was Ky. He'd just come to terms with the fact that she was probably dead and now, somehow, she was here in Fred's dog yard, and she was alive.

"It's me, Ky," he said. "Remember?"

She took one cautious step out of the barrel, then another. Jack saw the irregular lines of scar tissue on her flank and shoulder where the hair had grown in white. Big scars that mapped the enormity of her wounds and told of the terrible winter she'd passed before being caught in Fred's leg hold trap, yet the fear, pain, loneliness and hunger of the past year had all somehow been dominated by her fierce will to survive. She wasn't the young half-grown dog he remembered, the pup that had dogged his heels, posted a silent vigil on his bunk and watched over him protectively while he slept. She was a different dog now, just as he was a different man. The bond she'd forged with him in Afghanistan might have been eroded, erased and forgotten.

He held out his hand slowly so she could smell it. He watched her taste the air. Her eyes were bright on his face, her expression intense. Her entire body was taut and trembling. It was as if a strong electric current was running between them, connecting them. The experience was surreal.

"Remember, Ky?" he asked.

She moved toward him. Hesitant, crouching steps as if ready to spring away at any moment. There was no blind rush forward, no happy barking, no tail wagging, tongue lapping Walt Disney embrace. She felt her way back one wary step at a time, across the long year and the thousands of miles that had separated them since he'd put her crate on that cargo plane in Afghanistan. And then, finally, she was within touching distance of his outstretched hand. A hand that was empty. No food, no offering other than himself. She sniffed carefully and thoroughly and then studied him again for another long, intense moment.

She remembered.

His voice and his smell she remembered, and the memories were good. Her trembling became intense. The very tip of her tail moved back and forth. Her expression changed. Her ears flattened back, and her deep golden eyes began to shine. She let him touch her. He ran his hand over her head, down her shoulder, along her side. Felt the scars, the jutting bones, the rough fur. She made a small noise in the back of her throat, pressed closer, pushed her head against his chest, slid her muzzle under his arm and stood like that, pressed against him as close as she could get, trembling all over. He felt his eyes sting. His arms went around her, and he buried his face against her neck.

"It's okay, Ky," he said. "I'll never leave you behind again."

FRED WATCHED THE emotional reunion between the dog and the man and nodded thoughtfully. "She never got used to me," he said to Cameron. "I thought maybe by now she would have come to like me because I fed her, but her heart belonged to someone else. Now I know who."

Cameron wiped her wet cheeks. "Ky saved Jack's life twice in Afghanistan when he was deployed there. She's a very special dog. He just walked most of the Wolf River, looking for her. He knew she was still alive, even after all this time. He never gave up on her."

"She wouldn't have survived much longer if I hadn't caught her."

"You saved her life, Fred," Cameron said. "We can't thank you enough for doing that."

Fred sighed and rubbed his chin, watching the reunion between Jack and Ky. "Last winter was a bad winter. It was no good with the trapping, and I lost my best lead dog." For the first time his face looked sad. "Now winter's coming again and the fishing is poor. I don't know how I'm going to feed my dogs, and I don't have a leader to run with Mackenzie. I was going to teach that dog to run with the team this fall, see if she'd run up front. She's smart. She'd probably make a good leader."

"But she's Jack's dog. You can't keep her."

"I can't afford to buy another leader."

Cameron looked down at the month-old pup she cradled so protectively in her arms and gathered Lobo against her beating heart, wondering how she ever could have thought dogs weren't that important. She drew a deep breath. "Tell you what, Fred. I'll buy both dogs from you. Lobo and Ky. How does five thousand dollars sound?"

WALT PACED THE float plane dock not far from where he'd gassed up the Beaver for the return trip to Fort Simpson. He checked his wristwatch: 11:15 a.m. He'd arrived early, and Cameron was late. This disturbed him because she was never late. It was a sparkling clear morning, perfect for flying right now, but more bad weather was predicted for that afternoon. High winds and rain. He stared first upriver, then down. Then back up again. Then paced some more. The waitress at the hotel where he'd gone for breakfast confirmed that Cameron and Jack had left the evening before with Fred Andrew, that Fred took guests in sometimes when the hotels were full and he lived just a few miles upriver, not far below where the Wolf River came into the Mackenzie. But if Fred lived so close, where were they? Why weren't they here?

He paced and muttered under his breath and thought about Lori Tedlow, who was already waiting at his office. Maybe she was in labor now, having the baby on his office floor. She'd cried yesterday when he called her at her hotel to tell her about Cameron's phone call. She'd sobbed with relief when she learned her brother was okay.

"Didn't I say it'd all turn out fine?" Walt

had said when she showed up at eight o'clock that morning.

Now he was beginning to worry that he'd spoken too soon and jinxed himself. He glanced at his watch again. And then, finally, he heard the drone of an outboard motor over the light wind, and an aluminum skiff came around the bend in the river and headed toward the float-plane dock. Walt saw Cameron wave when she spotted him, and he returned the gesture with a grin of relief that faded rapidly as the boat drew near enough for him to see the occupants clearly. Cameron's appearance shocked him. He helped tie off the boat and steady it while she got out, followed by the now-bearded Jack, who was attached to a scrawny, skittish looking feral dog by a piece of rope. He was followed by Fred Andrew, a wiry, dark-skinned Dene wearing a perpetual smile in the deep creases of his face and a well-worn Red Sox ball cap over long dark hair.

Cameron introduced him to Fred, and he shook Fred's hand while looking between Jack and Cameron. His presumption that the two had shared a leisurely romantic tryst down the Wolf River had been shattered by their appearance, especially Cameron's. They both looked half-starved, and Cameron had a black eye and cuts and bruises all over her face. He gave her a careful bear hug, gave Jack his best steely-eyed stare and said to Cameron, "Maybe you should've brought them handcuffs along after all."

"Relax, Walt," she said. "I wouldn't be here if it weren't for Jack's help."

"Rough trip?" Walt asked.

"Yes, but successful. Jack found his dog. She was at Fred's kennel, and look what else we found." She pulled a fat squirming pup from inside her jacket. Walt stared.

"A wolf pup," he said, recalling all the wolves he'd shot in his younger years.

"Lobo's mother was one of Fred's best sled dogs, but she was killed by a grizzly."

"Is that right," Walt said. He knew a wolf pup when he saw one.

"So, Fred and I made a deal. I'll keep the pup, because it's too young and Fred can't take care of it, and he'll get a breeding to one of his bitches when Lobo's a yearling, because as it turns out, Lobo has really good bloodlines."

"Huh," Walt said, rubbing the stubble on his chin. "Well, you named him right, that's the truth." His eyes narrowed as he tried to envision a future for Cameron that included a one-legged soldier, a scrawny dog that looked like an underfed coyote and an orphaned wolf pup. He was having trouble trying to figure out how

Cameron would be able to fly full-time again when she'd taken on so much other stuff.

He looked at Jack, not feeling the least bit friendly toward this bearded, silent warrior with the haunted eyes who looked as beat-up as his dog but who still stood soldier straight, and had somehow captured the heart of his best pilot. "Your sister's waiting back at the floatplane base, and she could have her baby at any moment," he growled. "We better get a move on."

WALT FLEW BACK to the base, which was a good thing because Cameron fell asleep half an hour into the flight and didn't wake up until he landed. She sat up, wiped the sleep from her eyes and wondered why she felt so sick. There was a dull pain in her stomach. Or was it her heart? Matter of fact, she hurt all over. She felt awful and wondered if she was dying. As Walt taxied up to the dock, she saw a woman standing there, wearing a shapeless tan-colored coat that came to her knees and a bright red fleece hat pulled over shoulder-length dark hair. This had to be Jack's sister, Lori Tedlow.

Cameron glanced over her shoulder at Jack in the rear seat. Ky sat on floor between his knees, sphinxlike and unmoving. She forced a smile at him and faced front. The pain in her chest grew worse. Was she having a heart attack? She hoped so. Being dead would be better than feeling like this for the rest of her life.

She peeked inside her parka at Lobo. Sound asleep. Most laid-back pup, best traveler. Best buddy. She couldn't die of a broken heart. She had to take care of Lobo. Walt cut the engine when the float bumped the pilings, and looked across at her with a grim expression.

"Well, I suppose you'll be wanting a few days off to recover," he said.

"Jack!"

Lori Tedlow's shrill cry interrupted Cameron's attempt to tell Walt she wanted at least a week off so she could go back and pay Fred the money she'd promised him, then go see Minnie over in Yukon.

"Jack!" Lori was waving frantically, moving under the wing of the plane.

Cameron crawled into the back and popped the side door open. "Hold on," she called down to Lori. "Your brother's fine. Just give us a minute to tie the plane up." She avoided looking at Jack again because she felt very close to tears. This was it. This was the clean break. The Big Goodbye, and she hated goodbyes. Better to avoid them. She climbed out of the plane, pup still tucked inside her jacket, and her sore feet thumped onto the dock. She gave

Lori as much of a smile as she could manage under the circumstances.

"Hi, Lori. I'm Cameron Johnson," she said, sticking out her hand.

Lori took her hand, dark eyes brimming with tears. "Thank you so much for getting my brother back here safely. What happened to your face?"

Before Cameron could respond, Lori's gaze shifted. Her expression changed when she saw her brother framed in the plane's side door. She dropped Cameron's hand, visibly stunned by Jack's appearance. When she spotted the lean, skittish dog standing beside him, her eyes went blank and she would have collapsed if Cameron hadn't grabbed her arm to keep her on her feet.

"Ky's alive," Lori said, dazed. "I don't believe it. She's *alive!*"

"Walt, I sure could use a hand over here," Cameron said, struggling to prop up the very pregnant woman and hold on to Lobo at the same time. Walt finished tying off the plane and came to Cameron's aid as Jack climbed out of the plane, one arm hooked around Ky in a hip carry. He set his dog on the dock and looked at his sister.

"Hello, Lori."

"Jack," Lori said in a faint voice. "Please don't hate me. We thought she was dead, or we never would have left her there. I swear that's the truth."

"I know," Jack said.

Tears were running down Lori's face. "Oh, thank God you're safe."

"Where's that rich banker husband of yours? He owes this girl some money for putting her through hell."

"Clive's working. He couldn't leave the bank for so long. But don't worry, I brought the money and…" Her eyes widened, and even as Walt and Cameron steadied her, both hands went to her stomach.

"Oh!" she said. "That was a big one."

"A contraction?" Cameron asked.

"Yes. The biggest one yet."

"How many big ones have you had?"

"I don't know. I think maybe four or five."

"How far apart?"

Lori shook her head. "I haven't really kept count. I've been standing here waiting for Jack…"

"Is she in labor?" Walt looked like he'd rather be anyplace else.

Cameron shook her head. "How should I know? You're the one who knows everything about everything."

"I know CPR. I don't know anything about labor pains or delivering babies."

"If she's having that baby, we better get her to the clinic. I'll get your truck. You stay with her."

Cameron handed Lobo to Jack, wheeled and sprinted toward the office, climbed into Walt's truck and drove it down to the dock. She jumped out and helped Walt maneuver Lori toward the passenger side. "I'll call the clinic and let them know you're coming," she told Walt. She looked at Jack, who was still standing in the same spot. "You might want to help. She's your sister, after all, and this baby's going to be your niece or nephew. I'll watch Ky for you. They don't allow dogs at the clinic."

Cameron retrieved Lobo and for a moment thought Jack might not hand her the piece of rope tied to Ky's collar, but he did. Reluctantly. He helped Walt load his sister into the truck and then climbed in beside her while Walt got behind the wheel. He rolled down his window and caught her eye as Walt put the truck in reverse.

"Don't worry, I'll take good care of her," Cameron assured him. "She'll be fine with me and Lobo."

She watched as Walt drove up the ramp, pulled onto the road and accelerated out of sight in a cloud of dust. Ky lunged to follow the truck, and the rope nearly burned through

Cameron's hand. "Easy girl," she said, shortening the rope and winding it securely around her wrist. "He'll be back."

Hearing those words spoken aloud helped her more than Ky. This wasn't the clean break. The Big Goodbye. As long as she had Jack's dog, he'd be back.

CHAPTER TWENTY-THREE

LORI TEDLOW WAS rushed into the clinic and delivered into competent hands minutes after their arrival. The nurse practitioner was a calm, middle-aged woman who'd seen it all and had two assistants manning the clinic with her. She whisked Lori into the examining room. Walt didn't want to stick around. He wanted to go back to the floatplane base. He wasn't sure he'd tied up the plane properly in all the excitement, and had visions of it floating down the river to the Arctic Ocean. Besides, he couldn't think what to talk about with the scruffy soldier sitting beside him. He was just about to make his exit when his cell phone rang. He fished it out of his pocket with relief.

"It's Cameron," the familiar voice said. "Is the baby born yet?"

"We just got here. Give 'er some time."

"Is Jack there?"

"No, I dumped him out beside the road. Course he's here." He handed the phone to Jack. "Cameron."

Jack took the phone. "Hello...No baby yet, they're still examining her...Oh, no. You're kidding me. You're outside right now?...Okay, I'm on my way."

He handed the phone back to Walt. "She said for you to call her on her cell phone when and if the baby gets born. She's in the parking lot, and I'll be out waiting in her car. I guess my dog went a little crazy on her, tore up her car."

He pushed to his feet. Walt looked up at him. "Maybe you should just bring the dog and Cameron in here," he suggested. "You could all use a little patching up." At that moment the door to the examining room swung open, and the nurse poked her head out wearing a reas- suring smile.

"Your sister's fine," she told Jack. "She's not in true labor. She's just experienced a few strong Braxton-Hicks contractions, probably brought on by all the stress. We're discharging her, and she should be fine to fly home in the morning. She'll be out in a few minutes. She's getting dressed."

Walt jumped to his feet. "Cameron can give the both of you a ride. I have to check on my plane." He fled the clinic with relief and spot- ted Cameron's vehicle in the parking lot next to his truck. He peered in her open window, looking for the wild dog. It was cowering on the floorboards of the front seat. "Did you get bit?"

Cameron shook her head. "No, but look what she did to the inside of my car when Lobo and I were in the store buying groceries and dog food. I was gone less than ten minutes."

Walt looked. Cameron's SUV was always a mess. She stored everything in it. But there was a lot of fresh damage to the upholstery. Chunks of foam and fake leather were now mixed in with all the junk. The front seat on the passenger side had been demolished. He could see springs coiling up through the destruction. "Where's Jack?"

"He'll be out soon. He's waiting for his sister. Turns out she's not having the baby. It was false labor."

Cameron spied movement over his shoulder. "Oh good, here they come."

Jack spotted Walt and escorted Lori over to the SUV. He peered in the passenger window and took note of the destruction. He swore aloud. "Ky did that? All of it?"

"I'm responsible for all the junk, but she's responsible for the rest. She missed you," Cameron said. "Get in quick and love her up."

Jack opened the back door for Lori and then climbed into the front seat amid chunks of foam, arranging a few of the larger pieces to cover the springs. Ky crawled into his lap. "Damn, I'm sorry," he said, surveying the extent of the damage. "I'll have the seat replaced."

"Forget it. I only use the driver's side anyway. The rest is all just storage space. Lori, I'll give you a ride to wherever you're staying."

"I'd appreciate that," Lori said. She looked pale and tired but managed a small smile at Cameron, who caught it in the rearview mirror. "I'm staying at the Riverside Lodge. I booked a room there for Jack, as well."

"The Riverside?" Walt said. "That place don't take dogs."

Lori's face fell. "Oh. Well, I didn't think… I mean, I can call around, try to find someplace else that takes pets."

"I'll camp out in my car," Jack said. "All I need is a ride back to the floatplane base where I left it."

"But we need to talk first, Jack," Lori said. "It's important."

"You and Ky are welcome to bunk at my place," Cameron told Jack. "I have a shower with hot running water and a fenced yard for Ky and Lobo. I'll drop you off so you can visit your sister and pick you up when you call." Cameron looked past Jack to where Walt peered through the open window. "Thanks for picking us up this morning, Walt. We'll talk tomorrow about my extended medical leave."

"Medical leave?"

Cameron smiled and gave him a little wave. She started the old SUV and pulled away. Walt watched them out of sight. He shook his head, rounded his shoulders and shoved his hands in his pockets. Things weren't looking good at all. Extended medical leave? What did she mean by that? And the way those two looked at each other spelled bad news. The future of Walt's Flying Service had never been more up in the air.

Walt climbed into his truck and drove slowly back to the floatplane base, brooding. He pulled into his parking spot and cut the engine. He must be getting old. There was no more joy in the sunrise, just aches and pains and the feeling that his life was over. He climbed out, slammed the door. Walked down to the dock to make sure the plane was securely tied. It was. He stared across the river for a while, seeing only the mistakes he'd made over the years, then he sighed and walked back up to the office.

A car pulled in as he climbed the steps onto the porch. At least it wasn't Lori Tedlow. She'd be heading back to Montana in the morning, but he didn't feel the least bit sociable. A very well-built woman got out, dressed as racy as a greyhound, slammed the car door shut, then opened the rear door and reached inside for something, showing off the best looking ass north of the South Pole. Walt stopped in his tracks and stared. He rubbed his face. Was he seeing things?

"Jeri?" he said.

She straightened and looked over her shoulder with a toss of her head. "What's the matter, Walt? Have I been gone so damned long you don't recognize me anymore? I stopped by earlier but you weren't here, and the plane was gone so I went and got some lunch, then stopped by the store and picked up some stuff. You were out of everything, even toilet paper." She held up two grocery sacks. "I could make us a pot of coffee, if you want," she said, shutting the car door with a seductive swing of her hip.

Walt rubbed his eyes again to clear his vision, and when he spoke his voice cracked like an adolescent's. "I doubt I've ever wanted anything more than I want that," he said, and opened the door wide.

JACK CAUGHT BRIEF glimpses of the river between buildings as Cameron drove away from the clinic and headed down the main drag toward the outskirts of town. "Here's the River-side Lodge," she stated as she turned into the parking lot of an industrial looking building on the riverbank with alternating silver and red steel siding panels.

"It's not much to look at, but the food's not that bad," Lori said. "We need to talk, Jack. Please. Even if it's just for a few moments."

Cameron pulled the vehicle in front of the entrance and cut the ignition. The awkward silence that followed was all encompassing. "I'll wait right here and watch Ky," she finally said. "She'll be okay as long as I'm sitting in the car with her. Take your time."

Jack helped his sister out of the back seat and escorted her into the building. Lori kept one hand pressed into the small of her back and the other on his arm. They walked through the lobby and down the corridor to her room, which looked out on the river. Her suitcase was parked on a luggage rack, and the beige-colored room was neat and clean. She sat down slowly on the edge of one of the two double beds, cradling her immense belly.

"What did you want to talk about?" Jack asked.

Lori sighed. "I wanted to explain why I didn't tell you about Ky back when it happened. Mom was going to watch her while we went on our canoe trip, but she got sick and couldn't, so we took Ky along with us. And then when we came back, I was going to tell you what happened, but Mom made me promise not to."

"So now you're trying to blame this on Mom?"

Lori shook her head. "No, I'm not. Jack, Mom's still sick. Really sick."

He gave her a skeptical look. "I've been calling her all along, and she's never mentioned anything to me about being sick."

"She didn't want to worry you. She made me promise not to tell you, same as she made me promise not to tell you about Ky. When I visited you in the hospital, I was going to tell you then, but you told me to leave, and when I went back the next day, you were already gone.

"When you took off like that, Mom was worried you might be suicidal. We both were. That's why I hired Cameron to go after you. Jack, you have to come back home right away. Mom's been so worried she's never going to see you again."

Lori's words hit Jack like a burst of machine-gun fire. He sat down hard in one of the chairs. His head spun. Cameron had tried to tell him about his mother, and he hadn't believed her. He thought the whole thing was a ploy dreamed up by Lori to get him back to civilization as fast as possible. He stared at his sister.

"What's she sick with?"

"Leukemia. She was diagnosed two years ago, and she's had multiple treatments since then. That's why she didn't come see you at the hospital. It wasn't because she didn't want to fly—she was too weak from chemo to make the trip. It goes into remission, and she's good for a while, then it comes back and she needs more treatments. The doctors say she could live a long time like this, or she might not. The five-year survival rate is around 70 percent. She's been so stressed about you. Even if you don't plan to get out of the army, maybe you could tell her you were thinking about it. It would make her feel so much better. You almost died, Jack. She worries about you all the time."

He stared down at his hands, too stunned to speak, then raised his head, looked out at the river. Finally he looked at his sister. "Two years? She's been fighting leukemia for *two years*, and you didn't tell me?"

"She made me promise!" Lori repeated, pleading with him to understand. "She didn't want you to know about the cancer, she didn't want me to tell you about Ky. She felt guilty about Ky. She blamed herself for that dog going missing as much as we did. She said there was nothing you could do about any of it, so there was no point in telling you until you were back home."

"You should have told me everything. She's my mother, too. I deserve to know what's going on."

"Dammit, Jack, I wanted to tell you!" Lori burst out. "Don't you think I wanted to? I didn't know what to do. It drove me crazy that I couldn't tell you, but I promised her I wouldn't. I'm sorry if you think I screwed up. I did the best I could." She was crying openly now, nose running and tears streaming down her cheeks. Jack stood, got the box of tissues from the desk and handed it to her. She stripped out a wad, blew her nose.

He stood for a long silent moment beside her, then walked to the window and stared out. Lori looked up at him, wiping her eyes with a fresh tissue. "I told Mom last night that you were okay, but if you could call her and talk to her, tell her you're coming home?" she said in a wobbly voice.

He nodded again, staring at the water flowing past. "I will."

"She's feeling pretty good right now. The leukemia's gone back into remission."

"That's good."

"Please don't be mad."

"I'm not mad. I just wish you'd told me. I could have come home on emergency leave. I could have seen Mom. I could have found Ky a year ago when she went missing. She went through a year of hell."

"Yes, I know, and I put her through it and I guess you'll never forgive me for that, but you put us through hell, too, so let's just call it even. Please call Mom. And please don't be mad at Clive."

Jack turned to face her. "His bank tried to foreclose on the ranch. How the hell could I not be seriously pissed off at him?"

"He was only doing his job," Lori said defensively. "And it might not be a bad idea if she sold the place and moved in with us. The ranch is too much for her." She blew her nose. "My flight leaves at 8:00 a.m. tomorrow morning. I can reserve a seat for you."

"I'll drive back. My car's here, and Ky can ride with me. I have to go. I'll call you later tonight after I talk to Mom. My cell phone's in my rental car."

"Okay, thanks. And Jack?" She pulled an envelope out of her coat pocket and handed it to him. "This is for Cameron, for bringing you back to us. I'm really glad you found Ky. And I'm sorry about all of it. I really am. I love you. You know you've always been my hero."

He nodded, suddenly unable to speak. He tucked the envelope inside his pocket, gave her shoulder a squeeze and left her sitting on the edge of the bed, holding the box of tissues in her lap.

CAMERON GAVE HIM a searching look when he climbed back into the SUV. "Everything okay?"

He nodded as Ky dove into his lap. Cameron didn't ask any more questions, and he was glad. She started the car and put it into drive. "The Riverside's a nice hotel, but this other place I'm taking you to has a lot more character," she said as she pulled away. "You'll really like it. Has hot and cold running water and a shower, like I said, and a fenced yard for dogs, courtesy of the former tenant who had a couple of toddlers."

She turned down a side lane about a mile farther along, beyond the airstrip and in a residential area. At the end of the dirt lane, she stopped in front of a small pale green house trailer with a pitched roof, patches of rust along the skirting and a small porch off the side. A six-foot-high industrial chain-link fence surrounded the backyard. She cut the ignition and gave him a sidelong glance.

"Nice color," he said.

"Restroom green," Cameron said. "I re-

member that color from high school days."
She opened her door. "C'mon, I'll give you
the grand tour. You can let Ky check out the
backyard. I don't think she can jump that fence,
and even if she did, the only thing she'd do is
try to find you."

The first thing that struck him when he
stepped inside the house trailer carrying the
box of groceries was the smell of mold. The
second thing was a soggy ceiling tile that
dropped from above when she closed the trailer
door.

"Sorry about that. I should've warned you,"
she apologized, brushing pieces of tile off his
shoulder. "The ceiling tiles fall down all the
time, usually after a heavy rain. The roof leaks
pretty bad, and that awful smell is the mold in
the tiles and carpet. The landlord promised he'd
fix the roof and ceiling this summer, but I get
the feeling this project isn't high on his list of
priorities. You can let Ky out that door there.
She must have to pee. I'll fix them both something to eat. The bathroom's through there,
clean towels are on the shelf." She stopped with
an apologetic expression. "I'm babbling. Sorry.
If you don't want to stay in this dump, just say
so. It won't hurt my feelings. You could leave
Ky here with me tonight. I don't mind watching her if you'd rather stay at the Riverside."

"I wouldn't." He set the box of groceries on the kitchen counter.

"Okay."

They stared at each other for a long awkward moment.

"I hope you aren't still mad at your sister."

"No."

"Good. Because it's my fault she's not already home with her husband and her regular doctor. I promised I'd have you to the Mackenzie in four days, but you turned out to be a lot more difficult to corral than I thought you'd be." Lobo stuck his head out of the front of her jacket and yawned widely, showing pink gums studded with sharp little puppy teeth. "He's getting hungry. I better feed him."

She started to turn toward the box of groceries on the counter and then turned back. "You know, Jack, I've been thinking. About Ky, about you. If you're really set on going back to Afghanistan, I'll take care of her for you. Your sister's about to have a baby, she's got her hands full, but I can watch her. I have the perfect place here for dogs, the big fenced yard and all, and this trailer is such a dump my landlord can't possibly refuse pets. I'll take her for walks, and she'll get to know me and like me. I know she will. And she'll be good company for Lobo when I'm not home, and I'll take really good care of her and…and I'm babbling again. I'm sorry. I just wanted you to know that if you really want to go back on active duty, you don't have to worry about what's going to happen to Ky."

Jack felt Ky's body press against his leg and rested one hand on top of her head. He felt more tired and discouraged than he ever had. These weren't the words he wanted to hear from her.

"I'm heading back to Montana first thing tomorrow," he said. "I'll be taking Ky with me."

"Oh. Okay. I just thought I'd offer, that's all."

She turned away from him abruptly, set the pup on the floor and began rummaging in the box of groceries. She opened a can of dog food, mixed half of it with some milk and a few kibbles in a metal pie pan, then set it on the floor and watched Lobo immerse his muzzle and front paws in the pan as he ate with sloppy enthusiasm. She poured some kibble into another pot, added another can of dog food to it, mixed it up with a little water and put it on the floor in front of Ky. She filled a third cooking pan with water and added it to the canine collection at her feet.

Only when Ky and Lobo were eating did she look at Jack. "I'm glad you're taking your sister back home. That's nice of you."

"She's flying, I'm driving. I'm not sure when I'll be back."

Cameron shrugged. "Not a problem. I just wanted you to know that if you needed someone to watch your dog, I'm available."

Her words stung. He pulled the envelope out of his pocket and handed it to her. "Lori asked me to give this to you."

She took the brown manila envelope, lifted it up and down as if hefting the weight of it. "My bounty money."

"None of that belongs to Fred Andrew. I heard you offer your reward money to him in exchange for Ky, so he could buy a good lead dog, and I really appreciate you making that offer, but I gave him a fair amount of money while you were packing up your things at his place. That money from my sister is yours to keep."

"I don't want it." She held it out to him. "Put it toward your niece or nephew's college fund."

"You earned it, and then some. It's yours, and don't feel guilty about it, either. My sister hired you. She wanted you to have that money, and she and her husband are very well-off, in spite of what she might have told you. So go ahead and buy that red Jeep."

They stared at each other for another awkward moment. Cameron's eyes dropped to the envelope of money in her hands. "You better take the first shower. The hot-water heater doesn't work very well."

CHAPTER TWENTY-FOUR

CAMERON TOOK LOBO out into the fenced yard, then balanced precariously on the plastic lawn chair with the broken leg and struggled to breathe past the crushing pain in her chest. She'd just handed Jack every opportunity to tell her he didn't want to go back to Afghanistan, but he'd said nothing. Instead, he'd told her he was leaving for Montana in the morning and didn't know when he'd be back. And then he'd handed her the bounty money from his sister and said he'd paid Fred for Ky. His duty to her had been discharged. He was free and clear.

Lobo wandered about her feet in his determined puppy stagger, did his duty and then chewed with great determination on her boot laces. She heaved a heavy sigh and looked down at him through a shimmer of tears.

"He's killing me, but I can't let him know it," she told the pup. "I have to be strong."

Lobo was young and fat and healthy, but Ky's experience in the wilds had transformed her. Her ribs showed. Her scars showed. She looked like she'd been through hell. She needed lots of TLC, and she needed it from Jack. Nobody else could take his place. If he went back to Afghanistan, Ky would waste away. He had to know that. That poor dog hadn't even let him go into the bathroom to take his shower without trying to claw the door open in a panic. In the end he had to take her inside with him, leaving Cameron to listen to the sound of running water and feel jealous of a dog.

Cameron sat up straighter. She drew a deep breath and let it out very slowly. Jack couldn't go. He wouldn't. No matter how much he wanted to, no matter how much he thought he had to return to active duty to prove himself, he'd have to stay. After all he'd gone through to find his dog, he couldn't abandon her again. He'd said he was going to Montana, not Afghanistan, and he was taking Ky with him. He was abandoning *her*, not his dog, but at least he wasn't going back there again to be shot at or blown up and maybe killed. She should be grateful for that.

Cameron pulled the envelope containing the money out of her jacket pocket. She opened it, counted the hundred-dollar bills, all fifty of them, all in US currency. And there were three extra, a bit of a bonus even though she hadn't really earned it. Five thousand, three hundred US dollars in bounty money didn't take up much space. She tucked the bills back into the envelope, tucked the envelope back inside her jacket pocket and wiped the tears from her eyes. This money was supposed to have changed her life for the better. Instead, it made her feel like a cheap mercenary. It would have felt so much better to have given it all to Fred Andrew.

As for Johnny Allen's red Jeep, she couldn't care less.

WHEN JACK OPENED the bathroom door, the smell of food cooking made his stomach growl. Cameron was in the little kitchen, browning a package of stew beef in a cast-iron pan full of caramelized onions. She turned around when he came into the kitchen, spatula in hand, and her eyes widened. "You shaved!"

"Good or bad?"

Her head tilted slightly to one side as she appraised him. "You look very handsome."

He grinned. "What's cooking?"

"Moose chili. I ran into Tucker Gordon at the store when I was buying the dog food, and he insisted I take a package of his moose meat, since the store refused to sell it for him. I'm sure he shot it out of season, and it's illegal for the store to sell wild meat, but Tuck needed the money to buy some liquor. He's an alcoholic, and he was really suffering, so I bought it from him. Why don't you open the bottle of wine? If this is our last night together, let's make it a memorable one. Good meal, good wine, good company."

He opened the bottle of wine. "I can take over with the cooking if you want to take a shower," he said.

"It'll take at least half an hour for the water to heat back up. I'll get the chili put together, and it can simmer while I get cleaned up." She flashed him a smile. "Lobo's already gotten attached to Ky. He was wanting to get into the bathroom while the two of you were in there. Look at them cuddling together. Lucky for us they like each other."

"They're both half wild. Maybe that's the bond between them," Jack said.

"Or maybe it's because they were both abandoned."

There it was again. She drew that word like a gun.

"I'm not abandoning you, Cameron."

"I didn't say you were," she said, busily stirring the moose meat. "I was referring to the dogs. Why don't you pour the wine?"

He poured into the two glasses she'd set on the counter, still trying to fathom her mood.

"I'm not abandoning you," he repeated. "You think I'm running off to Montana and that's it, that's the end of us, but that's not the way it's going to be."

She turned to face him. "Jack, you can do whatever you want. I don't own you. You want to go, go."

"Do you want me to go?"

She didn't hesitate for long.

"No," she replied. "I don't want you to go back to Afghanistan, and I can't imagine why you'd want to go back there after what happened to you, and I don't want you to go to Montana, even though I know you have to. I want you to stay right here with me. But look at this place." She swept her arm out in an all encompassing gesture. "This is my life. I can't ask you to stick around here."

He ran his fingers through his damp hair, frustrated, wondering how he could make her understand. "A week ago, returning to my unit was all I wanted to do. But now everything's changed."

"What do you want to do now?" Cameron asked, turning back to the stove and focusing on the browning of the moose meat as if it was the most important thing in the world to her.

"I want to see if we can work things out between us," Jack said. "I want to see if we can manage something more than a clean break. What do you want?"

Her shoulders stiffened as he spoke. She stopped stirring the meat and turned to look at him, her dark eyes turbulent with emotion. "I want the same thing," she said. She was so beautiful, the way she was looking at him, standing there in her soiled and shredded trail clothes, covered with cuts and bruises, holding the spatula. He thought she was the most beautiful woman on the entire planet. Hell, he knew she was. He crossed to her, took her face in his hands and kissed her very gently on the lips.

"Then we'll make it happen," he promised. "But first I have to go to Montana. I'm not abandoning you, Cameron. Turns out you were right about my mother. She's really sick. I need to go see her, and I don't know how long I'll be gone."

CAMERON SUFFERED A new kind of pain while standing in the lukewarm shower. She'd almost gotten used to living with the pain, the difficulty breathing, the lack of appetite, the immense loneliness that she knew was going to fill her world as soon as Jack walked out of it. Now he'd turned the tables on her. Instead of wanting to be a pen pal, he'd told her he was coming back. She stood under the shower as the water grew cooler and wanted to believe him, but she knew men said things to women sometimes, things they didn't mean, in order to avoid unpleasant situations. They said things like "I'll call you," and then they never did.

Jack said he'd be back, but would he, or was he just trying to make their parting easier? And if he came back from Montana, then went back to Afghanistan, what then? Was she supposed to wait and wonder if he'd ever return? What they'd shared together on their wilderness trek had created a special bond between them, but who was she kidding, to think a worldly man like Jack would fall for a backwoods hick like her? He'd go to Montana to visit his mother and he'd call her every night, maybe, then once a week, then from time to time, until she no longer expected to hear from him.

The End.

By the time she exited the bathroom, dressed in clean blue jeans and a soft flannel shirt, she had gotten past the pain and panic and forted up inside herself again. She was strong. Whatever happened, she could get through this. She'd lived most of her life without Jack Parker, and she could live without him for the rest of it, if she had to. She wasn't going to beg and plead, she wasn't going to be clingy and needy.

She'd opened all the windows in the house

trailer upon their arrival, but it still smelled of mold with strong chili overtones. Had it always been this bad and she just hadn't noticed? She looked around, seeing the place with fresh eyes. The shabby furniture, the three cardboard boxes stacked in the living room with all her worldly possessions still unpacked. She could only imagine what he must think of anyone who lived like this.

Jack was standing at the stove, adjusting the gas burner. "That hot water felt good, didn't it?" he said when she came into the kitchen. "I need to make some phone calls to tell my mother I'm headed home and my sister to let her know I'll deliver her to the airport tomorrow morning. Her flight leaves at 8:00 a.m. I could get my car at the floatplane base tonight, if you'll give me a ride over. I left my cell phone in the car."

"Of course," Cameron said, reaching past him to turn off the gas burner under the pot of chili. "We should go right now, before supper." Truth was, she didn't want to sit around making awkward small talk with Jack as the clock ticked toward The Big Goodbye. Ten minutes later Ky and Lobo were in the backseat of the SUV, and she was driving Jack to the floatplane base.

"If you'd rather fly back with your sister,

you can leave your car here," Cameron said. "I could watch Ky for you." She knew she shouldn't have suggested that again, but she was moments away from begging and pleading with him not to leave her.

"My mother wants to see Ky, and I don't mind driving. She knows I'll be there in two days. I'll head south as soon as Lori's on the plane."

"You'll need to have Ky's rabies certificate faxed to the border crossing if you don't have it on you. I'm assuming she's up to date on shots."

"She is. Lori will know the name of the veterinary clinic and I'll give them a call."

Cameron fortified her inner defenses, reminding herself that she was a strong, self-reliant and independent woman. Strong. Self-reliant. Independent. She pulled into the floatplane base and parked next to Walt's truck. There was another vehicle in front of the office, one she hadn't seen for a while. She studied it for a moment, puzzled, then felt a jolt of happy surprise.

"Hey, Jeri's back! It's been hell around this place without her," she told Jack. "She was the brains of the outfit. I'll run inside and get your car keys. I want to say hi and make sure Walt gives her a big raise."

"I'd like to thank your boss before I go," Jack said, getting out of the vehicle. "Ky'll be okay for a few minutes. I'll stay on the porch where she can see me."

He was right behind her on the steps when the trailer door opened and Walt stepped onto the porch, pulling the door shut behind him. He looked a little disheveled and not all that happy to see them.

"Jeri's back," he told Cameron. "She's staying. We've talked things over and worked it all out."

"That's great, Walt, I'm really glad for all of us," Cameron said. "I'd like to say hi and pick up Jack's car keys. I also need to talk about my extended medical leave."

Walt kept his hand on the doorknob, blocking her entrance. "Can't this wait till morning? We're right in the middle of a serious discussion."

"Oh, for the love of bald-headed consumption, Walt," a familiar voice came through the door. It opened inward, pulling Walt off balance until he let go of the doorknob. Jeri smiled over Walt's shoulder. Her hair was mussed, her lipstick was smeared and she was straightening her clothing.

"Hey, Cameron!" she said, and gave her a big hug. "Good to see you, scars, bruises and all. Holy old boys, you look like you've been through hell, both of you, and you must be Jack Parker. I've heard all about you. Come on inside, have a cup of coffee. I'll make a fresh pot."

Jack looked over his shoulder at the SUV. "I better wait out here."

Cameron pulled him in behind her. "It'll be okay. Ky'll be fine for a few minutes."

"So," WALT SAID as Jeri handed the mugs of fresh brewed coffee to Cameron and Jack, who sat side by side on the sofa. "What's this about an extended medical leave?" He tried to sound nonchalant, but his words didn't quite come out that way. "You're one of my best pilots. Where's that going to leave me? Hunting season's right around the corner."

Cameron was staring at the mug in her hands, breathing in the smell of genuine Jeri-crafted coffee. She smiled with gratitude and raised her eyes to Walt. "I just need a little time off. I'd like to go over to Yukon and see a friend of mine, Minnie Parker. She's been like a grandmother to me, and she lost her husband awhile ago. You still have Mitch. He can fill in while I'm gone."

Walt sat at the desk, in the radio seat. He rubbed his face and looked between Jack and

Cameron. "You mean, this extended leave has nothing to do with the two of you running off together?"

"No," Cameron said, looking puzzled and a little embarrassed. "Jack's leaving for Montana in the morning to visit his mother, and I'm driving to Whitehorse to see Minnie. I'll be gone another week or so, then you'll have me back full-time."

"Well, I'll be damned." Relief flooded through him. "I'm glad to hear it. I was sure you'd be flying off into the sunset with the Lone Ranger. Guess I read you two all wrong."

"Let me get this straight," Jeri said, balancing on the arm of Walt's chair and draping her arm over his shoulder. "This has nothing to do with taking a medical leave?" Cameron shook her head, and Jeri looked relieved. "Good thing. Walt's policy expired last week. It's going to take me some fancy finagling to get him back in the insurance company's good graces. There's lots of stuff that needs fixing around here. It'll take me a month or so to get things back in order. Take your time, Cameron. You could use a long vacation, from the looks of you. You both could. Walt told me what you've been through." She gave Jack a shrewd appraisal. "So you're heading south tomorrow. Montana's a long haul."

"Not that far, and it's all downhill," Jack said.

Jeri laughed, but she'd gotten that scheming look that always put Walt on guard. "Walt tells me you're in the army?"

"That's right, but I've decided on a change of careers. I'll be getting out on a medical discharge."

"What will you do then?"

Walt was disgruntled at Jeri's line of questioning. Who cared what the Lone Ranger was going to do with his life? He had Cameron back. That's all that mattered. And he didn't like the way Cameron was looking at Jack just now, like he'd just given her a giant diamond or something.

"I guess that's up to Cameron," Jack said. Walt glared. This was getting out of hand. "I'd like another cup of your coffee, Jeri," he said. "Anybody else want a refill?"

"What's that supposed to mean?" Cameron asked, looking at Jack.

"I said I'd come back here and I meant it."

"Oh," Jeri said. Now she was wearing that dreamy, romantic look. "Guess you weren't wrong about them after all, huh, Walt?" She prodded him with her elbow. "Seems to me your drive to Montana would be easier with some company, Jack. Cameron should go along with you, meet the rest of your family. Then maybe the two of you can head north again, go over to Yukon and visit with her Grandma Minnie."

"Hold on a minute," Walt said. "That sounds like a long road trip."

"It's August," Jeri reminded him. "We have about four more weeks until winter shuts everything down up here except the hunters. That's just about enough time. It would be a wonderful trip through some beautiful country. I say, gas up and go. Mitch and Walt can do the flying while you're gone, and I'll man the office. You're only young once, isn't that right, Walt?"

Walt stared. "Whose side are you on?"

"And another thing, Walt," Jeri continued. "That hovel Cameron's living in should be condemned. She needs better housing. That should be part of her new pay package."

"Pay package?" Walt was dumbfounded. What had come over her? A few moments ago they'd been going at it, hot and heavy on the couch. Now she was acting like the CEO of Tim Hortons.

"If you want Walt's Flying Service to survive, you need to run it like a business," Jeri said. "You have to hire the best pilots you can, and pay them the best you can. Cameron's by far the best pilot you have, but Mitch makes more than she does because he's a man. That sort of discrimination has to stop."

"Mitch makes more than me?" Cameron asked. "How much more?"

"I left you because you didn't appreciate me," Jeri said to Walt. "I landed a good paying government job in Yellowknife because I'm talented, smart and a good worker. I was handed all the benefits from the get-go. You should've seen the office where I worked. Unlike you, the government spares no expense, but I'll be the first to admit that money isn't everything. It's not even close. I was miserable there. I missed this place so much. I even missed *you*, Walt. Hard to believe, isn't it? So I quit that easy government job, and I came back. I'm staying, but this time around things are going to be different. I'm not going to be your coffee maker, your errand girl, or your bed warmer. I'm going to be your wife, and I'm going to run this place the way it should be run, before you run it right into the ground. And, Walt, I promise I'm going to make you the happiest man north of 60."

She bent and kissed him full on the mouth, and he stared at her afterward and forgot all the arguments he was going to make. "We're getting married?"

"You're making an honest woman out of me,

in exchange for me saving your failing business. It'll be a good partnership. As for the two of you," she continued, shifting her attention to Jack and Cameron, "Jack knows what I'm talking about when I say life's shorter than you think. Don't waste a lot of time chasing after things that don't matter. Find the things that really matter, and hang on to them. Hang on tight and don't let go."

She got up, grabbed a set of keys off the bulletin board next to Walt's radio chair and tossed them to Jack. "Now vamoose. Have a good trip, and we'll see you both when you get back. Right now, me'n Walt need to finish our serious discussion."

CAMERON AND JACK exited the office trailer and stood for a moment on the porch. They cast sidelong glances at each other, then looked at the SUV. No further damage had been wrought by the dog sitting erectly in the passenger seat, waiting for Jack. It seemed Ky was settling down.

"I'm glad Jeri's back," Cameron said, "but I can't help but feel a little sorry for Walt."

"Jeri's just what Walt needs." Jack descended the steps, his car keys in hand. He paused when he reached the bottom. "About that four-week road trip," he began.

She stopped beside him and felt the familiar tightness in her chest that made it so hard to breathe. "Oh, that Jeri. She likes to kid around."

"Sounded like a good plan to me," Jack said. "I'll see if I can arrange an extended leave to see my mother, maybe even enough time for us to go visit Minnie and see that lodge you like so much. And I'll start the ball rolling on my discharge."

Cameron was astonished. Had she read him all wrong? Did he really want her tagging along when he went to visit his mother in Montana? Did he really want to go with her to see that lodge of Minnie's in Yukon?

"Are you really getting out of the army?" she asked.

"I am," he said. "I don't know how long the discharge process will take, but I'm coming back here. I don't know why you don't trust me. Maybe it's because of Roy, maybe it's because of your mother, I don't know. I only know Jeri gave us some good advice, and I think we should take it. We should head south together tomorrow morning. It sure as hell beats that clean break you were so set on. So what do you say? Want to see Montana?"

Cameron struggled to breathe. She wanted to cry, but she couldn't. She wanted to speak but couldn't do that either, so she nodded, because a nod was all she could manage.

"Good. Now that that's out of the way, what do you say we go back to your place and have a serious discussion of our own?"

She nodded again through a blur of tears, laughing and crying at the same time.

He drew her into his arms, and she hung on tight. She clung to him because she needed him more than she'd ever needed anything or anyone. Until Jack Parker had walked into her life, she'd been as lost as his dog, and hadn't even known it. Jeri was right. She had found what really mattered, and she was never letting go.

* * * * *

LARGER-PRINT BOOKS!
GET 2 FREE LARGER-PRINT NOVELS PLUS
2 FREE GIFTS!

HARLEQUIN®

Romance

From the Heart, For the Heart

YES! Please send me 2 FREE LARGER-PRINT Harlequin® Romance novels and my 2 FREE gifts (gifts are worth about $10). After receiving them, if I don't wish to receive any more books, I can return the shipping statement marked "cancel." If I don't cancel, I will receive 4 brand-new novels every month and be billed just $5.09 per book in the U.S. or $5.49 per book in Canada. That's a savings of at least 15% off the cover price! It's quite a bargain! Shipping and handling is just 50¢ per book in the U.S. and 75¢ per book in Canada.* I understand that accepting the 2 free books and gifts places me under no obligation to buy anything. I can always return a shipment and cancel at any time. Even if I never buy another book, the two free books and gifts are mine to keep forever.

119/319 HDN GHWC

Name	(PLEASE PRINT)

Address	Apt. #

City	State/Prov.	Zip/Postal Code

Signature (if under 18, a parent or guardian must sign)

Mail to the **Reader Service:**
IN U.S.A.: P.O. Box 1867, Buffalo, NY 14240-1867
IN CANADA: P.O. Box 609, Fort Erie, Ontario L2A 5X3
Want to try two free books from another line?
Call 1-800-873-8635 or visit www.ReaderService.com.

* Terms and prices subject to change without notice. Prices do not include applicable taxes. Sales tax applicable in N.Y. Canadian residents will be charged applicable taxes. Offer not valid in Quebec. This offer is limited to one order per household. Not valid for current subscribers to Harlequin Romance Larger-Print books. All orders subject to credit approval. Credit or debit balances in a customer's account(s) may be offset by any other outstanding balance owed by or to the customer. Please allow 4 to 6 weeks for delivery. Offer available while quantities last.

Your Privacy—The Reader Service is committed to protecting your privacy. Our Privacy Policy is available online at www.ReaderService.com or upon request from the Reader Service.

We make a portion of our mailing list available to reputable third parties that offer products we believe may interest you. If you prefer that we not exchange your name with third parties, or if you wish to clarify or modify your communication preferences, please visit us at www.ReaderService.com/consumerchoice or write to us at Reader Service Preference Service, P.O. Box 9062, Buffalo, NY 14240-9062. Include your complete name and address.

HRLP15

LARGER-PRINT BOOKS!

HARLEQUIN

Presents®

PASSION GUARANTEED SEDUCTION

GET 2 FREE LARGER-PRINT NOVELS PLUS 2 FREE GIFTS!

YES! Please send me 2 FREE LARGER-PRINT Harlequin Presents® novels and my 2 FREE gifts (gifts are worth about $10). After receiving them, if I don't wish to receive any more books, I can return the shipping statement marked "cancel." If I don't cancel, I will receive 6 brand-new novels every month and be billed just $5.30 per book in the U.S. or $5.74 per book in Canada. That's a saving of at least 12% off the cover price! It's quite a bargain! Shipping and handling is just 50¢ per book in the U.S. and 75¢ per book in Canada.* I understand that accepting the 2 free books and gifts places me under no obligation to buy anything. I can always return a shipment and cancel at any time. Even if I never buy another book, the two free books and gifts are mine to keep forever.

176/376 HDN GHVY

Name	(PLEASE PRINT)	
Address		Apt. #
City	State/Prov.	Zip/Postal Code

Signature (if under 18, a parent or guardian must sign)

Mail to the **Reader Service:**
IN U.S.A.: P.O. Box 1867, Buffalo, NY 14240-1867
IN CANADA: P.O. Box 609, Fort Erie, Ontario L2A 5X3

**Are you a subscriber to Harlequin Presents® books
and want to receive the larger-print edition?
Call 1-800-873-8635 today or visit us at www.ReaderService.com.**

* Terms and prices subject to change without notice. Prices do not include applicable taxes. Sales tax applicable in N.Y. Canadian residents will be charged applicable taxes. Offer not valid in Quebec. This offer is limited to one order per household. Not valid for current subscribers to Harlequin Presents Larger-Print books. All orders subject to credit approval. Credit or debit balances in a customer's account(s) may be offset by any other outstanding balance owed by or to the customer. Please allow 4 to 6 weeks for delivery. Offer available while quantities last.

Your Privacy—The Reader Service is committed to protecting your privacy. Our Privacy Policy is available online at www.ReaderService.com or upon request from the Reader Service.

We make a portion of our mailing list available to reputable third parties that offer products we believe may interest you. If you prefer that we not exchange your name with third parties, or if you wish to clarify or modify your communication preferences, please visit us at www.ReaderService.com/consumerschoice or write to us at Reader Service Preference Service, P.O. Box 9062, Buffalo, NY 14240-9062. Include your complete name and address.

LARGER-PRINT BOOKS!
GET 2 FREE LARGER-PRINT NOVELS PLUS
2 FREE GIFTS!

⊞ HARLEQUIN®

INTRIGUE

BREATHTAKING ROMANTIC SUSPENSE

YES! Please send me 2 FREE LARGER-PRINT Harlequin® Intrigue novels and my 2 FREE gifts (gifts are worth about $10). After receiving them, if I don't wish to receive any more books, I can return the shipping statement marked "cancel." If I don't cancel, I will receive 6 brand-new novels every month and be billed just $5.49 per book in the U.S. or $6.24 per book in Canada. That's a saving of at least 11% off the cover price! It's quite a bargain! Shipping and handling is just 50¢ per book in the U.S. and 75¢ per book in Canada.* I understand that accepting the 2 free books and gifts places me under no obligation to buy anything. I can always return a shipment and cancel at any time. Even if I never buy another book, the two free books and gifts are mine to keep forever.

199/399 HDN GHWN

Name _____ (PLEASE PRINT) _____

Address _____ Apt. # _____

City _____ State/Prov. _____ Zip/Postal Code _____

Signature (if under 18, a parent or guardian must sign)

Mail to the **Reader Service:**
IN U.S.A.: P.O. Box 1867, Buffalo, NY 14240-1867
IN CANADA: P.O. Box 609, Fort Erie, Ontario L2A 5X3

**Are you a subscriber to Harlequin® Intrigue books
and want to receive the larger-print edition?
Call 1-800-873-8635 today or visit www.ReaderService.com.**

* Terms and prices subject to change without notice. Prices do not include applicable taxes. Sales tax applicable in N.Y. Canadian residents will be charged applicable taxes. Offer not valid in Quebec. This offer is limited to one order per household. Not valid for current subscribers to Harlequin Intrigue Larger-Print books. All orders subject to credit approval. Credit or debit balances in a customer's account(s) may be offset by any other outstanding balance owed by or to the customer. Please allow 4 to 6 weeks for delivery. Offer available while quantities last.

Your Privacy—The Reader Service is committed to protecting your privacy. Our Privacy Policy is available online at www.ReaderService.com or upon request from the Reader Service.

We make a portion of our mailing list available to reputable third parties that offer products we believe may interest you. If you prefer that we not exchange your name with third parties, or if you wish to clarify or modify your communication preferences, please visit us at www.ReaderService.com/consumerchoice or write to us at Reader Service Preference Service, P.O. Box 9062, Buffalo, NY 14240-9062. Include your complete name and address.

HILP15